UNEXPECTED
LIGHTNING

Praise for Cass Sellars

Lightning Chasers

Lightning Chasers "is a rewarding read, and Sellars ensures you feel the emotions in the story. It is a murder investigation, and whilst it is not too difficult to work out who is probably responsible, the investigation and the relationships amongst the friends are what sets this apart...The romance between Syd and Parker retains the fire from the first book, and our journey with them as their relationship continues to grow is one of the high points of the book."—*The Lesbian Review*

Lightning Strikes

"*Lightning Strikes* is a really lovely story of two people arriving at a point in each of their lives when they need to make a change. Parker is fresh out of a disastrous marriage with no intention of being in a relationship any time soon. Syd is a player who has never considered monogamy her thing. But you can never predict the moment when Lightening Strikes...They made a perfect couple, and I felt invested in their story."—*Kitty Kat's Book Review Blog*

"*Lightning Strikes* is a butch/femme romance that is just so extraordinarily good...This is a beautifully written, scintillating, seriously hot book that is a real page turner and, I will say it again, is a ROMANCE! I have no hesitation in recommending this book, go and buy it. It is one of the best books I have read this year."—*The Lesbian Review*

By the Author

Lightning Strikes

Lightning Chasers

Unexpected Lightning

UNEXPECTED LIGHTNING

by
Cass Sellars

2019

THIS TRADE PAPERBACK ORIGINAL IS PUBLISHED BY
BOLD STROKES BOOKS, INC.
P.O. BOX 249
VALLEY FALLS, NY 12185

FIRST EDITION: FEBRUARY 2019

CREDITS
EDITORS: VICTORIA VILLASEÑOR AND BARBARA ANN WRIGHT
PRODUCTION DESIGN: STACIA SEAMAN
COVER DESIGN BY MELODY POND

Acknowledgments

Ruth and Vic, thank you for making me better at the process.

Thank you, Rad and Sandy, for your insight and vision.

Thank you, Dee and Cara, for investing with me.

Thank you to the readers who genuinely wanted to read the next one.

One never knows how important the journey
until the destination becomes imperative.
So thankful for the reminder that lightning often appears
when the storm is the most silent.

Chapter One

Parker Duncan brushed eraser dust from the blueprints and used the dawning light to mark up the plans for the new office space overlooking Silver Lake. The challenges at Davidson Properties made the synapses fire. She was also using it as a distraction from thinking about Sydney, away far too long on a New York business trip. The past two years with the handsome, consummate ex-player was the best decision she never actually made. Sharing a home with Syd felt exciting and new and like something that had always been. She snapped herself out of her daydream when she caught movement in the hallway.

Since it was only seven a.m., she was mildly shocked when Quint Davidson, the CEO of DPI, strolled into her office. She was used to the cocoon of her solitary early mornings lasting until at least seven thirty.

"Morning, Parker, how's it coming on the CacheTech expansion?" The ruddy-faced fifty-four-year-old fell into her guest chair and pulled an ankle over his knee.

She couldn't help but chuckle at his socks, which were covered in magenta farm animals. "Surprisingly well. I think they're so happy to be expanding instead of fighting the media, they're fairly amenable to anything."

Quint nodded approvingly and glanced over to Parker as if gauging her reaction to the uncomfortable recall. CacheTech Incorporated had been involved in a substantial scandal the prior year, one that nearly cost Parker's partner her life. She flinched involuntarily at the memory of seeing Syd unconscious after a CTI truck ran her and their friend, Lieutenant Mack Foster, off the road. Quint gave her a reassuring smile.

"You do good work, Parker, but you probably know that already. You know how this place runs as well as I do."

Parker relished being a key player, and his praise was always welcome since she hoped to move up in the company soon.

"Which makes the favor I'm about to ask even more audacious." He shifted uncomfortably in his chair. "I hate to ask this, but..."

"Give me the bad news. I can handle it, Quint." She smiled genuinely and knitted her hands in front of her as he continued to verbally squirm.

"I know you can." He inhaled deeply and started to speak. "Brenda is redoing the house...again. Consequently, there are more hard hats in my home than on our jobsites right now. I'm fairly sure someone's erecting a tomb in the basement, but I don't want to say anything in case I can use it to sleep in peace and quiet one day."

He dragged his thumbs over his eyes, causing her to recall the last unannounced catastrophe his wife had made of their home, requiring a lengthy stay in a hotel and a visit from city inspectors who discovered their general contractor had received no permits.

Parker laughed and watched with genuine affection as he appeared to take a millisecond nap. "Does this mean that you want me to come over and pick wallpaper with you or that you want to hide at our house until it's over?"

He looked relieved. "Well, since you're feeling so charitable...maybe you won't mind hosting the CTI launch party a few weekends from now?" Davidson crinkled his nose and continued when Parker didn't flinch.

"They were promised a not-so-formal gathering for the key project stakeholders at my home—and now yours—if you agree.

At the same time, they can meet and greet all the players from our office. It won't be more than a hundred invitees, and you know that fifty won't even show. We'll pay for everything, and I'll even get a service to come clean up after, if you want. I'd have it myself, but there's just no way…"

Parker held up her hand. "Quint, it's not a big deal. I'll check with Syd, to be fair, but I can't imagine it will be a problem. Don't worry."

He visibly deflated with relief as the words seemed to drain some of his stress.

"Jenny will host with me, and you can do the schmoozing part that we both hate, deal?"

He smiled brightly. "Deal. But we only have two weeks. They're hand-delivering the invites so we'll be sure they're in the right hands in time. Tess will get you the RSVP updates as they come in. The caterer is already locked in, and we can have them deliver the bar setup whenever you want. I'll even give you the Monday off afterward so you can recover."

"Appreciated but not necessary. As long as I can work from home when I need the quiet, the deal is more than fair."

"You could show up here once a month, and I'd be fine." He took a deep breath and reclined in his chair. "However, Frank Meyers would have no one to secretly drool over, so morale might take a plunge." He offered a crooked smile as Parker shook her head. He slipped a folded list from his back pocket and handed it to her.

"I think he only pretends to be devoted to me to get to Jenny." Parker took the list and placed it on her desk. "Actually, I think he just needs to find a woman to listen to his annoying line of bull without severing all hope of a carnal liaison." Parker found the wormy account executive fairly harmless, and he bent her assistant director's ear much more often than hers. Meyers had landed the CTI contract through sheer luck when the new operations manager at CTI, now a good friend of hers, had called Parker for advice on the office expansion.

Quint laughed as he unfolded from the chair. "I owe you big, Parker. Actually, Brenda owes you big. After she finishes paying off my therapy, I'll get her to pay up." He shook her hand warmly.

"Go! I have work to do, and the boss is a real hardass." Parker laughed as he saluted and left.

Parker heard Jenny's chirpy greeting as she passed Davidson in the hall and dropped her purse on the table in the waiting area. Her tiny blond best friend was as eternally chipper as she was incredibly efficient. They made a fabulous team, running the real estate and HR departments as if they had been at it for decades.

"Morning!" Jenny Foster beamed as she rounded the desk and hugged Parker.

"Hello, Mrs. Foster. How was your weekend with the family? We've missed seeing you lately." For the mother of an eighteen-month-old little girl, she looked pretty good.

"She misses you and her Sy-ee." The glint in her eye was evident as she repeated her child's nickname for Syd. Jenny gushed as she opened her phone to display the latest picture of Olivia Grace gnawing on Mack's cheek.

"You were born to be a mom, Jenny." She took in the image of the two people Jenny loved more than anything on the planet.

"I think I was." She took a last moment to smile at the photo before she put the phone in hibernation mode. "So, to what do we owe a visit from the boss of bosses?" She jerked her head toward the hallway.

"More work. The CTI reception slated for his house was derailed by Brenda's latest remodel, so assuming Sydney agrees, you and I are hosting the soirée at the loft." She sat back and waited for Jenny to process.

"Well, then. I assume someone else is paying, and we get to be creative?"

Parker could practically see the ideas sifting through Jenny's mind. "Indeed. His new assistant will get us the final RSVP list while you and I convince Sydney that this is a fabulous idea."

"Shall I assume you're going to make her a fancy dinner and provide some sort of athletic sexual favors?" Jenny stood and straightened her skirt as if preparing for a royal visit.

"I have at least twenty-four hours before Syd comes home from Albany to devise that plan." Parker jotted a few notes on a scrap of paper and shoved it into her purse. "I'll just make her think it's a great idea and then hit her with the sexual favors." She rubbed her hands together with mock deviousness.

"I don't think anyone wants to face you in battle, Park. I'm just going to tell whoever to roll over. It's easier." She laughed, looking back over her shoulder as she strolled to the door.

"You give me way too much credit, Jen. How is tomorrow at six for dinner?" She took out the red grease pencil and went back to marking up her plans with the furniture she had ordered.

"We wouldn't *dare* miss that performance." She picked her bag up and stopped to lean back into the office. "Three candidates for scheduling manager and four for the accounting clerk positions will be here starting at ten. Can you sit in? I'm guessing twenty-five minutes apiece, and we might be making offers to two schedulers, at least temporarily."

"I'll meet you in the conference room at five till, and we can split them up. You talk to them first? I'll do the seconds and start them on paperwork."

"Love ya, mean it." Jenny blew Parker an exaggerated kiss as she stepped away and into her adjacent office.

CHAPTER TWO

Sydney Hyatt had just finished emptying her overnight bag when the large oak sliding door creaked past the frame and admitted the woman who made her world turn. She abandoned the planned trip into her home gym in favor of Parker's embrace.

"I missed you so much."

The low, husky timbre of Syd's voice seemed to seep into Parker's skin. She dropped her purse and let her laptop bag fall against the floor next to it.

"Oh my God, I'm so happy to see you." She threw her arms around Syd before accepting Sydney's hungry mouth over hers.

Syd growled in response when Parker returned a harder kiss. She smoothed her hands over Parker's back and lifted her to perch on the kitchen island. Parker locked her legs over her hips and squeezed Syd's body into hers.

"I will take that greeting any day." Syd breathed the words along Parker's neck, stopping to nip at her earlobe.

"You'd better. People at work aren't nearly as receptive when I do this to them." Parker gave Sydney a wicked smile as she squeezed her thighs harder around Syd's waist.

"I guess they should learn to take it when they can." She continued feathering kisses along Parker's shoulder. "Especially since their days would be numbered if I found out they touched you even once." Sydney was only half kidding about the bodily injury she could do to someone who laid a finger on the woman she very completely considered hers.

"My personal bodyguard? I feel very privileged." She issued the words playfully and tapped a series of kisses along Syd's jaw.

"Come clean, now. Tell me why I'm supposed to be ready by six." Syd fought the fluttering sensations brought on by Parker's attentions so she could focus on whatever they were supposed to be doing.

"Well, Mack and Jen are coming for dinner, and you shouldn't be all sweaty from a workout when Olivia uses you for a jungle gym."

Sydney often waffled between enthusiastically embracing the child that habitually climbed all over her and retaining her determination not to be melted by it.

"Now, help me make a salad, and I'll be back right after I change." Parker peeled off her black silk suit jacket and began to walk down the hall as she unbuttoned her blouse.

She laughed when Sydney slid behind her on the hardwood floor and skated her hand around Parker's rib cage. She ran her tongue over Parker's skin and heard a moan escape in answer.

"How is it that you're this hard to resist after two years?" Parker dropped her head back, and Syd caught the scent of her favorite perfume.

"My goal is fifty years, so I'm just getting warmed up." She slid Parker onto the king mattress still unmade from the night before. She drew her hungry mouth over Parker's skin as she tossed her blouse to the floor. Parker sighed and pressed her sensitive breasts against Syd.

"We should be making dinner, Syd." Parked groaned into Sydney's ear. "But I want you."

The words woke her body from the slumber that came from being without her for too many days. "I thought about this all the way back from Albany." Syd stripped away the rest of Parker's clothes.

Parker straddled Syd's hips and watched her hands skim across her flesh, multiplying the intoxicating sensations.

Syd met her eyes. "Kiss me, now."

Parker smirked at the command, playfully turning her head. "Make me." She saw the air of challenge overtake Syd, who playfully flipped Parker beneath her.

"I told you to kiss me." Syd crushed her mouth to Parker's.

"What do I get in return?" Parker's eyes were heavy, and she prickled with the heat Sydney was creating within her.

"To feel me make you surrender." Her touch was firm, her eyes intense. She slid her hand over Parker's breast and then along the curve of her stomach.

"Very sure of yourself, aren't you? We'll see." She had barely finished her sentence when a guttural moan escaped her throat in response to Sydney's hand claiming her at her core. Her fingernails glanced over Syd's back.

"I am. I'm even more sure that you need me to make you come." The words were hungry and insistent and, for Parker, incredibly accurate. Sydney moved her hair, exposing Parker's collarbone to Syd's teeth.

"Yes, please." Parker shifted abruptly and within moments felt the wave consume her. Parker recovered her focus and grinned at how pleased Syd looked with herself. Parker skimmed her teeth along Sydney's neck, and she exhaled hot breathy edicts near her ear.

"So, now I get to remind you how much you miss what I can do for you." The words were a reminder that her stronger, powerful girlfriend could be undone by her as much as the reverse was true.

"You know how I like that."

CHAPTER THREE

So, to what do we owe this midweek honor?" Lieutenant Mack Foster looked over the fresh salad and basket of garlic bread. "Real homemade food even. Something has to be wrong."

"That's what I said. There must be some sucking up scheduled in exchange for a high-stakes heist or a tear-jerking chick flick." Sydney pinched off a piece of the butter-sodden garlic bread just in time to receive a corrective smack on her arm from Parker. She feigned shock as she mischievously stepped out of reach and defiantly continued to chew.

Jenny rolled her eyes as she let Olivia Grace slip from her hip. "Could you try to have a little faith in us? We only ever want jewelry and foot rubs." Jenny looked over at Parker, who smiled at her.

"Actually, we really only want the foot rubs. They're a lot cheaper than jewelry anyway." Parker beamed at Sydney as Olivia crashed headfirst into Sydney's shins and raised her stubby arms over her head. "Sy-ee up!"

"You are ruthless, O.G." Sydney was clearly trying to look unfazed as she swung the child into her arms and nuzzled her neck, eliciting an eardrum-shattering squeal from the toddler.

Parker's heart swelled when she saw the child in Sydney's once reluctant arms. They didn't want children together, but Syd's tender side touched her heart every time.

"Didn't I forbid everyone from referring to my child as the Original Gangster? Uncle Allen is in so much trouble for starting that." Mack tried to look stern, but Parker knew she was overcome by the existence of their miracle baby, finally theirs after three tries and two heartbreaking losses.

"By the time she's old enough for it to matter, no one will remember who that was anyway; we're just old." Jenny snuggled into the circle of her wife's arms and kissed her. "And don't worry, I'll make sure she visits you in the home."

"Considering I only have two years on you, you might be right next to me." Mack swayed Jenny against her as they seemed to get lost in each other. Parker recalled Jenny clinging to Mack at a hospital not long ago and knew well the teasing was part of the strong bond they shared after Mack could easily have been taken away from their family.

They sat at the rarely used dining table in order to accommodate Olivia's highchair that clipped onto the tabletop next to Jenny's seat. Sydney passed the salad and looked expectantly at Parker as she began to eat.

"Okay, we're sitting. What's the story?" Syd chewed slowly as Parker began to formulate a strategy for the conversation.

"Well, Quint came into my office the other morning and asked a big favor. I told him I thought you would be fine with it, but then I got the RSVP list today, and suddenly, I'm not so sure." Parker's run-on sentence rushed out as she caught Jenny's eye, silently pleading for help.

"Invite list. So, I'm assuming, then, that the big favor is a function of some kind, am I correct? And we are having it here?" Syd took another bite of lettuce she had folded onto her fork.

"Yeah, sorry. I forgot to start there. We're just starting the renovation for the CTI expansion on the lake. Quint promised them a summer kick-off party at his house, but Brenda unexpectedly derailed it all with some big remodel that won't even be ready until late fall at the soonest. So, he asked me…us, if we could have it here, and Jenny and I could host."

Sydney looked amused.

"It would just be CTI people meeting DPI people and a couple of the key vendors and partners. Which," she stopped to take a new breath, "is where the iffy part comes in." Parker bit down on a rounded fingernail as Sydney grinned at her, obviously waiting for the punch line.

"Yes?" Sydney laid her fork on the plate and folded her arms, thoroughly enjoying the show.

"It seems that PRG is the advertising/PR firm doing CTI's rebranding, which means Richard and Allen would be invited..."

"As well as Dayne Grant, right?" Sydney shifted slightly as she processed the thought of Parker's ex-wife being inside her home. The first time Sydney met Dayne, she made a targeted play for Parker and proposed that she and Parker get back together.

"Right," Jenny piped up, obviously trying to slightly lessen the pressure Parker was feeling. A party was one thing; possibly dealing with Dayne's misbehavior was quite another.

Sydney picked up her fork and pierced a firm cherry tomato. "How many other guests do they expect?" She didn't look up from her plate.

"A hundred are invited, but it's unlikely that we'll have more than fifty actually show up. DPI will pay for everything, and he even offered a service to come clean the next day if we wanted... you wanted. But it's only two weeks away, so it will be a bit of a rush." Parker stared at Sydney, clearly trying to decipher Sydney's mood as she crunched contemplatively through her salad.

Syd carefully placed her fork on the plate and took a bite of bread, slowly swallowing before she spoke.

"So, let me get this straight." Her voice was stern, and she narrowed her eyes. "You want us to host a huge work party in our home and allow your arrogant ex-wife to come poke through our medicine cabinet and paw through your underwear drawer?" Syd winked covertly at Mack, catching the mischievous glint in her eye as Syd pretended she had significant concerns at the prospective evening. Jenny shifted her stare between Parker and Sydney nervously, as if expecting an angry eruption.

She started to speak as Sydney moved from her chair and walked over to Parker's. Mack started laughing when it was obvious Syd couldn't bite her tongue or fight the smile any longer. Syd kneeled in front of Parker, grinning.

"I have told you a million times that I'm not threatened by the woman who let you get away, Park." She held her fingers and kissed them lightly. "I was just teasing you. I couldn't care less if she is here. That is, unless you have renewed feelings for her, in which case I'll just have her taken out before the party. Problem solved."

Parker noticeably relaxed into her chair and tapped Sydney on the forehead with a scolding finger. "Not nice, you know. I really thought you were mad." Parker tilted her head onto Sydney's shoulder before kissing her cheek.

Sydney took Parker's face into her hands and looked at her seriously. "Name one time I've actually been mad at you in two years."

"Well, there was the time when I let a stranger into the building who turned out to be Becky."

"Doesn't count. I hadn't swept you off your feet yet." Syd tried to remain light when she thought of Becky Weaver holding a knife to Parker in an effort to get to Sydney.

"Good point. Then, I guess never." She brightened and stroked her fingers down Sydney's arm. "You sure this will be okay?"

"Certainly. As soon as you convince me that I won't find you groping her in the bathroom, we're all set." Sydney straightened and winked at Jenny, who stifled a laugh while Sydney sat back in her chair.

"Seriously, love? Just think of how many other *choices* I will have that night. Why eat the same dessert twice?" Parker teased Sydney, who knew she had it coming.

"Point taken. And it might just be the reason we finally get you that 'Property of Hyatt' tattoo on your forehead." Sydney winked while she corralled the final mouthful of salad onto her fork.

"You two are like a comedy team. If this business thing ever fails, you could always hit the road together." Mack shook her head and heaped pasta onto her plate, creating a tiny pile without sauce for Olivia.

"Bite your tongue, Foster. Parker isn't allowed to leave DPI until I do." Jenny poked at her wife before turning her attention to her daughter.

"You're just afraid of being the sole object of Frank's attention. At least he *pretends* to talk business with *me*." Parker rolled her eyes and rubbed her bare foot up Sydney's calf.

"Who is Frank?" Sydney looked at Jen, who was trying to corral an escaped noodle before it hit the floor under Olivia's chair.

"Ugh. Just a nerdy guy in sales. He can't hit on Parker overtly, so he pretends to talk to her about work and tells *me* about his female conquests because he thinks we're buddies or something. He can barely concentrate when she's in the room because he's staring at her boobs, and as soon as she walks away, his eyes are glued to her ass."

Jenny shook her head and cut another noodle for Olivia, who seemed to be more enthralled with squeezing the pasta between her fingers than eating it.

Sydney raised her eyebrow at Parker. "Maybe we need to schedule that tattoo sooner than we thought."

Parker smirked. "My dear, Frank Meyers is a tiny little man nearly half my age who has a better shot with *you* than he has ever had with me."

"Well, there goes my appetite." Sydney theatrically dropped her garlic toast onto her plate to a renewed round of laughter.

"Please be sure to identify him if he comes to the party. Syd and I can make a point to introduce ourselves." Mack smirked, catching her de facto partner's eye. They had worked together on several unofficial cases and had nearly been killed together in Sydney's rolling Porsche. The resulting bond was unbreakable.

"Oh, no. You two will probably make him wet his pants before his first cocktail." Parker wagged a finger at them. "He's harmless and a little sad, but he's no threat to either of you. Besides, Jenny is the only person he can look in the eye, so his staring at other people's body parts might just be a coincidence." Parker ducked as Jenny threw a balled-up napkin across the table at her.

"All that said, Jen and I will plan it over the next week and handle the final details on Thursday and Friday from here, if that's okay with you, love?"

Syd nodded as everyone began stacking their cleaned plates. "Sure." Syd lifted some dishes from the table. "Just tell me what I need to do."

"Be my bodyguard and grope me in the bathroom, of course," Parker said seriously as she walked into the kitchen.

"Finally. A job I'm completely qualified for. Score one for me." Syd snuck a kiss and returned to collect the remaining remnants of dinner.

Jenny kissed Olivia loudly on the cheek before scooping the cold pasta out of the corner of the highchair tray. Syd loaded the dishwasher and drained the remaining wine into Parker's glass.

"Thanks for dinner, and sorry for the mess the little gangster made." Jenny balanced Olivia on the island as Mack took a wet towel to her fingers and face.

"You are more than welcome always, you know that. Let's meet in the morning, and we can get started, okay?" Parker turned to hug Mack and nuzzled Olivia before they packed acres of baby things into their car and headed home.

She and Syd were finally alone together. "Thank you for being the best girlfriend and being understanding about what will happen to your place for forty-eight hours." Parker heaved herself onto the countertop and pulled Sydney to her with her legs.

"Park, this is *our* place. Why would you ask my opinion instead of just telling me how it's going to be?" Syd sifted her fingers through Parker's hair. Parker closed her eyes when Sydney began rubbing the tension from her neck.

"I guess the Dayne thing was the extra monkey wrench in it this time. I just didn't want you to feel like you had to say yes if it made you uncomfortable." Parker stroked Syd's arm.

"I promise to tell you when something makes me uncomfortable if you'll promise the same."

"Deal." Parker leaned against Syd and breathed in the scent of her skin. "I love you more than I ever thought possible."

"Best part of my day is when you tell me things like that. I love you." She wondered why Parker still couldn't think of this as their home. Syd thought the years of compulsive independence might take a few more years to completely unravel. She was willing to wait.

Chapter Four

Parker looked up from her desk and unexpectedly saw Syd's face. She grinned as she recalled the hours spent rolling around with her the night before.

"I don't believe you've ever been to this office during business hours, Ms. Hyatt." Parker stood and stepped from behind her desk.

Syd cocked a khaki-clad hip into the door frame and hooked the arm of her sunglasses into the collar of her casual black T-shirt.

"I thought you were running a successful business helping overworked legal professionals put away the bad guys." Parker regarded her curiously.

"Indeed I am. But I heard the love of my life works here, and I just needed to see her beautiful face." She winked playfully as Parker stood and moved around her desk.

"What is happening in here, may I ask?" Jenny appeared around the corner wearing plum-colored platform heels and a perfectly hued sheath to match. She snaked an arm around Sydney's waist and accepted a chaste kiss on her cheek. "You should train my wife to come visit me in the middle of the day, Syd."

"She wants to, Mrs. Foster, but she just can't trust herself to be restrained around you." Syd winked at her, locking her arms around Jenny.

"Dear heavens, you are a lucky girl, Park. The charm just leaks out everywhere." Jenny waved her hand over Syd's body and shook her head in mock resignation.

"Trust me, I know. It's dangerous, especially when you don't know what the ulterior motive is." Parker deposited a quick kiss on Sydney's mouth as she glanced down the executive hall behind them. She was careful to shield her personal life at the office, since she knew well that HR was subject to extra scrutiny. She didn't care who knew she was a lesbian, but she always avoided overt PDAs in the office.

Parker heard footsteps, and Jenny leaned back to see better down the hall. She gestured and mouthed "Frank" to Sydney, who didn't turn around.

Frank Meyers stood twisting the toe of his loafer against the grain of the carpet until Jenny released Syd and spun to greet the account executive.

"Afternoon, Frank. How are you?" Jenny said enthusiastically.

Sydney slowly pivoted to appraise her wife's biggest fan.

"Hi, Jenny. I just wondered if you have everything you need for my new employees. I'm getting backed up and hoped they would be able to start this week." He peered around Jenny, presumably to catch sight of Parker. "Hi, Parker. You look very nice today." He dropped his eyes to the floor before obviously skating them up Parker's body.

Syd glanced back at Parker, who returned a warning look at Syd before she replied.

"Thank you, Frank. I saw your new hires this morning with the two new accounting guys doing tax forms and getting the tour from Quint. So, you should—speak of the devil." Parker gestured behind him where Quint was leading the new employees. "Here they are now. Perfect timing."

Quint led a wiry man in his thirties wearing worn gray pants and a yellow oxford into the crowd. A younger, dark-complexioned man in a cheap suit followed closely behind. Two bookish and pale men over forty stood close to one another as if forming a shield in the face of suspected fire.

Jenny stepped forward to shake their hands. "How is your first day so far, everyone? It's quite an honor to get the tour from the CEO on your first day. I'm still waiting for mine." Jenny smiled broadly at Quint, who looked at her fondly.

"I'm just waiting for a break in my schedule, Jenny. I think 2022 will be your year." He laughed at the mock huff and Jenny's well-known inability to keep a straight face.

Parker stepped past Syd and welcomed them each to DPI. She knew Syd would bring Frank up later. Syd was protective of her to a fault, somehow charming and mildly suffocating at the same time.

Quint held a hand out toward Sydney. "How are you, Ms. Hyatt? I wanted to say thank you again for agreeing to host our little shindig. Very generous of you."

"Call me Syd, please, and you're very welcome. My pleasure." Sydney shook his hand and smiled. "Well, if you'll excuse me, I'm headed to Maclean for a meeting with the DA, so I should be prompt. Nice to see everyone." Syd hugged Parker and accepted a quick peck from Jenny, who headed back to her office with Frank in tow. The new employees followed in a single line behind him.

Quint walked with Syd to the elevator, seemingly relieved to relinquish his tour guide duties. Syd glanced back at Parker before Quint began quizzing her about how she recreated crime scenes for juries and prosecutors trying a case. He seemed genuinely fascinated, and Sydney offered him a private look inside the DRIFT studios before the party.

Parker took stock of the visit and decided to be happy she'd missed her enough to stop by instead of wondering if she just wanted to be sure Parker was where she said she would be. She reasoned that Syd's concern wasn't about her potential infidelity but an undeniable need to make sure she was safe. And she couldn't fault her for that.

CHAPTER FIVE

Parker felt as if she'd spent twenty-four hours pointing and adjusting and shifting the entire contents of the loft. She stashed a myriad of precious knickknacks and personal photos into boxes to accommodate a makeshift bar and multiple surfaces for hors d'oeuvres, petit fours, and an ice sculpture boasting the CTI logo that Brenda Davidson had insisted on. Parker tended toward the understated where Brenda liked to scream things just a bit too loudly for Parker's taste.

Jenny plodded into the living room wearing only a camisole, cotton shorts, and a scowl. "I need help. Mack won't be back from dropping Olivia for an hour, and I don't think I packed the right outfit. I'm panicking."

"Well, Frank will love you just as you are, Jen." Parker laughed as Jenny stomped her foot. She huffed and turned back toward the bedroom just in time to smack into Sydney as she was buttoning a white Lanvin shirt.

Jen gasped at Sydney, who lost hold of a cufflink. "I'm so sorry, Syd. I didn't see you!" Jenny scrambled to pick up the platinum lightning bolt that skittered across the old concrete floor. She retrieved it and appraised the item that matched Parker's necklace.

She turned to Parker with a smile. "I take it these are from you, Park? Nice job." She placed it in Syd's palm. "You two are so damn cute together, it's almost nauseating. Parker, I need your closet before I have a meltdown." She shifted focus again.

"All yours, Jen. You'll be beautiful as always," Parker called after her, running a finger over the charm at her neck that reminded her of their journey and what Sydney meant to her. She stepped over to take the cufflink Sydney held and attached it to her right sleeve.

"I love you." She whispered the words as she felt Syd's arms stretch around her, holding her tightly. She closed her eyes and recognized the ever-present butterflies in her stomach.

"I love you, too. You'll be fabulous tonight, as always." Syd nipped at her bottom lip before she kissed her gently.

For the moment, Parker forgot her hosting duties and allowed herself to get lost in Syd's arms, grateful for the temporary distraction. After a few deep breaths, she straightened and stepped back, snapping once again into hostess mode.

"Did you see the *ice sculpture*? Take pictures this evening because I can assure you there will *never* be another one of those in here." She shook her head and dragged herself away as she went to finish her makeup. "Unless, of course, your new girlfriend gets one."

"Since there will never be one of those, I think we're safe to assume this will be the last ice sculpture," Syd called after her as she walked down the hall. Since Jenny and Mack had agreed to stay over, Parker was grateful she and Syd wouldn't be left to entertain any stragglers alone.

Within a half hour, Jenny seemed to have recovered her calm when she whirled into the kitchen in her straight black skirt matched with a robin's egg blue blouse she had snagged from Parker's closet. She had swept her blond hair into a deconstructed ponytail and donned long teardrop earrings. Her ubiquitous heels finished off the look as she twirled in front of them.

"Very nice, Jen. You threw that together fast." Parker smiled.

"I'm going shopping in your closet more often! You're not so bad yourself. Where did you get that?" Jenny turned Parker to get a better look at her gunmetal gray suit in raw silk. "Very fancy."

"Syd went shopping the last time she went to New York and surprised me with it." Parker watched Syd answer the door for a member of the catering staff, and her pulse raced.

"You're a lucky girl, but then, so is Sydney." Jenny hugged her best friend and switched gears. "So! I've put our overnight bags in the closet and tidied up the spare room in case you get any wanderers. Besides, I don't want Dayne going through *my* underwear." She laughed, and Parker stuck out her tongue in reply.

"Seriously, where are we, what's happening, what can I do?" Jenny adopted work mode.

Over Jenny's shoulder, Parker saw Mack in charcoal pants and a lighter gray silk shirt tap shoulders with Sydney, who was lugging a full tub of beer. Parker nudged Jenny. "Go kiss your wife, and then get a glass of wine. The show starts in ten."

Brenda Davidson was the first to arrive, sweeping into the loft in a form-fitting red sundress and kitten heels. Quint followed behind in a tight black suit that might have been more appropriate on him if he were a few decades younger. Brenda bought all his clothes and repeatedly tried to outfit him like a GQ model, which made him look as if he tried too hard, when in fact, he didn't try at all.

Brenda turned in the sweeping foyer and openly appraised the twenty-five-foot ceilings in the vaulted space. Syd explained the history of the Meridian Street Warehouses, which had been repurposed from old industrial units to live-work condos. Despite the conversion, they had kept the basic integrity of the structures, which impressed many a guest.

"These are fabulous! I love what you've done with the décor." Brenda flattered Sydney, who nodded a polite thank you. Parker heard her say that the best part of living in the warehouses was that she'd met Parker there. Syd spoke to Brenda as if she was the most important person in the room. She could coolly finesse any situation if she so desired, an attribute Parker had always found sexy. Parker recalled that Sydney's talents had worked on her when she bought the unit across the hall. She now rented it to their friend Mia Wright, but it would always be the catalyst that brought them together, and it made this building that much more special. It felt like home; Syd felt like home.

Syd led the Davidsons on a brief tour. Parker shot her a withering look when she heard her speaking enthusiastically to Brenda. "Parker was just mentioning what a stroke of genius the ice sculpture was. She couldn't stop talking about how much she liked it."

"Ass," Parker mouthed and shook her head. Syd shot her a grin behind Brenda's back.

Within the hour, the loft had swelled to capacity as sixty-five guests dined on tasty amuse-bouche delivered on silver trays by traditionally uniformed waiters. Parker hadn't stopped greeting and hosting from the kitchen for even a moment while Jenny worked the door, introducing strangers to each other before sending them off toward the bar or a food station.

Parker glanced up at the office loft and saw several of the wall screens now bright with crime scene photos. Quint looked spellbound as Syd played one of the reconstruction videos Parker recognized from a case Mack had worked with her last year.

Parker turned from the kitchen just in time to see Dayne sweep into the foyer in her signature black Armani with Julie Thomas—the woman Parker had found Dayne on top of on their anniversary—tightly clinging to her elbow. Her eyes darted around the room, and Dayne seemed to pull away, perhaps trying to lessen Julie's grip. Jenny offered a gracious greeting and pointed them toward the back corner for a drink before she spun around as if to evaluate Parker's reaction.

Parker lifted a large glass of wine and gave her a knowing smirk. She mouthed, "It's fine," to Jenny when she looked mildly concerned. Parker turned away and suddenly found herself cornered by Frank Meyers in a too-shiny gray suit and a melon colored T-shirt. She tried not to conjure *Miami Vice* images as she spoke to him.

"Well, hello, Frank. Where did you come from all of a sudden?" Parker purposefully walked him backward to remove herself from the tight space behind the island, arriving at the bottom of the loft stairs in full view of everyone else.

"Oh, I haven't been here long. I just wanted to tell you that you look gorgeous, Parker."

The nervous tone in his voice made Parker feel a bit sorry for the awkward man who tried so hard to sound cool and confident despite never quite managing it.

"That's very kind of you, Frank. Perhaps there will be some new people you can meet here tonight." She hoped her encouragement sounded positive instead of dismissive.

"Actually, I already have my eye on a really pretty girl with long blond hair standing by the bar."

Parker stepped around him to see the girl Frank had set his sights on. She arrived at the curvy figure of Sydney's ex, Darcy, now the manager of the Silver Lake Crime Lab. She was also the girlfriend of CTI's operations manager and very much a lesbian. Poor Frank seemed to be attracted to women he definitely had no chance with.

"Ooh, Frank. I'm sorry, but Darcy is already spoken for. You know Taylor Westin from CTI, right?" He nodded and looked momentarily crestfallen. "That's her partner, Darcy Dean." As if privy to the conversation, Darcy threaded her fingers through Taylor's and leaned into her.

"Oh well, it wasn't like I have time for a long-term thing anyway." He attempted to scramble up some bravado as he touched her arm. "I'll just have to wait until someone nice like you comes along."

Parker heard heavy footfalls on the black metal steps behind them and felt Sydney's presence before she saw her.

"Hello, Frank, I met you the other day at the office." Syd spoke a little too sternly as she reached out to shake his hand. "I'm Sydney Hyatt."

Mack stood close behind her as Quint Davidson rushed down past them to greet the newcomers he had been neglecting in favor of marveling at Syd's computer toys. Frank offered Sydney his hand, and Parker watched his entire body move with the force of it.

"And this is Lieutenant Foster."

Parker paused and looked carefully at the duo. Sydney never introduced Mack that way in social situations. Equally amusing was the fact that Mack didn't offer her first name as she took her turn to shake Frank's hand. "Jenny Foster is my wife."

"Okay. Nice to meet you. Well, I guess I should mingle." Frank backed away and rushed off to be swallowed by the crowd. Sydney traded knowing looks with Mack.

Parker folded her arms across her chest. "Shall I get out the rulers for the dick-measuring contest later?" She scolded them in a harsh whisper.

"Nah, we don't want to embarrass everyone else, Park." Mack tried to look serious when Sydney stifled a laugh and turned to Parker.

"Don't be mad, Park. He just needed to know you weren't available." She slid her palm down Parker's back. "Now, we'll go charm our guests, and I'll keep my euphemistic appendage in my pants, I promise." She squeezed Parker's waist for just a second before she and Mack moved into the crowd. Parker reminded herself to tell Jenny the episode she'd missed and would have thoroughly enjoyed.

Within minutes, Frank entered the kitchen, quickly followed by a harried Jenny and new hire Ben Barrett, who was carrying a small glass of club soda.

"What happened?" Parker asked when Jenny held Ben's sleeve aloft.

"Apparently, Ben stood too close to a meatball-wielding

woman and ended up wearing it on his shirt." Jenny guided him toward the sink and dipped a bar towel in the cup. Ben looked awkward as Jenny worked the soaked fabric under the faucet.

"How are you enjoying yourself otherwise, Ben? Are you managing to meet some people?" Parker watched him straighten and take a deep breath as if pleased to have a new topic.

"Yes, ma'am. It's a little overwhelming, but it's a great party." He seemed to relax as Jenny unhanded him only to reach back and take another shot at the faint legacy of barbecue sauce still marring his broadcloth dress shirt. "It helps that Chris is new, too."

Chris lingered behind the trio with a can of ginger ale wrapped inside a meticulously folded napkin. "Nothing from the bar tonight, Chris?" Sydney asked as she strolled in.

"No, I don't drink. My church forbids the consumption of alcohol, sir." He choked out a quick correction. "I mean ma'am, sorry."

"No worries. You certainly aren't the first." Sydney sipped her scotch and smiled at the rigid, timid man Parker was fairly sure would be swallowed up by the Washington DC area construction business in short order. She watched the crowd in amusement before one of the waiters brushed past her and rushed into the kitchen.

"Miss Jenny, I'm sorry, but I think the blenders blew a fuse. Maybe if you have a surge protector, we can stop it from happening again."

Jenny smiled at him. "Sounds like a good idea, Adam. Syd, can we use the one in our room? I think there's only a lamp plugged into it."

"I'm on it." Syd turned and headed to the spare room for the item with Adam following close behind.

"Hey, Adam," Jenny called after the retreating duo. "How about just one blender at a time from now on, just in case?" He smiled and nodded as he walked more quickly to catch Syd.

"Why am I here again?" Parker smiled at her when Jenny

sent Ben and Chris back to the living room. "I really should have gone for a massage and a pedicure tonight." She glanced idly at her toes. "You're a one-woman machine, and I feel like window dressing."

"Bite your tongue; I could never do this without you." Jenny smiled at her.

Eddie Mayhew, the accounting manager, led his two new hires into the kitchen; neither seemed to have any problem with alcohol consumption. Randy and Steve each held huge daiquiris in warring hues of melon and fuchsia. Parker surmised that perhaps the drinks were what had put the 1940s electricity on the fritz. The new employees hadn't really needed to meet the CTI management, but Parker thought it was a nice way to bring them on board and let them get to know everyone.

Parker and Jenny engaged them in idle chatter before Parker managed to extricate them from the conversation in favor of a new tray of hors d'oeuvres.

Jenny's voice was barely above a whisper as she looked past Parker and toward the hallway. "That looks like a dangerous combination."

Parker followed her stare and saw Syd in quiet conversation with Dayne. Parker watched them sip their drinks.

"Well, maybe this is the bridge to harmony." Parker tried not to sound dramatic as she watched her girlfriend and her ex-wife carefully.

"From your lips…" Jenny left to resume her front door post. Parker swept abandoned cups and plates into the bin before turning to see Dayne walking toward her.

"Hey, Princess!" She smiled broadly and offered a casual side hug.

"Dayne, it's probably better if we avoid old nicknames, okay?" She didn't like it much when Darcy called Sydney by a long-ago nickname, so she couldn't imagine Sydney would appreciate the converse.

"Sorry, you're right. Julie might not think much of it either."

She stepped back and swept her eyes over Parker. "You look really happy, and this place is awesome. Sydney mentioned you're officially living together now? I'm really happy for you, Park." Dayne was rarely sincere unless it suited her purposes. but Parker almost believed her ex-wife actually meant it this time.

"Shall I assume you and Julie are in a good place, too?" Parker watched Dayne's face warily. She had spent ten years learning to spot her ex-wife's lies; she just hadn't been very good at figuring them out *before* the blade had landed in her back. She had sharpened her skills since then.

"We are. It's pretty relaxed; nothing permanent for a while. I'm still getting over the love of my life, you know." Dayne gave her the look that used to win Parker over every time.

Parker nearly pointed out that the so-called love of her life had caught her straddling Julie on the afternoon of their tenth anniversary, but she decided to change the subject instead.

"So, are you heading up the CTI campaign with Richard?" She hadn't spoken to her best friends Allen and Richard since they arrived hours ago, but she had seen Brenda speaking intensely to Allen while Richard was obligated to glad-hand the crowd on behalf of PRG.

"Nope, this one's all Richard; the boss just wanted a good showing for tonight, and I figured this is the only way *I'd* get an invite to Sydney Hyatt's house."

Parker laughed at the very true statement and caught Sydney out of the corner of her eye moving around the loft above them. "Well, I suppose we should head into the crowd. I don't think I've made it out of the kitchen all night." She tossed a dish towel over the edge of the sink.

Parker twitched involuntarily when Dayne suddenly placed her hand over her lower back. Parker deliberately walked ahead of her until she was out of her reach. Dayne was swallowed by the crowd, and Parker steered toward Allen, who was still being held hostage by an enthusiastic Brenda.

"Hi, Biscuit." Parker tapped a kiss on his cheek when he

smiled at his old nickname. Parker had coined it as he chased his Bichon Frise through the streets in their apartment complex waving dog treats. He hugged her enthusiastically.

"Brenda and I have just been discussing the crushed velvet French maid wallpaper she's putting up in her new powder room; doesn't that sound just *delicious?*" His grin bordered on manic, and Parker fought to stifle a laugh.

"Wow, Allen. And you've been looking for new ideas at *your* house, too. It sounds like this was fate." Allen's face was beet red, nearly matching his bowtie and signature red high-tops he wore with his cream linen suit. Sweat beaded on his face. and he dabbed an olive-green cocktail napkin over his skin.

Brenda was clearly delighted by the concept and squeezed his hands in hers. "You call me anytime, and we'll do a day at the design store." She kissed both his flushed cheeks and glided away to speak with an arriving executive from CTI.

Allen wordlessly guided her to the bedroom and shut the door. The empty room was cool and blissfully quiet.

"French maids? Really?" Allen flopped back on the bed and let the breeze from the ceiling fan brush over his flushed skin.

"I'm assuming you know the ice monstrosity out there was her idea, too." Parker sighed and tilted her face to the breeze.

"No kidding. If you copped to ordering that, we would have to break up."

"I would deserve nothing less." Parker joined him on the bed.

"So, how does it feel having your ex-wife and her wonder mistress in your house?" He giggled as Parker tried to relax against the pillow without wrinkling her skirt.

"Not bad, I guess. She and Syd were having some convo in the hallway, so I can't wait to get the scoop on that." She looked at the nightstand clock and groaned. "It's already ten; maybe everyone will start to head home." A wave of fatigue washed over her.

"Um, free booze and too much really fabulous food? You might be in for a late one, Park."

They both jumped as the door opened, and Sydney stood at the threshold. She looked relieved when she saw Parker. "Hey, baby. I just thought something might be wrong. You okay?"

Allen launched himself off the bed and gently patted Sydney's shoulder. "She's tired and antisocial. She's all yours." He spun out of the room on a cloud of renewed energy, and Parker fell backward, caring much less about potential wrinkles.

Syd clicked the door shut and reclined to pull Parker against her. "Want me to chase everyone out, and you can help me melt the ice sculpture?" Sydney held the hair off Parker's neck, letting the air from the fan hit her skin.

"You mean the damn thing isn't slush yet?" She closed her eyes and audibly breathed in Syd's cologne. "By the way, you are entirely gorgeous, in case I forgot to tell you."

"You could be accused of being significantly biased, but thank you." Syd dropped her hair and smoothed it over her back. "How about we do one more round together? The group is starting to thin. I heard your gentleman caller tell Jen he was taking the new guys out to score some women. And yes, that's a direct quote."

Parker grimaced. "There was so much wrong with what you just said; I don't know where to begin." Parker chuckled wearily into Syd's neck before allowing herself to be pulled to her feet. Sydney leaned in for an excruciatingly slow kiss until Parker moaned gratefully, grasping at her shirt.

"Meet me back here in an hour. I have something for you." Syd propelled Parker gently into the hall and the melee.

To Parker's delight, the caterers had begun loading equipment onto a flat cart headed toward the exit.

"Just found out that the caterers were only contracted until ten thirty. I think the end might be near," Jenny reported, looking as if she was done in, too.

"I might just do the happy dance in a minute," Parker said as Allen waved and blew kisses from the center of an exiting crowd that included Darcy and Dayne. Chris Newkirk waited alone on a barstool while Frank, Randy, and Steve appeared to be plotting their night. Ben looked on inattentively from the edge of the conversation.

By eleven thirty, every last body was gone, and the hum of the evening started to defuse. Jenny leaned back into Mack's shoulder and was swept into her arms. "I haven't touched you once in many hours, Mrs. Foster. I plan to remedy that now." Jenny laughed and reclined limply in Mack's arms.

"I'm too tired to resist; you may have your way with me, Lieutenant." She gestured grandly as she was led through the open door to the spare bedroom, her shoes dangling limply from her fingers.

"Good night, guys," Syd called before steering Parker down the hall.

"Syd, shouldn't we clean up a bit?"

Syd shook her head, and Parker didn't argue. Sydney opened the bedroom door, and it snicked quietly shut behind her. Parker shuffled immediately to the walk-in closet and kicked her gray pumps into a corner of the floor. She skimmed the suit jacket down her arms and released the catch on the skirt.

Sydney closed in behind her and tilted Parker's face to hers. She began teasing the skin at her throat with her teeth, leaving trails of goose bumps in her wake. A shiver rushed up Parker's spine when Syd relieved her of the rest of her clothes. The moves were swift, and Parker was left in only her bra and underwear.

"This could be very dangerous in my present delirious state, my love." Parker's voice was breathy and weak as she responded to the touch of the only woman who had ever made her melt in seconds.

Wordlessly, Sydney slid her bra straps from her shoulders and shifted her nearly naked body to the floor, continuing to nip sensitive paths that burned into Parker's skin. Parker arched against her as she watched Sydney's gray eyes turn black with desire.

"God, Syd, I..." Parker's words were quelled by Syd's insistent mouth pressing roughly onto hers.

"I need you. Now."

Sydney's words tore through Parker as Sydney dragged the lacy G-string from her hips. Parker succumbed to the cresting waves rushing at her, threatening to overtake her without so much as another touch.

"God, love, this is going to be so fast. You're making me crazy."

"No, baby. Slow." Syd's deep voice was thick with need. "Not until I say. I need to touch every part of you." Syd skidded her teeth over the pebbled point of Parker's breast, capturing the other between her fingertips. Parker cried against the splinters of impending ecstasy she couldn't staunch.

"Syd, I can't. Please, I need to feel you."

Sydney raked her fingers slowly from her chest, gliding her hand toward Parker's hips. She glanced over her hard center, stilling her thumb before continuing her maddening manipulations. Parker ached to feel more and thrust harder against her.

Syd continued to tease her, to scrape her teeth along Parker's throat, slowing her touch every time Parker neared her punishing edge. Parker felt Sydney respond with renewed command when Parker's flaring rhythms multiplied in response to Sydney's direction. Syd surged against her, suddenly plunging harder into her and over the searing swells of need. Syd pressed her lips against Parker's ear. Parker could always be impaled by her words, compelled by her voice. She closed her eyes against the firing sensations.

"Look at me."

Parker struggled to focus. She breathed heavily against her imminent surrender as Syd pushed her nearer and nearer to her all-consuming edge. Parker was shocked by the powerful sensations that began to rock over her, causing her breath to catch as she gripped Syd's skin, soundly biting her neck in a primal answer.

"Right there, baby." Sydney's words were fierce and commanding. Syd was visibly shaken as her own orgasm clearly took her by surprise. Parker felt her surge past her edge when her teeth again found the sensitive skin behind Syd's ear.

"Fuck." Sydney's mouth swallowed their moans as the quaking sensations ripped raggedly at them both. "Now. With me. Now."

"Don't let go, Sydney, please." She knew Sydney waited for the sating words she couldn't help but issue each time they found themselves feeding their mutual addiction. Parker breathed unevenly until the spell of the hungry moment waned. She watched Sydney silently war against some invisible force as her eyes struggled to focus on Parker's face. She closed them instead. Parker drew a line down her cheekbone and over her shoulder.

"I think I might have bitten you." Parker grinned sheepishly as she tried to locate evidence of the offense.

"I think I might have liked it just a little." Sydney dropped her head onto Parker's chest again as a shudder washed over her hot skin. Syd kissed the place under her lips.

"So, do you want to tell me what that was about?" Parker lifted Syd's face and brushed her lips against Sydney's softly. "Don't get me wrong, I'm not complaining in any way because it was hot as hell." She again eased her mouth over Sydney's, still immersed in the lingering intensity that hung heavily between them. "I just know you, and that wasn't your normal MO, sweetheart."

Sydney shifted Parker against her, cradling her body and pressing her mouth into Parker's mussed hair. "I just don't want to ever forget who we are. Why we are. I know we joke about being each other's property and things like that, but you *are* mine, *only* mine."

Sydney's fingers pressed deeply into Parker's back, and jagged air escaped her lips.

Parker pulled tighter into the embrace and searched Syd's face, attempting to gather clues. "Of course I am. What did I miss, love?" Parker was suddenly anxious to connect at the place where Sydney had traveled. "Tell me, please."

"Nothing, baby. I just think how beautiful you are and how many people could imagine themselves in my place. Just tonight…Dayne and this Frank guy. I watched Dayne touch you in the kitchen, and I could feel it…here." She tapped a fist to her chest. "Literally feel it. I just need to know that you have what you need from me."

Parker looked incredulous, and she locked her eyes on to Syd's. "Sydney Hyatt, you are my life. I would give up anything I have, *everything* I have, before I could be without you. Don't you know that by now?" Her words were replicated by her desperate grip of Sydney's crumpled shirt.

Syd shook her head. "I know that. I'm being stupid, I guess." She forced her eyes to refocus on Parker and brushed a tender kiss over her mouth. "I love you like a crazy person, and I've nearly lost you twice in two years. I guess I get scared that if I'm not paying attention, something could take you away from me. Then, apparently, I turn into a raging lunatic that devours you in the closet at midnight. Do you forgive me?"

Parker offered her a peaceful smile. "What exactly should I forgive you for? Loving me in a way people would trade their souls for? Or ravishing me in a way I never thought was possible before you crashed into my life?" Parker leaned back against the wall and pulled at Sydney to compel her to shift with her. "I'm fascinated by you every day. I just *see* you, and you make me melt. Syd, I honestly walk into a room with you, and I feel like the princess in a fairy tale."

"Even when I need to possess you and consume you at the same time for no logical reason whatsoever?" Sydney stroked Parker's calf.

"Yes, especially then. You look at me, every day, like I'm made of gold. I know every part of you. You only came for me two years ago, but I've known you forever." Syd relaxed against her as she spoke. "I know that sounds ridiculously clichéd, but I believe it's true."

"Someone screwed up somewhere because I don't deserve you." Syd's smile accompanied a wink as she turned to hold Parker to her again. "But I'll never let you go."

"Better not," Parker whispered. "Now, do you also want to tell me what you were thinking when you practically broke down the door in here tonight?"

Syd pressed a delicate kiss over Parker's throat and fought an involuntary wince. "Shall I assume from the question that you won't accept that I was just worried that you might be sick or something?" Syd squeezed her eyes shut and tilted her forehead against Parker's shoulder in an attempt to shield her embarrassment at the impending revelation.

"You assume correctly, my love." She teased her fingers through Syd's black hair and waited quietly.

"Um. It could have been possible that I saw you walk out of the kitchen with Dayne's hand on you, and when I came down to look for you, the door to the bedroom was closed, and I momentarily went blind and deaf and irrational and…"

Parker pressed a finger over her mouth and stemmed the rushing tide of words escaping from Sydney's lips. She framed Sydney's face and drew a thumb across her clenched jaw. "So, what you're saying is that you thought that I gave up the most amazing thing I have ever had so I could risk being devastated again by a woman I don't even like anymore, in our bedroom, thirty feet from where I knew you were?"

Syd recognized a familiar sadness that she was anxious to banish. "Something like that…"

"And you know me better than that, as well." Parker smiled and at once lightened the mood that cloaked Sydney's emotions. "What did you two talk about tonight, anyway?"

"Actually, she just thanked me, us, for inviting her here. She said she wanted me to know that she was very happy with Julie and that she was sorry for trying to drag you back to her at New Year's…you know, nothing I actually *believed* or anything, but she gave it a shot." Sydney smiled and pulled Parker over to lie on top of her.

"You know, I'm still hopelessly naked, and you're wearing far too many clothes." Parker kissed a path from her shoulder to her ear, worrying at the few buttons that held Syd's shirt closed. "I would like to show you how much I love you on our very soft mattress. What do you think?"

"I think I can't wait." Sydney pushed herself up from the floor and pulled Parker to her feet. Parker helped her shed the rest of her clothes and joined her in the cool sheets before she slid her mouth between Sydney's thighs.

CHAPTER SIX

Morning, sweeties. Sleep well?" Parker shuffled into the kitchen to find Mack poking through a sad leftover fruit tray while Jen hunched over what appeared to be life-renewing coffee.

"Actually, I was accosted repeatedly by my wife, so I had little sleep," Mack grumbled into the bowl of fruit and popped a red grape theatrically between her lips.

"Sounds devastating." Syd smirked as she poured coffee into a mug and flipped the power switch on the tea kettle. "Luckily, we dropped off as soon as our heads hit the pillow."

"I call bullshit." Jenny's indelicate growl seeped from beneath the curtain of tousled hair that fell across her sleepy visage. "I went to the bathroom twice, and I believe I heard lusty noises coming from your room both times."

"Voyeur." Parker folded around Sydney, who was more than grateful for the reassuring embrace.

Jenny took another sip of her coffee and slid a small, sealed envelope across the island to Parker, who looked at her inquisitively.

"Shouldn't you be sending thank-you notes to Mack?" Parker slid a finger under the flap.

"Found it in the bathroom. It's addressed to the Lady of the House, so I suppose it's a toss-up, but I thought I had a better shot with you, Park." Jenny's eyes were becoming clearer as she looked imploringly at Sydney and skated her empty mug across the polished stone countertop.

Syd refilled her cup and watched as Parker opened the mysterious envelope. A fold of faux parchment held a short, handwritten note in an untidy hand:

To my exquisite hostess:
A precious time, a lovely night
A gorgeous girl, a ray of light
Thank you for your help and fun
All the world knows you're the one.

Parker read the words aloud before gesturing with the paper. "I have to admit it's a little creepy, but I'm sure someone's just trying to be nice."

"Maybe Frank finally wants to see something other than your boobs." Jenny poked at Parker, who chucked the note on the counter.

"Very funny." She glanced up at Syd, who felt surprisingly sedate.

"What can I say, you're adored by millions. Of course, if I find out who wrote this, I'll be forced to remove his very non-euphemistic appendage from his body." Sydney's words were light, and she allowed the shadow of concern to pass quickly.

"Of course you will, love. I would be insulted if you didn't defend my honor in such a subtle and refined way." Parker smiled at Sydney, reconnecting at the place they'd found each other just a few hours ago.

By the time the cleaning crew arrived, Parker had repacked a variety of leftovers into to-go boxes for Mack and Jen and helped them load their bags into the car. Jenny waved enthusiastically as her wife backed their Murano onto Meridian Street headed to pick up Olivia.

Sydney threaded her fingers through Parker's and dusted a kiss over her temple. "What do you think about a walk?"

"I think I like the way you think." The morning was still quiet, and the cloying heat and accompanying humidity still hovered a few hours away.

"Thank you for last night. I guess I lost it a little bit." Syd slid her lips over Parker's hand as they walked across the grassy hill outside the loft.

"Sweetheart, you didn't lose anything. I wish I could make you feel half as desired and needed as you make me feel. I love you for that."

"You make me feel like a god somehow. You're my everything, always." She looped her arm around Parker's shoulder. "Now, let's talk about your secret admirer." Sydney still seemed relatively undisturbed by the note. "Do you think it could be Dayne?"

Parker chuckled at the vision of her ex-wife creating something not offered on designer-laden pages in some overpriced catalog.

"Love, Dayne couldn't write poetry...even bad poetry like that, with a how-to manual and a gun to her head."

"Well, there's an interesting thought." Syd's sarcastic comment received a scolding nudge from Parker. "What about Frankie Farmer?"

"Maybe someone has a crush on *you*, my love. Remember, I can still recall women lining up for you at the Pride." Parker prodded at Syd's womanizing past.

"*Lady of the house, gorgeous girl*, remember? People have called me a lot of things, but there is no way you can push this off on me, and you know it."

"Okay. You're right. Let's chalk it up to too much free liquor and talk about our very lazy day on the couch watching bad movies while you rub my feet."

"I like the way you think. Will there be cake, too?" Sydney tickled Parker from behind and gave chase when she squirmed away.

"Play your cards right, Hyatt, and I'll give you anything you want." Parker had never meant anything more completely.

Mia was in the lobby when Sydney rushed a laughing Parker through the door of the building.

"Hi, Mia. Want to come in for some coffee?" Parker pulled her into a brief hug and led them into the loft. "We missed seeing you last night."

"I came by, but there were so many people, I decided to leave. I guess I wasn't really up for a crowd, so I didn't stay long."

"Sorry, we didn't see you. I totally understand, believe me. I had to fight the urge to come hang with you at your place. Sorry we didn't notice you come in." Sydney issued a casual squeeze and directed Mia to the kitchen.

"You're always welcome, you know," Mia said. "You both are; I mean, it is your place, technically."

"Nope, it's your home, Mia." Parker appraised their friend carefully, knowing the journey to process Sandy's death had been a rough one. "I hope it feels like it."

"Getting there. Sandy is with me every second, but it feels like this is where I'm supposed to be."

After Parker put on a movie, Mia finally settled onto the couch with her coffee, and Parker wondered if she ever thought of her girlfriend without being reminded of the fact that a criminal's bullet took her away. She seemed to relax and perhaps, for a moment, not fight against the memories of her former life. Parker stretched out on the sofa and eventually felt Sydney doze off beside her, and it wasn't long before her own eyes closed. When the movie ended, Parker felt Mia drop a blanket over their legs and slide out quietly.

CHAPTER SEVEN

Parker spent Tuesday afternoon plowing through work that had been put to the side in the wake of the party and tackling the next major projects on her list. She packed blueprints and sample books onto a cart and prepared to drag them to her car.

Jenny stopped outside her office carrying a huge bouquet of white lilies.

"Wow, Jen, what did *you* do after you left our house this weekend?" Parker tucked her nose into the fragrant bouquet and savored the perfume as it floated around her.

"More like what did *you* do? Mack knows better than to drop two hundred bucks on *your* favorite flowers. Sydney, however, follows no such rules. Nice job at whatever it was." Jenny plucked the card from the plastic fork and handed it to her before she carried the vase into Parker's office.

Beautiful like a flower

The simple, typewritten note had been entered on the florist's generic, all-occasion card and addressed simply to Davidson Properties–Human Resources. She took another moment to admire the bouquet before checking her watch and hurrying down to the parking lot. She had finished loading her car and pulled into traffic before making a call Sydney. She heard her voice mail pick up as she remembered that Syd had another meeting in Maclean.

"Hi, my love. Thank you. I adore you. I'm headed to CTI, see you tonight."

At the future CTI Sales Building, Parker traded her heels for a more sensible pair of boots and began trudging over the muddy approach to the jobsite. A roll of blueprints tucked under one arm, she carried the hair-smashing hard hat she loathed under the other.

Terry Carver was leaning over a makeshift plywood desk and drawing exaggerated circles with a red pencil. The cacophony of distant saws and drills told her that the demo for the retrofit project was well on its way.

"Looking good, Terry." Parker took in the nearly cleared space that would eventually house CacheTech's sales and marketing departments.

"Getting there. Demo's always the easy part. I do have a question for you while you're here." He tapped his red pencil on the papers in front of him. "The plans call for an open conference room in the back, but I have two support columns in the middle here." He pointed to two dotted squares on the print. "If we have to jack in an I-beam over that kind of expanse to carry the load, it's going to add thousands to this job, not to mention delay us a few weeks."

Parker placed her armload of work documents onto the table and reluctantly set the hard hat over her hair. "Why don't you show me, and then tell me what our options are?"

She followed him down a lengthy hall and back to the corner of the aging building. Sheetrock dust painted her once black pants with clouds of white chalk. The building was one of the first in the business park built in the late 1980s, so it had a long way to go before it melded with the modern style of the neighboring CTI headquarters tower. The location had been too convenient to pass up, so the company spent the money to do the retrofit before someone else snatched up the premium real estate. As they rounded the corner, Parker saw the reason for Terry's concern.

"I've already ordered a twenty-two-foot table, Terry. If we tried to put it in here right now, we would hit that column dead center." She turned and eyed the adjoining spaces that were already open. "Why can't we flip it and use the other corner for my conference room and keep this for the offices?" She finished the question as a jackhammer began on the floor above them.

Terry leaned closer and yelled, "Because you're the only person who can sweet-talk that snotty architect into being redirected. Since there's already a beam on that side, it's a completely logical option."

Terry smiled ruefully, reminding Parker of the tumultuous relationship the foreman and the architect had forged over many years of projects.

"Well, if you're asking me to talk to him, I will. Otherwise, it will be impossible to accommodate what CTI wants. Apparently, these weren't noted correctly on the as-builts, so we have no choice but to make a change."

"Make sure the change order comes from him and not my side," Terry said emphatically, still yelling to be heard over the din.

"I'll handle him, Terry. He's not that bad."

The jackhammer quieted, allowing for Terry's reply at a normal volume, but his tone remained flat. "Yes, he is." He managed a smile, conveying that he would try to be malleable in the face of an anticipated battle.

Parker heard a deafening roar engulf the building before vibrations from crumbling rock and crunching metal sent clouds of dust and rubble raining over the first floor.

Terry grabbed Parker's arm and curved over her, moving them into the support of a doorway. A terrifying avalanche of debris fell around them, engulfing the space in a cloud of white. Parker folded her arms into her chest in an unconscious effort to make herself a smaller target and crouched in the corner Terry had forced her into.

She felt a heavy thud at her shoulder. A chunk of concrete smashed into Terry's cheek as he attempted to shield them, and though he grunted in pain, he didn't move away from her. The concrete chunk bounced off her upper back, and she winced, curling tighter against him. For what seemed like an eternity, Terry crouched above her. His weight at Parker's back felt claustrophobic but she didn't dare move. The noise finally settled into a disturbing hum. She remained frozen in place, waiting for some reassurance that it was really over.

The floors were now carpeted with pebble-sized chunks of powdery concrete mingled with a few larger sections scattered through the expanse. Several erratic fingers of twisted metal angled awkwardly from the ceiling where the rebar had been ripped from its place. The floor above the main hallway, where they had been standing only seconds before, had collapsed. Parker could see into the second level and out through the spaces where the windows would one day be. She shuddered at the thought of what would have happened if Terry hadn't moved them.

She had no concept of how long they had been inside, but loud voices and yelled instructions were swirling past her. She felt Terry move away and pull at her shoulders, directing her to skirt the area that had collapsed. Sirens wailed from a distance as he attempted to rush her out of the way and toward the exit. She pulled back in order to get her own bearings and balance, suddenly needing to just stand on her own.

"We need to get out of here now!" Terry shouted despite the fact she stood next to him. She nodded, braced for another round of debris. She ran in a crouch while he pulled at the side injured by the falling concrete. His cheek sported a jagged gash, and muddy streaks of blood ran over his jaw. They finally reached the front lobby as firemen in full turnout gear clogged the entranceway.

"Everyone out?" A man carrying some claw-like tool looked at Terry. "How many more?"

"I had six on the second floor and one on three. Stairwells on the east end are the only egress from the upper levels." Terry coughed as the rolling dust was worsened by the booted feet of the first responders.

"Go now. We'll get them out." He motioned outside before turning away from them.

"No argument here." Parker felt for her keys in her pocket and headed for the clear air outside. She was covered in the gray soot billowing out of the building's many glassless window openings. Parker removed the hard hat and chucked it into the grass. She imagined that her hair was half its normal color and a dusty mess below the reaches of the helmet. She fought the shaking of her hands and refused to succumb to the shock of what could have happened. A crowd from CTI headquarters stood outside, and numerous cell phones were raised, no doubt in video mode.

Parker looked over Terry's ruddy complexion sifted with the gray dust. He took out a neon green bandana to wipe his face, offering it first to Parker. She shook her head but took it from his fingers.

"You have a serious gash here. Does it hurt?" Parker turned his chin, allowing the sun to illuminate his damaged skin. Years of unfettered exposure to the elements betrayed his forty-year-old face, making him seem much older.

"Parker, I've been doing this job for twenty years. I don't even notice unless I see a body part on the ground." Terry looked back at the building, clearly itching to go find his team.

"There's a lovely visual. Is it okay if I dab it a little?" She found the cleanest part of the cloth and pressed it over his cheek. "Thanks for the assist back there. I have to admit, this is my first concrete storm."

"Sure." His voice was tense as he appraised his project. "I'm going to be up to my ass in questions and paperwork."

"You didn't do anything wrong, Terry. No one even knows what happened yet. Try not to worry." She squeezed his shoulder gently as she attempted to reassure him, trying to ignore the throbbing of her own injury.

"Davidson will have my ass when he knows one of his people ended up hurt." He shook his head and stared apprehensively at the door.

"I got a bump on the shoulder and a serious dry-cleaning bill—not to worry. Quint will know you had no responsibility in this. So will everyone else because I'll tell them." Parker would make sure her boss knew it was just a freak accident.

Finally, they glimpsed firefighters as they began bringing out dusty, dirty workers they had lowered from the precarious second floor, none of them with even a scratch.

A filthy man still clutching a sledgehammer approached and spoke to Terry. "Apparently, we were just at the wrong place at the wrong time, boss. Chain reaction to Waterman's jackhammer. We didn't think it would cave like that."

"Think we know we have a problem now." Terry sighed and rubbed at his eyes.

"Yup. I'm going to say the answer is…not so good." Terry's worker coughed. "Hey, you should get your face checked out."

"I told you." Parker turned to look at him, concerned that the blood was still streaking down his cheek.

"In a minute. I want to talk to the guys first." He walked to an assembly of his workers pouring water from thermoses over their faces.

By four p.m., the building had been officially locked down in preparation for OSHA and city inspectors to arrive. Parker sighed as yellow caution tape boasting the words "Do Not Enter" wound unevenly around the building like the ribbon on a questionable present. Her busy week would now be bathed in red tape and damage control. She had provided her statement so authorities could begin to decide whether the structure was safe or should be condemned. Parker cringed at the possibility.

Her arm had become ridiculously tight, and trying to stretch against the painful stiffness wasn't doing anything to change it. As she walked to her car, she caught a black sports car in her periphery as it jerked into the fire lane. Parker recognized the image racing in her direction.

Sydney slammed to a stop, jumped out, and crushed Parker against her. Parker fought against the cringe-inducing pain in her shoulder as Sydney took in the filthy streaks covering her face.

"What the hell happened? Are you okay? I saw your car on the news, and then Taylor called me from CTI. What the hell?" Syd was visibly trying to steady her shallow breaths as she scanned Parker for injuries.

Parker offered a weary smile as she allowed Syd to move her behind the Audi. "The concrete floor in an upper hallway collapsed. The guys who were working up there think they hit a weak spot with a jackhammer. They'll do density calculations on the existing materials and see what happened. The building's old, so it may have been age or a problem from when it was built."

"Where were you?" Sydney clearly wasn't interested in anything other than Parker's potential injuries.

"I was with Terry Carver in the back hall, and he managed to duck us into a doorway. He shielded us, mostly. I'm fine, love, really." She attempted a grin, which Sydney ignored.

Syd's expression suggested she wasn't convinced. "Where are you hurt? Did you let them check you out?" She glanced back at the cluster of idling emergency vehicles including two ambulances.

"There wasn't any need. I just took a chunk on the shoulder, and I might have a bruise. It hit Terry right in the face, poor guy. Everyone else is okay, thank goodness." She glanced at the crowd staring back in their direction. "Quite a show for the CTI people, huh?"

Syd ignored her weak attempt to distract her and moved the lapels of her torn jacket from her neck, attempting to appraise the angry places on her skin. "Why does the universe keep reminding me that I could lose you in a second?" She dropped the statement absently as she moved Parker's hair and pressed gently along Parker's shoulder.

Parker looked guiltily at Syd who, only a few days ago, offered that as her biggest fear. "Nothing happened, love. It's okay. I'm okay."

Sydney let the ripped jacket fall to the ground.

"My ass. You're not okay, Park. There's blood and a pretty deep cut back here. Come over to the EMTs with me. You have to get this cleaned up before it gets infected."

"What is it? I can't see." Parker tried to angle over her shoulder to see what Sydney looked so horrified by. Of course, she maintained the opinion that Sydney would fuss over a hangnail if Parker looked the least bit uncomfortable. Still, she couldn't angle to look at the injury.

Sydney caught Parker's face in both her hands. "Please, Parker. Humor me."

Her anguished expression made Parker want to do anything to erase it from her face. Parker nodded and leaned gratefully against Sydney's shoulder, suddenly exhausted. "Come meet Terry first. He's the one who got us to a safe place today." Sydney held Parker so tightly Parker was afraid she would might add another bruise, but if it reassured Syd, she would take a thousand bruises.

"Terry, how are you?" Parker squeezed his arm. The construction foreman sported a small butterfly bandage on his cheek; dried blood still streaked over his jaw.

"Hey, I'll live to fight with the authorities for the rest of the week, right?" He offered her a crooked smirk.

"Terry Carver, I wanted you to meet my partner, Sydney Hyatt. I told her you were the one who got us to the safe zone in there."

Terry looked at Sydney and then back toward Parker. "Partner?"

"Her girlfriend." Sydney shook Terry's limp hand. "Thank

you for keeping her safe. I can't tell you how much I appreciate it." Sydney began to move Parker toward the ambulance when the fire inspector started lobbing new questions in his direction.

"No sweat," he called after them, still sporting a strange expression as he watched them walk away.

"I don't think he knew you were a carpet muncher, my dear," Syd whispered in Parker's ear.

Parker slapped her stomach. "Classy, Hyatt."

"I'm just saying that I think you might be starring in his naughty dreams later." Sydney stopped her in front of the ambulance and swept her long hair away from the wound. "But luckily, I don't believe he'll be in yours."

"You're the only person in my dreams, love. Now, let's get this over with so we can go home."

Syd answered Parker's phone when Jenny and Mia called, both reporting being glued to the news coverage. Parker grimaced as the EMT blotted disinfectant onto the abraded skin and taped a large square of gauze over the wound. Parker caught Terry staring at her oddly when Syd pulled her to her feet, lending credence to Syd's characterization of him.

"You sure you can't just leave your car, and I'll bring you back in the morning?" Syd clearly wanted Parker safely with her.

"I'm sure. I want to go home, and I may even stay home and work tomorrow. I'll call in a combat-recovery excuse." She smiled.

"I'll follow you. Stop if you're hurting, okay?"

"We live twenty minutes from here. I'm fine, love." Parker pulled against her when they stopped at her car, and Sydney opened the door.

"Hey, I just remembered. Thank you for the flowers today. They were beautiful." Parker dropped heavily into the seat and started her car when Sydney grabbed the closing door.

"What flowers?" She folded onto her heels and stared at her.

"The lilies." She gave Sydney a curious look. "Two dozen

lilies came from Hinter's Florist by the office." She waited as if she expected Syd to cop to a joke. "You didn't send them?"

"No, I didn't send them." Sydney was deadly serious and had that look Parker associated with her protective mode. "We need to talk when we get home, okay?"

Parker nodded, vaguely confused at the implication of a second anonymous offering inside of a week.

❖

"Of course it's weird, Syd. It's just not *criminal* weird." Mack spoke quietly as if not to be overheard in her office.

"I know it's not criminal *yet*, Mack, but you would be freaking if this were Jenny, and you know it." Syd watched Parker's taillights closely as she followed her in the waning afternoon light.

Mack sighed loudly. "You're right, I would. I can't do anything official, but I'll check on a couple of things and call you back. Just don't get crazy. She's okay."

"I can't imagine what you mean, Foster. I'm the picture of cool." Syd chuckled as she allowed emotions she didn't feel to color her tone. She didn't want Parker to hear the worry she felt. She disconnected as they pulled into the lot in front of their home and scanned the dark lawn surrounding the old warehouse buildings.

"Stop," Parker said as if she could read Syd's face like a large print child's book. "This isn't like Becky Weaver."

Sydney struggled against the memories and the ever-present guilt. "I know. We're good. Let's go in." Syd shifted her focus to the contents of Parker's trunk. "What do you need?"

"Just my purse and my laptop bag. The rest I won't need until the building is cleared."

"And I guess you think I'll let you go back in there? Crazy woman." Syd shook her head, her delivery only half joking.

"Do you plan to roll me in bubble wrap and Styrofoam peanuts?" Parker grinned up at Syd, who was again holding her tightly around the waist.

"Well, not the peanuts, they make such a mess. I'm nothing if not practical. People can just visit you here every other Wednesday between two and five." Syd punched the door code into the panel and replaced her arm around Parker's body when she saw her stretch her neck awkwardly.

"That sounds suspiciously like prison, love."

"Let's call it protective custody, okay? I sound less crazy that way." Syd decided she didn't care how it sounded if it meant the woman she loved was out of harm's way.

"If you say so." Parker groaned when she sat on the bench in their room, and Syd removed her boots.

"As much as I want to fall into bed, I desperately need a shower. Feel like chaperoning me in there? You never know what I could get up to on my own." Parker slid her palms up Sydney's chest, running her lips softly over her collarbone.

Sydney sighed. "Yes. I think it's for the best. I suspect I'll have to review the conditions of your incarceration."

She steered Parker toward the bathroom. Parker was fiercely independent, often a source of tension in their relationship, but Syd felt Parker lean against her, indicating she could use a little caretaking this time. She was grateful for the opportunity rarely granted.

CHAPTER EIGHT

S o, I did a routine check on Becky but, Syd, right now, it's just a weird note and some flowers. Don't overreact. In fact, don't react at all until you have to. This may be the end of it."

Syd knew Mack's placating tone was meant to stanch Syd's tendency to overplay her protective role where Parker was concerned. "Not planning on reacting, but I just need to know that it wasn't her."

"Good. Now you do. You can go to your cushy home office and stare at her through the window in case the air-conditioning gives her goose bumps or something."

"Bite me, Foster." Syd smirked, knowing she would likely do just that since Parker was now home for the balance of the week.

"Hey, one more thing. I have a homicide investigators conference in Richmond next week. I wondered if it would be okay if Jen and the baby stayed with you guys starting Tuesday. Just in case something happens."

"Well, I don't know…goose bumps?" Syd toyed with the pen on her desk. She could always count on Mack to get her to take things less seriously. This time, however, she felt a heaviness she couldn't quantify. Something told her that a simple note and an unattributed gift of flowers were more than they appeared to be.

"I deserved that," Mack replied.

"Yes, you did. And of course she can. Park will love it, and with Mia across the hall, I can begin to establish my harem."

"Well, it's up to you what you do on your last day on earth if you ever touch my wife, Hyatt." Mack's warning tone was meant to sound ominous, but Sydney laughed.

"We'll see her Tuesday night, then. Let's all do dinner when you're back." Sydney shoved project files into a desk tray and stretched her legs under the desk.

"Be good. Call me if something else happens."

"You'll be the first, but you probably already knew that." Syd placed her phone face down on the counter and glanced at Parker through the window of her office. She watched her tap data into her laptop, attempting to embark on a normal day, but she wondered if she was replaying yesterday's events as much as she was. Syd wanted to believe she was just being overprotective, but her instincts told her something was off. She'd be on edge until she figured out what it was.

After two hours of work, Sydney went downstairs and heard Parker talking emphatically.

"No, really, I'm fine. Just a scratch and a bruise, and it's a good day to work from home."

Sydney climbed onto the low back of the sofa behind Parker and stretched her legs on either side of her, surreptitiously checking the state of Parker's shoulder injury while she was occupied. Parker reclined contentedly into the V of Syd's thighs and closed her eyes when Sydney massaged her temples.

"Call me if you hear from the inspectors, okay? Yeah, you can tell him I'm fine. Thanks." Parker chucked the phone on the cushion and looked behind her.

"Shall I assume your protective little friend was asking about you for the next installment of his fantasies?" Syd looked down at her, dropping a lazy kiss on her forehead.

"You're very committed to your dim view of the world, Ms. Hyatt," Parker teased as they indulged in the midafternoon moment they rarely experienced together.

"So, I'm wrong, then?" She leaned slightly over Parker and rubbed unhurried circles over her arms.

"No, not wrong. Just a presumptuous eavesdropper. I thought you were working, anyway." Parker closed her eyes as Syd continued the massage.

"I was. But with you at home? That's like trying to be on a diet in a chocolate factory. Temptation's everywhere." Syd tried to stay playful, but touching Parker was building a fire.

"Do you practice that, or are you really that charming?" She laid her head on Sydney's knee.

"Actually, neither. But I came down to tell you that Jenny's coming to stay with us next week, if that's okay, of course. Mack's going to Richmond, and she thought it would be good for her to stay here."

"Has she asked Jenny?" Concern crossed Parker's face.

Syd shrugged. "No idea. She hasn't mentioned anything to you, I take it?"

Parker shook her head. "No. Not yet, anyway. I just don't want to be part of making her feel like a child. If she wants to be here, I'd love to have her, but Mack needs to let that be her decision. She can be a little overbearing."

"Understood. You call it. I'm just an innocent bystander." Sydney raised her hands in mock surrender.

"My love, you haven't been an innocent anything in a very long time." Parker twisted up to kneel in front of Syd. "But I happen to love that about you."

"Does that mean you can take a naughty break and meet me in the bedroom?" Syd captured Parker's tongue in her mouth and kissed her languidly until her lips burned hotly against Parker's skin.

"I guess it's lunchtime somewhere." Parker pulled Sydney onto her and compelled her to stretch out over the sofa. "Welcome to my home office."

"Thank you. I think I'd like to order all the services you offer here."

Parker snaked her legs around Syd's waist and began grinding her pelvis against her.

"Damn, baby." Syd shook her head in mock warning. "You're in so much trouble now."

She pulled Parker's shirt away from her body, revealing the soft skin she wanted to devour. Parker pushed Sydney's top toward her neck, and Syd ripped it away. She shivered at the burning contact with Parker's skin. Ravenously, she sucked a hard nipple against her teeth, and Parker again tilted her hips into Syd's body.

When she heard Parker moan for her, Syd slid down and tugged her pants off. She glided her lips and tongue over Parker's taut flesh, bending to course her teeth over her sensitive inner thighs and, finding her target, lapping her tongue over her.

"What did I do to deserve this?" Parker growled seductively, arching against her. "What do you want, Hyatt?"

Sydney grabbed her hips, smirking confidently as she pulled Parker toward her waiting mouth. "Baby, I just want to make you scream." Sydney designed her teasing and lazy strokes to push Parker to her edge, but she planned to control when she allowed her to crash over. Syd would get Parker to beg for release but deliver it when she commanded. They both thrived on the mutual game.

Parker glanced her nails along the corded muscles in Syd's arms, "Please, Sydney, now, please."

Sydney smiled as she decreased the intensity and stroked more slowly inside her. She adored the broken moans and the halting breaths she could prompt from Parker.

Syd found the sensitive place within Parker that she craved and watched her face, her eyes fluttering against the colliding sensations.

"You want to come, baby?" Syd asked after a few minutes of making Parker writhe.

"God, yes."

Sydney fought a greedy smile before continuing her manipulations. Her eyes, though, lingered on Parker's face. Parker screamed Syd's name as her punishing drop from the edge consumed her.

Sydney snaked up Parker's side and continued to bite against the hypersensitive skin and tight muscles in her neck. She clawed her fingers into Parker's hair and captured her mouth, bruising a kiss over her lips.

"Oh my God, Sydney. Are you buttering me up for something? What do you want?" She breathed raggedly as her eyes returned to focus on Syd's face, and she pressed her hand between Syd's legs.

"I already got it." She delivered a satisfied smile. "I told you...I just wanted to make you scream." She felt the satisfaction that came with connecting with Parker on a physical level, but she would admit, only to herself, that she breathed a little easier knowing she was safe at home instead of out of her protective reach.

CHAPTER NINE

Syd watched as Jenny pulled into the parking lot beside Parker's convertible. She couldn't help but smile at the slightly frazzled look in Jenny's expression. "Boy, am I glad to see you." Jen traded a quick kiss with Sydney and handed her Olivia and a diaper bag. "I never imagined that I'd need this much stuff for four nights away from home until I had a baby."

"See, O.G.? High maintenance already." Sydney laughed as Olivia plucked at Syd's T-shirt. "Leave it for now, and I'll come get the rest in a bit."

Jenny gratefully nodded and heaved a duffel bag over her shoulder. "It's nice of you to have me stay, Syd. I want you to know that I'm perfectly capable of taking care of my child on my own, but Mack thinks I need a chaperone."

"Maybe Mack wants everything to be easier for you, just in case you need a break." Syd pulled Jenny against her in a comforting embrace.

"Perhaps you're just trying to stick up for her, like always." Jenny laughed and leaned against Syd.

"Perhaps I am, or maybe, we like having you and Olivia over here. Ever think of that?" Sydney moved her arm from around Jenny and reached over her to hold the foyer door where Parker stood with her arms open for Olivia.

"Hi, my girl," Parker sang, and Olivia leaned over to be swept into Parker's arms.

Syd deposited the bags on the guest bed and returned to find Olivia scooting along the rug in the living room and Jenny examining Parker's shoulder.

"Nice, huh?" Syd grimaced. The black and blue patch had flowered into a much larger bloom across Parker's upper back, but the cut itself looked as if it was already healing.

"Park, you were really lucky it wasn't any closer to your face. Quint freaked when he heard about it. He ran into my office while I was meeting with Frank and the new schedulers; he practically knocked me over. I stumbled into poor Ben trying to stay upright." Jenny chuckled when she recounted his shell-shocked reaction.

Syd stared at the injury. "She wasn't lucky enough for me. Did she mention she was banned from leaving the house from now on? It's a fairly new thing, so she might not have told you yet." Syd winked at Jenny when Parker shot her a warning look. Syd ducked quickly out the door to Jen's car to avoid the pillow Parker was aiming in her direction.

"Why were you meeting with them?" Parker inquired as she knelt to roll a ball with Olivia. She was already out of the loop, and she hated that feeling.

"Seems someone in accounting entered their salaries wrong, and Frank caught it when he was reviewing the data during their orientation week. I handled it, so no big deal." Jenny motioned as if she was swatting an annoying insect.

"I needed to be in the office today instead of sitting here on my butt. We're going to get very behind with the delay at CTI." Parker frowned as she began making notes on a legal pad while Olivia crawled over to take colorful blocks from a canvas bag.

"We are not behind. Besides, I brought a ton of work for us to do tomorrow. We have no meetings, so we can get a lot done from right here, Park. We'll be fine."

Parker knew she was a chronic workaholic, and she drove herself hard. She tried not to focus on the work potentially piling up on her desk. However, she had to admit that the stiffness in her entire body made working from her couch a welcome relief and a nice respite. And it gave Syd a little time to hover and feel needed. She knew that had been a relationship complaint from more than just Syd. She had a hard time needing anyone.

❖

Sydney met Parker and Jenny in the lobby as they were strapping Olivia into her stroller. "Jen has convinced me that she handled everything urgent from today, so we're going to try and tire Olivia out on a walk. Want to come?" Parker wrapped her arms around Syd's waist and stood on her toes to kiss her.

"Why don't I take the stuff in, set up the crib, and order us Chinese food so we can all relax when you get back?"

"You're a genius." Jenny smiled gratefully.

"You keep telling her that, will you?" She turned to Parker and spoke sternly. "Please, don't walk near anything, over anything, under anything, or talk to strangers." Syd was only half kidding, and she went back into the loft amidst the duet of groans and "Yes, Dad" comments lobbed in her direction. She dialed the Chinese restaurant from memory and began to attack the engineering marvel of the portable crib.

Syd heard the heavy front door slide open from her spot on the bedroom floor just a few minutes later. "Back already?" she called toward the living room.

"It's Mia. Anyone home?"

Syd leaned out of the door to the spare room and watched Mia tentatively step inside.

"Just me. I'm back here, Mia. Come on in." Syd continued to fuss with the small rubber feet designed to prevent the light crib from sliding across the floor.

"Planning something I don't know about?" Mia smiled.

Syd was contorted on the concrete floor, bracing the crib with her thighs.

"That would be a huge *no*. You know better than that." Syd unfolded her body and stood to offer a greeting hug. She felt Mia hold on to her a little tighter than usual.

Syd stepped back to face her. "Do you want to talk about it?"

Tears started in earnest where they had only hinted before. "I just miss Sandy some days more than others, I guess."

Syd wrapped her arms around Mia's shoulders and stroked her back.

Mia reached around Sydney's waist and squeezed. "Sorry to be a drip. I guess some days it's easier not to be alone."

"Mia, please, don't apologize, I'm glad I was here. One of us is always around, or at least most of the time. You can come over and just hang out. It's okay. Parker loves having you here and so do I." Syd released her hold on Mia, who looked embarrassed. She drew her thumbs gently under Mia's watery green eyes and studied her carefully. "Want to stay for dinner? You know I always over-order on the Chinese."

Mia smiled back and nodded as they finished building the crib together.

Within an hour, Olivia was set for the night thanks to the sleep-inducing stroll down Meridian Street and a warm bath. Syd sipped a scotch from a cut-crystal rocks glass and watched out the window. She hoped to intercept the delivery driver before he rang the buzzer, possibly disturbing the baby. When she saw a sweep of headlights over the grass, she rushed to the door, leaving Jen, Mia, and Parker watching the news from the sofa.

Syd handed over the cash and took the stuffed brown bag from his arms. She looked at him strangely as he handed her a white envelope as well.

"Found it by the cars, figured it was yours...probably blew off the windshield or something." He shrugged and thanked her for the tip before walking back to the lot.

Sydney set the bag on the floor and examined the envelope, which just said, "Unit A," and tore the side seam open.

I see your heart, in your blue eyes
To feel you makes my pulse rate rise
Until the time we touch again
And I reveal my thoughts without this pen

She can't feel you the way I do
Her sick ways are not for you
I'll feed your soul and set it free
You'll love your life, your place with me.

Sydney felt acid rise in her throat as she processed the third such move in a sick game she and Parker didn't want to play. Parker poked her head out the door as Sydney slipped the note inside the bag.

"Are you making that stuff out here? We're hungry." Parker smiled as Sydney picked up the brown bag and walked inside.

"Just making sure it was all in there." Syd followed Parker into the kitchen and slid the food onto the island. She turned and glided a hand under Parker's hair, kissing her lightly. "Go sit, and I'll bring it in." Syd managed a smile as Parker turned for the living room. She shoved the envelope into a plastic bag in the kitchen drawer where she kept her Sig, reminding herself to move the gun into a higher cabinet since Olivia would be there for most of the week. Parker wasn't likely to go into that drawer, so it would buy her some time.

"Dinner is served." Syd carried a stack of plates and the heavy bag into the living room. Parker had cleared the coffee table where they gathered for the informal feast.

"Take our picture, Syd." Jen shuffled nearer to Mia and Parker. "For Mack."

Syd snapped the picture of the cozy trio, noting that Mia seemed a little lighter since their earlier conversation. She texted the picture to Mack.

Harem growing by the minute. Sorry you're missing it, but I can handle things here. We need to talk.

Mack answered immediately:

At homicide seminar learning new ways to torture you, Hyatt. Tell Jen I'll call later. I'll call you soon.

Jenny was the first to roll back onto the sofa, groaning in resignation. "I'm done. I eat another grain of rice, and I will explode."

Mia joined in and laid her plate on the table. "Yup, full, to say the least. I'm supposed to work early, but I might still be in a food coma." She smiled at Sydney and used Parker's shoulder to push herself off the couch. "Please, let me give you some money for dinner."

Syd stood and stacked her plate on top of Mia's. "Not a chance; we ordered this before you even stopped by, so you owe nothing."

Mia took Jenny's plate and reached for Parker's.

"Thanks, Mia. You don't have to go, you know." Parker's smile was gentle. "We would love to have you stay."

"Rain check? I really do have an early meeting." Mia moved toward the kitchen and set the plates on the island. "Thanks for dinner, Syd. I needed it." She seemed far away for just a moment before looping her arms around Sydney's neck.

"Any time, Mia, you know that."

Mia tapped an appreciative kiss on Syd's cheek and waved before sliding the large door closed behind her.

Jenny launched herself from the couch and collected a handful of takeout boxes by their thin wire handles, creating an awkward bouquet in her fingers. "I am going to call my wife and hit the sheets myself. Thank you both for dinner. And thank you for doing the crib, Syd; you rock."

Jenny hugged Parker before she shuffled toward the spare room. Parker watched Syd rinse dishes and arrange them in the dishwasher while she placed leftovers in the fridge. "You've been far away all night, love. Is something bothering you?"

Sydney sighed heavily and walked to the drawer. She knew keeping Parker in the dark wouldn't last long. She pulled out the envelope and held it up. "How well do you know this Terry guy from the construction company?"

Parker shot her a puzzled look and focused on the envelope Syd held by the outer edges. "Why? What's that?"

"The guy that delivered the food found it near the cars and brought it to me." She let the folded parchment slide out onto the counter and opened it by the corners. Parker leaned over to read it, threading her arm around Sydney and tensing as she recited it aloud.

I see your heart, in your blue eyes
To feel you makes my pulse rate rise
Until the time we touch again
And I reveal my thoughts without this pen

She can't feel you the way I do
Her sick ways are not for you
I'll feed your soul and set it free
You'll love your life, your place with me.

Parker swallowed loudly, trying to stem an involuntary shudder. "You think this is Terry?"

"Who else has 'touched you' lately? He looked all crazy when he saw us together and figured out who I was to you. I joked about it then, but now, I don't think it's funny. In fact, I don't want you anywhere near him until we find out what's going on." Sydney's jaw clenched, and she swiped her fingers roughly through her hair.

Parker winced at the directive, and Syd took notice.

"Baby, this isn't me being bossy or macho; this is scary shit. You can't take letters left on your car and in your house lightly." She held Parker's shoulders and pulled her hard against her chest.

"I know. I am a little alarmed now. Especially for you. Whoever this is knows who *you* are. You deal with bad people, criminal situations, a lot. It could be anyone."

"He *touched you. Blue eyes.* It happened after all those people were here. It's about *you.* Did he come to the party? That Terry guy?" She watched as Parker mentally checked through her memories of the CTI party night.

"He would have been invited, but no, he didn't come, I'm pretty sure."

Jenny opened the door, holding her toothbrush and heading for the bathroom.

"Jenny." Parker called to her quietly and motioned her toward the kitchen. "Did Terry Carver come to the CTI party here?"

"No, he had to go to his niece's wedding, I think. Why?" She looked at Parker strangely.

"Syd got this note tonight, and well, you read it."

Syd spun it on the counter with the end of a pen, clearly intending for her to read it without touching it.

"Ooh, very creepy, guys." She frowned and backed away from the letter as if it was contagious. "Wait, you think this is Terry Carver?"

"Well, no. I don't know. It could be just coincidental, I guess." Parker shrugged.

"The fact is, he was in the building with her during the collapse, hence the *touching* part, and when he figured out Parker and I were together, he kind of acted…off, I guess. But it's got to be the same person who left the one at the party. Can you think of anyone else that would be obsessed with her?" Syd pulled the note back to face her and reread the words that made her cringe.

"He just doesn't seem like the kind. But then, who does?" Jenny watched Syd use a napkin to refold the note into the envelope. "Should I mention it to Mack?"

"I'll make a report and turn it over in the morning. We can talk Friday when the training is over. I don't want to put this on her when she's trying to concentrate." Syd stared at the envelope while she spoke, trying to find any pieces that might fit together.

"I'm sure it's just some weird crush thing, but we can

brainstorm in the morning, Jen. Go to bed, go tell Mack good night, and don't worry about all this, okay? It'll be fine."

"I know it will. Love you, guys." Jenny's smile looked forced when she resumed her trip to the bathroom.

"Let's do the rest of the dishes in the morning?"

Parker's banal expression did nothing to dispel Sydney's feeling of dread.

Syd pulled her gun from the drawer, and Parker's stare become stony. "Please, don't give me crap about this, Park. Not until we know what's happening?"

"Okay. I get it. I just hate that we're here again."

Syd knew Parker was thinking about the last time she saw her point a gun at the man who had nearly killed her and Mack in Syd's car. Parker would understand it, but the thought stole a little bit of their peace.

Sydney shut the blinds in the bedroom and laid the gun on the nightstand. She reclined on top of the bedspread fully clothed and watched as Parker slipped out of her shoes. "Can you come and lie with me for a second?"

Parker crawled onto the bed and hooked her leg over Sydney's thigh. She welcomed the flush of warmth that flooded her skin when Parker pressed her body tightly against her.

"How can this happen? Haven't we been through enough together already?"

Syd pulled Parker closer instead of answering.

"Don't check out on me, okay? I don't want to have to guess what you're thinking. I need us to be in this together."

Syd knew it was typical to get lost in her own intense thoughts, and she needed to reassure Parker that they were a team.

"We are in everything together. I'm just trying to figure out whoever this may be and why they're doing it now. Who is new in your life that doesn't know about me, or who is around you more than they were before? Can you think of anyone like that?"

"No, I really can't, and for that matter, Terry has been around almost as long as I have, and we've never been anything but professional with one another. Can we just put it away for tonight? I just need you...without all of this." Parker slid onto Sydney and kissed her neck.

"No fair. I have no defenses for that, but of course, you know this." Syd allowed the eerie feeling to slip away as she rolled Parker's body under her own and took her mouth.

"I need to feel you." Parker breathed into her skin, and Syd closed her eyes to the dangerous train she saw speeding toward them.

CHAPTER TEN

Wednesday morning, Jenny carried a sleepy Olivia into the kitchen and sat her on the edge of the island to shift an escaping sock back onto her pudgy foot. "So, did you have creepy dreams last night, like I did?"

"Something like that, when I managed to sleep. I just can't figure it out, and you know that makes me crazy." Parker grinned ruefully.

Syd jogged down the metal stairs from her office wearing black dress pants and a beige button-down shirt. Her suit jacket was tailored to her broad shoulders, a look Parker adored. She dropped her empty cup on the trivet near the coffeemaker.

"Good morning, Jen. Good morning, Gangster Baby." She kissed each on the cheek and then gave Parker a lingering kiss.

"You're certainly in a different place this morning. How long have you been up, anyway?" Parker had rolled over at 4:45, concerned to find Sydney's side of the bed cold and empty. She'd fought the urge to look for her, assuming that the habitual night owl was hard at work in her office.

"I started work about four, I guess. I had a lot on my mind, and I wanted to check on some things." Syd offered Jen a mug of coffee and topped up Parker's tea.

"Things like what?" Parker eyed her suspiciously.

"Well, I just wanted to make some notes. I cross-referenced some names from the guest list and looked at some new people in the neighborhood, stuff like that." Sydney replenished her coffee and slid the note into a plastic zip bag, joining it with the one from the night of the party. "I need to drop the note at the station first thing."

"Why don't you just become a private investigator?" Jenny sipped her coffee and kept a steadying hand on Olivia.

"Already am." Syd turned to place the bag in the center of her portfolio.

"Huh?" Parker looked at her as if they'd just met. "What do you mean 'already am'? You've never even mentioned that once."

Syd shrugged. "It's not anything that's ever come up. Anyway, I thought we talked about it before. I got my license when I started the business, thinking I might use it as an extra source of income—as a fallback of sorts. I've never needed it, as it turns out."

"What else don't I know about you?" Parker smiled, fascinated that she was still learning about her girlfriend. She would always be impressed by her. Awards lined the shelves in their living room, speaking volumes about the talents Sydney possessed, first as a general media editor and now working with district attorneys to help make their cases. It didn't really surprise her that investigative work had always been in her blood. "Do you sneak out and do drag in DC while I'm sleeping?"

"No, baby. You know that would cut into my gigolo time, and that's where the big money is." She winked at Parker casually, but the look on her face said she knew they would protect each other no matter what. "You're both staying here today, right? No field trips planned?"

"No, love. We shall be locked in just like our warden says. Where are you going?"

"Just to the PD and to run some errands, you know, do a little research. I'll let you know if I find anything. How about I bring home salads from Amici's for lunch? Sound good?"

"I'll take that! Sounds great to me." Jenny swept Olivia off the counter and into the playpen in the living room.

Once they were semi-alone, Sydney's expression became serious. "I know you're perfectly capable of taking care of yourself, but it makes me feel better if you let me do it just a little, okay? Consider it relationship charity."

In response, Parker brought Sydney's lips to hers. "We have a lot of work to do, so we'll be here with the baby. We won't even take her out for a walk until you get back, deal?"

"I love you more than anyone ever will." Sydney held her close and whispered into her hair.

"I know that. I love you, sweetheart." Parker kissed her deeply, letting the heat linger. "Come back soon."

Sydney parked next to a graphite gray Mercedes sedan in the nearly empty PRG parking lot. She scanned for Richard's car, but since she wasn't planning a lengthy visit, she was almost relieved by its absence. She waved confidently at the front desk attendant and walked purposefully toward the elevators. She'd learned that if you acted as if you were supposed to be somewhere, people would rarely assume you weren't. She didn't want her visit announced, not until she could do it herself.

The account executives all shared the fourth floor with a bullpen of assistants and proposal writers occupying the center of the space. The early morning buzz was still mellow, and Richard Dailey's office was still dark. She knocked on the frame of the open door of the next office. She noted the curious look on Dayne Grant's face as she stood and walked around to meet Syd in front of her desk.

"Got a minute?" Sydney stood behind the guest chairs, a convenient buffer, and Dayne extended her hand. Sydney shook it firmly.

"Uh, sure. Have a seat?" She gestured to the stiff side chairs and leaned casually in a half sit against her desk.

"I'm fine, thanks." Sitting would have meant taking the submissive position to Dayne, which Syd would never do; she preferred to move when she spoke anyway.

"To what do I owe this visit? I'm thinking this isn't a social call." She was tall and wore her spiky blond hair cut short over her ears, which displayed two large diamond studs in each, the same as when Syd had first met her nearly two years ago at Richard and Allen's annual New Year's Eve celebration. She wore expensive olive green linen slacks and a short-sleeve silk sweater. Dayne was known for her extravagant taste in clothing and for getting what she wanted at any cost. Of course, that was how Parker got hurt. For just a few seconds, Sydney bristled at the memories of what she knew of their past.

"No, it's not a social call," Syd finally responded. "I need to ask you a question I'm pretty sure I already know the answer to, but I have to eliminate some angles." She unzipped the portfolio.

"Sounds fairly ominous. I'll do what I can." Dayne watched Sydney warily.

"Other than the night of the party at our place, have you had or attempted to have any communication with Parker?" Sydney sounded as if she was conducting an admission-seeking interview rather than garnering help from an acquaintance, but she couldn't help it.

Dayne frowned and shook her head.

"Written her any notes, sent her gifts, or anything at all or had anyone else do it?"

Dayne shook her ahead again. "No. Nothing."

"Julie, maybe?" Syd focused on Dayne's eyes to see if she could detect deception.

Dayne chuckled and pushed herself off the desk. She glanced at the folder in Syd's hand. "I can assure you, if I ever arrived at such a thought, Julie would *not* be the person I would go to for that. She would be more likely to send Parker one of my recently removed body parts." Her tone was edgy and suggested the existence of some serious tension in the relationship. "Want to fill me in?"

"This isn't public knowledge." Syd would trust Dayne with the information in order to gauge her reaction.

"And I won't make it any. I know you don't believe that I want Parker to be happy, but I do. I wouldn't do anything to hurt her."

Syd thought that she had done enough when she was caught cheating on her with Julie. "Since I assume that Julie wasn't the first, you can understand why it's not easy to believe that."

The fact that Parker had no names for the numerous casual flings that came before Julie didn't mean she wasn't aware of them. It didn't lessen the fact that they had existed, and Syd knew it had seriously fractured their ten-year relationship.

Dayne sighed. "True then and a fact now. I'm just not sure putting a finer point on that would help Park."

"You can't believe that she doesn't know." Syd allowed the conversation to leave its intended track momentarily.

"Maybe I just hope that the past, my mistakes, can just stay there."

Dayne shrugged, and Syd saw no point in continuing the dialogue about ancient history since she wasn't there to dredge up the dusty memories that contributed to Parker's divorce.

Sydney slid copies of the two notes from her portfolio and handed them to Dayne, knowing Mack probably wouldn't approve. "There was a delivery of two dozen white lilies in between those two, as well."

After of few minutes scanning and then rescanning the notes, Dayne focused on Sydney with a curious expression and handed the plastic-encased pages back.

"You don't know me well enough to know this, but those aren't me. First of all, I suck at poetry and wouldn't even attempt to write something like that…even that lame. I tend to be a little more direct than that, which is something you *do* know about me." Dayne's wry smile indicated that she recalled her past bad behavior as clearly as Sydney did. "I can promise you that those didn't come from me."

"Any chance Julie would try to complicate things for Parker?"

Dayne shrugged. "It's a fair question, but no. And she would never spend that kind of money on a 'stay away' gift. She is the tightest person with a penny I've ever met, which makes our relationship challenging at times. She's also very eloquent, good with words and appropriate sentiment. This sounds like a guy to me. Sparing with words, badly assembled. Almost elementary."

"It does to me, too," Syd conceded, "but I had to ask. This guy could be dangerous, and I want to be one step ahead of him, and so far, I'm not." Sydney placed the notes back in her portfolio and drew the zipper over the edges.

"I get it. I would have done the same thing. Probably less politely than you did." Dayne walked to her window and stood next to Sydney where the city moved below them. Without looking away from the view, she said, "I really do get it. This scares the shit out of you, and you're on a mission to protect her." Dayne's words were measured, as though she knew she might be entering territory where she wasn't welcome. "If I had to guess, you've put everything else on hold, but you haven't told her that yet."

"There's nothing to tell her." Syd shifted uncomfortably and worked to police her expression. She didn't want to give away her guilt at hiding anything from Parker.

"Sure, there is. You're pissed off that someone got this close and more than a little scared. Which is why you're armed." Dayne nodded at the small of Sydney's back, and Sydney was thrown off by the detection.

Dayne answered the unasked question. "My job is relationship management. Which is just a talent for figuring out what causes people to make the decisions they do. You're wearing a jacket in ninety degrees, and it's not because it matches your pants. Parker is the reason you get up every morning, and that scares the shit out of you, too. I believe you would break someone's neck if they hurt her, and I understand that, as well. She has that effect on the people who love her because if she loves you, she would give up anything to make sure you were happy."

"Are you speaking theoretically, or are you still one of those people?" Syd crossed her arms over her chest.

"Do you want me to lie?" Dayne stared out the window as a bus narrowly avoided a bicyclist running a light.

"Not particularly." Sydney grazed fingers through her hair, uncertain what she'd do with a genuinely honest response.

"I would take her back before you could blink if she would have me." Dayne spoke matter-of-factly, staring out the window instead of looking at Sydney. "But I don't believe that's an option."

"Does Julie know that?" Syd carefully processed Dayne's admission, and it reinforced her assertion that she would never completely trust Dayne.

"On some level, she knows. I tell her I love her because I do, but she's looking for me to make it permanent, and I'm not ready for that yet. At least I'm not as ready as she is. Sometimes I wonder if it's more about making sure I *don't* think about Park than it is about making a firm commitment to *her*." Dayne grinned wryly and looked at Sydney. "And I have no idea why I just told you all that."

Syd wasn't sure either. "Maybe Julie knows you've never really been in that place with her. It's pretty hard to compete with a ghost." Sydney slipped her portfolio under her arm and stood squarely in front of her. Syd didn't look away as she continued to speak. "Question for you…how would you envision the status of your relationship with Parker had she not caught you with Julie, or was that the plan all along?"

"Subconsciously, I guess it was the plan. Maybe I thought her catching me was easier than me telling her I wasn't happy. Since I didn't do a very good job keeping it in my pants, I suppose getting caught was inevitable."

"That was a cowardly way out. If it doesn't seem to be working with Julie, aren't you just as likely to do it again?" Sydney was mildly amused by the conversation about relationships between the two of them, since Dayne was an unfaithful cad, and until Parker, Sydney was a womanizing commitment-phobe.

"I know that. It's all on me, and I'm trying to work it out before she does get hurt. But understand, trading one relationship for another was never the plan. I think I'm a different person now, but I know what happened was my own fault." She took a deep breath and sighed. "A word of unsolicited advice for you?" Dayne looked as if she was waiting for some indication that Sydney would listen but continued anyway. "Don't do all this behind Parker's back. I get coming here, but you need to loop her in before she starts to feel like some hothouse orchid, too fragile to handle information about her own life. Especially if it crosses into her business, she won't appreciate anyone else knowing where you are on this before she gets to manage the information."

"I hear you. Thanks for the talk." Sydney constantly weighed the risk to her relationship against the risk to Parker, but she never gave it words and certainly wouldn't start now with Dayne.

She walked toward the door before Dayne's voice stopped her.

"And, Sydney?" Dayne's sharp green eyes were unfocused as she spoke a little more softly. "I don't make the same mistake twice. Especially when it costs me something that meant as much to me as I realize Parker did. If there was ever a chance to fix what I broke, I would take it."

"There won't be." Syd walked briskly out the door without looking back. Dayne would never be in a position to win Parker back as long as Sydney drew breath. She pushed the interaction aside as she formulated her next steps, happy she could cross the arrogant Dayne Grant from her list of suspects. It felt at once like a relief and a setback.

❖

Syd spent more time than she liked in line for lunch. She deposited a bulging bag of colossal salads and warm French bread into the passenger seat and drove in the direction of the loft. She had intentionally not called or texted Parker, taking Dayne's words to heart by not hovering over her. She ignored the twinge of guilt she felt, using that as a convenient excuse to not reveal where she'd been. Her cell rang, and she hit the answer key on her dash.

"So, I've already done a little checking for you." Mack launched into her speech without any greeting.

"I thought you were busy learning how to be a better cop at the cop convention?" Syd joked when Mack took a breath.

"I am, but I realized I was already brilliant at it, so I called in a favor during a bathroom break. Becky is still in the Lakeside Mental Treatment Center. Weaver's mother recommitted her after she applied to have her name changed…to Hyatt, believe it or not. So, it's fairly reasonable to assume that she isn't Parker's latest fan. In fact, her doctor told me, unofficially, of course, that she doesn't remember anything about that night or even who Parker is. She keeps waiting for you to come pick her up for your wedding. He doesn't expect her to be released anytime soon because he still believes she's holding on to some pretty deep-seated delusions, particularly where you're concerned."

"Wow. How did I not see any of that?" She recalled the seemingly normal, albeit too eager, woman who followed her home from the bar one night.

"The doc said he thinks she's had issues for a long time, and you were just part of the perfect storm for the break that put her over. She was part of three significant breakups where the other person left her, and her mother dealt with it by trying to invalidate the importance of the affairs and trying to set her up with men. The last woman abused her pretty badly, and she never really recovered."

"I guess you just never know what people are dealing with." Sydney felt bad for the experience that had altered Becky but not enough to forgive her for hurting Parker. "So, I dropped everything off with Sgt. Hicks, including the second note." Sydney was prepared to fill her in but expected that Jen already had.

"He wrote a report, so we have it on file. I'm hoping it will be a waste of time, but at least we'll have it in the system if something else happens."

"I wish I had as much confidence about that as you do. I cleared Dayne off the list of possibles this morning. I'm pretty convinced this isn't her thing."

"I'll let you tell me about that later. I would have loved to be a fly on that wall," Mack said sarcastically.

"We were civil and fairly transparent about what was permissible and likely." Syd was cryptic in favor of a later conversation. "Can I tell Parker about the Becky information? I don't want to look like I'm keeping things from her." She would never credit Dayne for her moment of clarity, but the admonition hadn't hurt.

"Well, look at that; someone's wising up."

Mack's appraisal reminded Sydney that she had habitually kept Parker in the dark for her own perceived safety, which had, more than once, caused conflict.

"Don't patronize me, Foster. Can I tell her or not?" Syd turned into the lot and found her customary spot.

"Yeah, just keep it quiet otherwise, so I don't burn my favor, okay? I now have to go be schooled on the nuances of sociopaths and Miranda challenges. Have a better time than I will."

"Ugh. Enjoy. See you Friday." Syd punched the disconnect button on the dash and dragged the bag of food out of the seat.

When she entered the apartment, the tension in the living room was palpable as Parker paced with a phone pressed to her ear.

"I understand that you're concerned about the building's safety, and so am I, but surely we can get the inspector to sign off before next week. If not, we run the risk of not being dried in before the bad weather hits." She balled her fist and tapped it repeatedly onto her thigh as she walked up and down the hall.

Olivia was sleeping in the playpen as Jenny held another phone to her shoulder and took notes on a yellow legal pad.

"How hard is it to enter two salaries in the system? They're five-digit numbers, Eddie. Payroll drops tomorrow, and if we can't fix it before then, I'm coming down for live checks. This makes *me* look bad because I'm the one who hired these guys."

Sydney unpacked the boxes and laid silverware on the island, musing that she wouldn't volunteer to tangle with either of the angry women in her living room. They both appeared flushed as they clicked off their calls and rounded the corner into the kitchen almost simultaneously.

"Rough morning?" Sydney shoved the salads across the island and hoped for some calm.

"People are idiots, that's all." Jenny shook parmesan over the bright green leaves and reached for the packet of creamy Italian dressing.

"Agreed. I need to run to the office this afternoon and sign off on some city forms so I'm not the one to hold up the inspections for CTI." Parker popped open a salad container with a little more force than necessary.

Sydney's head snapped up at the announcement.

Jenny held up her hands. "Don't worry. I have to go, too, since putting numbers in a computer seems to be a challenge for accounting. We'll be there thirty minutes tops and come right back." She smiled sheepishly at Syd. "That is, if you'll be here and keep an eye on Olivia? Otherwise, it will take *much* longer." She shoved a huge bite of lettuce into her mouth and waited.

"That is devious and manipulative, Mrs. Foster. Both traits I admire in a woman." She stood behind Parker and dropped her arms around her waist. "I'll watch her if you promise you call when you get there and text when you leave."

"That seems like overkill, but okay." Parker shrugged, obviously trying to work through her conflicting emotions.

"Speaking of devious and manipulative, I've eliminated Becky and Dayne from the list of possible note writers." Syd walked casually back to her food and started stabbing at the greens.

"Would you like to enlighten us on just how you did that?" Parker shot Syd a serious look.

"Mack checked on Becky, who is still in the hospital. According to Mack, she will be for a while since her mother signed her in again when she applied to have her name changed."

"To what?"

Sydney had hoped to skim past the question. *Obviously not going to happen.* "Hyatt, it seems."

Parker stared at her for a moment and simply shook her head. "We'll talk about that one later. What about Dayne?" Parker moved lettuce around the plate, not actually eating anything.

"I saw her this morning. She was one of my errands." Sydney watched Jenny glance at Parker as if expecting to be ringside for a significant reaction.

"Why wouldn't you tell me that this morning?" Parker dropped her fork along with the pretense of trying to eat. "Did you think I would try to stop you?"

"Yeah. I don't know. Maybe. Maybe I wasn't all that sure I would actually go." Syd leaned onto her forearms and faced Parker's annoyed stare. "I know you're pissed, but I needed to rule her out, even though I know you already had. The upshot was that she said she didn't write them or send you the flowers." Syd looked mildly irritated when she spoke again. "She also said that if she had a glimmer of hope with you, she would try to win you back."

"Well, isn't that a dumbass thing to say to your ex-wife's girlfriend?" Jenny looked disbelieving.

"Fairly dumb, yeah. We have an understanding that there would be no such opportunity, and I suggested she focus on Julie, who seems devoted to her for some reason." Sydney glanced toward Parker, who pushed her food to the center of the island and walked away. Syd shot Jenny a confused look and began to follow her.

"Give her a minute, Syd. You kind of overturned the applecart on her. Let her process before you go smother her."

"You think I smother her?" Sydney's voice ratcheted up a few notes as she took in the accusation.

"First, I think you want to protect her, but you've dumped all kinds of information on her after you've already had time to process it. Give her a second. Think about it; she has to process that her ex-wife wants her back and told her replacement as much. Then her kidnapper—your insane, one-night-stand-stalker—suddenly wants your last name and is still too unstable to be released from the institution."

Syd exhaled loudly. "I didn't want to keep her in the dark because that makes her mad, Jen."

"Of course it does; just give her a minute before you go stomping back there demanding that she get to the place you already are." Jen waggled a fork in Syd's direction. "Walk back there calmly and be a little sorry for whacking her in the head with all the info without notice. And don't piss her off. She needs to not be crazy when we drive to the office."

Syd stopped to consider how she was supposed to deliver a lot of important information without doing it all at once. She still had some things to learn, apparently. She headed to the bedroom and found Parker perched on the edge of their mattress wearing a pressed dress shirt and thin cotton dress pants. Sydney sat next to her and slipped a hand under her knees, pulling Parker's legs over her lap.

"Jenny says that basically, I'm an idiot, and I threw out a bunch of information without warning. I'm sorry."

"You didn't say anything that wasn't true. I just wasn't expecting it." Parker traced her fingers over Sydney's forearm. "I just can't believe Becky is still obsessed with you and that Dayne was arrogant enough to tell you that about me." She shook her head and tilted it on Syd's shoulder.

"At least she was honest. It wasn't a bad conversation; she just made sure I knew where she stood in case I dropped the ball anywhere. Not that I think you would go back for any reason."

"No, I wouldn't. She's still just as entitled—as evidenced by your conversation. What's worse is that Becky hasn't gotten any better and is still obsessed with you. It's terrifying to think that she could try to get to you again." Parker's sigh was heavy. "Why can't we just be alone and quiet and happy?"

"Because we have pasts, and the world isn't always as it should be. We *are* happy, we'll get through this, and I'll make sure you're safe." Sydney slid her arms around Parker and tilted her face against Parker's cheek.

"Who's going to make sure you're safe, Superwoman? The note made it sound like they're angry at you, not me."

"We'll both be careful until we figure out who this is, okay? I'll be fine, too."

"Fine. We'll talk about it later. I'll be back as soon as I can." She kissed Sydney, lingering over her lips.

"Call me, please. I love you." Sydney reluctantly let Parker slide away from her and walk toward the hall.

Syd watched them pull out of view in Jenny's car and thought she might not breathe until they were back. A soft knock jolted her out of her thoughts.

"Hey, Syd." Mia grinned at her from the hallway. "Just wondered if you had time for coffee?"

"Sure, you just missed Park and Jen. They're driving to the office, and I'm in charge of the littlest Foster." Syd swept an arm toward the playpen where Olivia still slept quietly.

"They're sure taking a chance, aren't they?" Mia grinned. "Parker's really lucky to have you to depend on if she needs it. You're the best."

"Whoa. My press has certainly been exaggerated. I'm just lucky that she still wants to be here." Syd walked to the coffeemaker and started a pot, trying not to wake the baby as she collected the abandoned salads and sealed their containers. "Mia, I know you can't think about it now, but you'll have that with someone again. It'll just take some time."

"I can't imagine being with someone like that. All I see is Sandy. I still think I feel her at night, and then I wake up, and I have to remind myself that she's gone." Quiet tears overflowed onto her cheeks, and Sydney felt inadequate to help with that amount of grief. She held Mia from her perch on the barstool and waited until she heard a deep breath and felt her straighten.

"You're going to get pretty sick of me, you know." Mia dragged a napkin over her face.

"I have a beautiful woman telling me all her secrets and keeping me from screwing up baby duty? Not a chance, doll." Syd kissed her forehead and returned to pour coffees. She caught Mia staring absently, likely fielding memories of her life with Sandy before she was shot.

Olivia abruptly voiced her desire to be part of the conversation.

"Got it," Mia said, and she happily swung the baby up and into her arms.

Sydney received Parker's arrival text while Mia was spooning organic apple puree into Olivia's waiting mouth. They managed to empty an entire jar into the child and constructed a pyramid from her bright plastic toys until she was sleepy. Mia rubbed her stomach soothingly until Olivia dropped to sleep again beside

Syd, who still felt the weight of the mystery surrounding them and stared at the rough beams that stretched across the ceiling. Her need to safeguard their life together would always supersede her work or her independent life.

❖

Parker slid through the door with an armload of folders. She motioned to Jen to be quiet when she glimpsed the trio in the living room. Sydney lay asleep on the flokati rug with Olivia's head against her shoulder. Mia slept perpendicular, with the baby's feet resting in her hands.

"Well, that's about the cutest thing I've ever seen." Jenny set her box of work on the couch and picked up her stirring daughter before she disturbed the duo. "I'm going to give her a bath before we go for a walk. You handle our two worn-out babysitters," Jenny whispered, whisking a groggy Olivia into the bedroom. Mia woke and sat up, focusing on Parker, who smiled at her.

"Good nap?" Parker spoke quietly as Mia brushed her hands over her slightly rumpled clothes.

"Actually, yes, and surprising after two cups of your girlfriend's coffee. But I need to get back to work before my boss notices my computer's been off for too long." She hugged Parker and headed for the door. "She's great with that little girl, but I think she wants to keep it a secret."

"I won't tell if you won't."

Mia yawned and waved as she slid the door shut behind her.

Parker slipped off her shoes and tiptoed to stand over Syd. She straddled her and then gently lay on top of her long body and tucked against her neck. She smiled as she felt Sydney's arms slide around her back.

"I'm supposed to be babysitting, not feeling up my woman in the living room." Syd smiled and rolled them sideways. "What happened to you texting me when you left?"

Parker smiled and nuzzled into the warmth of Syd's neck. "I did, but you must have missed it while you were sleeping with other women."

"Oh yeah. That might have been it. You caught me." Syd's dark eyes fired at Parker as she ran her teeth along her uninjured shoulder.

"Enough, we have a walk to take and dinner to prepare. You act like you're sexually deprived," Parker teased, wishing they were alone.

"I am. I need you all the time." Syd winked and nipped Parker's bottom lip gently. "Everything okay at the office?"

"Yeah. I told Quint about the notes and the flowers. He said he would do whatever we needed, and he would keep an eye out at the office. I have to handle a personnel situation tomorrow, so I'm going to go in early." When Sydney looked at her curiously, she continued. "It seems the new guy, Chris Newkirk, cornered Jenny and told her that Mike in sales is playing music that is offending him from a religious perspective because it's secular music, and he likes the all-Jesus-all-the-time station. So, I'm going to go play preschool referee to two grown adults who can't figure out how to share the sandbox."

"I think I would rather deal with my criminals and lawyers all day. At least I know what to expect most of the time." Syd rolled up before pulling Parker to her feet. "What would you like for dinner?"

"I say we do an empty-the-fridge exercise. We have a ton of leftovers, as well as cheese and fruit that will all go bad if we don't eat it. Go tell Mia to join us if she wants while I change?"

"Done. I love you, in case I haven't told you today." Syd smiled.

Parker fought the uneasy feeling that came with returning to the office. It was silly, she thought. There were tons of people, and she had never felt unsafe before. She dearly wished for the *before*; she should have appreciated it more.

❖

"Why do I always feel like I'm about to explode when I leave here?" Mia groaned and carried her plate into the kitchen.

"At least we made a serious dent in the fridge space. I was starting to be afraid to go in there." Parker stacked dishes and walked in behind Mia.

"I hate to eat and run again, but I have a deposition with two warring families at seven, so I'm aiming for the shower and then bed. Thank you for having me." She hugged Jenny and then Parker.

"You're family, Mia. You don't have to thank us." Syd walked her to the door and accepted a tight hug before she made her exit.

"Someone's a little attached to you, love," Parker whispered when Sydney locked the door behind her.

"Huh?" Syd was uncomfortable at the perceived inference and began to protest, "Baby, I haven't done—"

"Love, that wasn't an accusation. I think it's sweet. She feels like she can lean on you, like she can talk about Sandy. She needs that." Parker's smile was reassuring, not accusing.

Jenny led a tottering Olivia into the kitchen. "You look tired, Park. Why don't Sydney and I take Olivia for a walk, and you go have a nice bath?" Jenny topped off Parker's wine and handed her the glass.

"That sounds good," Sydney agreed. "You stay here and relax."

"I think I'm in love with both of you now. I can't think of anything that sounds better."

Sydney gathered Olivia into her arms and moved for the stroller.

"Go." Jenny shooed Parker toward the tub and walked out the door with Syd.

"Thank you for going with me, Sydney, not that I gave you much choice."

"Are you kidding? I get to spend time with Gangster Baby and her mom, and you made Park rest for five minutes. I should be thanking you." Syd was quiet for a moment, hesitant to ask Jenny about Parker's state of mind. "Is she okay, you know, after today?"

"Yeah, she's good. She's happy you're keeping her in the loop. The Becky stuff freaked her out a little, but she's fine now. She's just worried about work crap and dealing with that new guy tomorrow. She has to be careful that she doesn't get DPI in some religious discrimination hot water, that's all."

"I can see why she'd rather do the construction stuff sometimes. At least there's less human drama." Syd dealt with human drama, too, but the dynamics Parker had to deal with seemed somehow more irritating.

Jenny turned the stroller around at the end of the block when Olivia's eyes became heavy. "Between Frank's ogling and the new guy's fanaticism, the fact that Ben never says anything makes him the most normal of the bunch." Jenny shook her head.

"Thanks for being her right hand. She couldn't do any of this without you."

"Well, thank you for making her so happy. She adores every cell in your body, Sydney. I've known her for a long time, and she's so happy with you." Jen steered back up the hill toward the sidewalk. "You're good for each other, and I love you both."

Syd felt her thin arm slide around her waist, and Syd stopped to hug her. "I'm glad you're here, and thank you for knowing when I need a push in the right direction."

Syd held the front door, and Jen steered the stroller inside. "That's what friends are for, right?"

Syd brushed her teeth and found Parker wrapped in a silk robe on the cool sheets of their bed.

"Thank you for a wonderful little rest. I feel magnificent."

Syd stripped off her pants and tossed the shirt onto the pile. "And you look just as magnificent. What else can I do for you?" She grinned mischievously. Pulling the sash away from the robe, she kissed along Parker's ribs.

"That's a really good start." Parker arched against Sydney's demanding mouth and exploring fingers. "Don't stop."

CHAPTER ELEVEN

Parker gratefully accepted a to-go mug of tea from Sydney. She could still feel Syd's body under her hands, succumbing to her the night before.

"You were amazing last night. You do amazing things to me." Parker felt Sydney's strong hands under her hair, gently exposing the flesh at her neck, which she kissed softly.

"I can't get enough of you ever, baby. Come home soon, so we can do it again." She smiled and caught her in a long, slow kiss before Jenny coughed from the hallway.

"If I'm interrupting early morning kitchen sex, you'll have to forgive me; someone is hungry." Jenny looked down at Olivia, who was headed straight for Syd's legs.

"Sy-ee up!"

Syd pulled the toddler into her arms and addressed her seriously. "How about a tasty array of pureed organic crap in a jar? Yum."

"Yum," Olivia parroted.

"Well, I'll leave the gourmet selections to you. I have to go deal with less mature humans in their twenties and thirties." Parker kissed Olivia's round cheeks and accepted another from Sydney.

❖

"Good morning, Chris, please have a seat. I'm sure Mike will be here any minute." Parker gestured to the pair of gray fabric chairs in front of her desk.

"I would like to ask you something before he gets here." Chris's formal tone put Parker on guard.

"Go ahead."

"Do you believe in God?" He leaned over his knees and offered a concerned stare.

Parker took a deep breath before she replied. "Okay. Chris, you need to understand a few things. First of all, my religious beliefs are none of anyone's business unless and until I choose to share them in a suitable setting. Second, it is highly inappropriate to discuss those things in *this* setting. If you have human resources concerns, Jenny or I are the proper people to talk to, but only about *your* concerns, not our personal lives or anyone else's beliefs. DPI respects your freedom to exercise your religion, but you can't push that on anyone else at work. Do you understand?" Parker held his gaze to make her point.

"Yes, and I don't. But I shouldn't be expected to drink at parties or listen to secular music if it offends me. Or accept other things that aren't right." He looked as if he were pouting.

"Agreed. That's why we're having this meeting." Parker noticed Mike heading toward her office. "Good morning, Mike. Please, close the door behind you."

Mike slid the remaining visitor's chair a few feet away from Chris's before he sat. Parker took a long breath. "Okay. Mike, I understand that there was some conflict yesterday concerning your music being too loud."

"I never even touched the volume, Parker. It has been that way for *two* years." Mike looked incredulous at being sent to HR for something so minor.

"I understand that it has never been a problem before, but we have to be sensitive to other people who work around you. I'm going to have to ask you to refrain from playing music while Chris is in the office, or perhaps you could wear headphones in one ear so that it doesn't prevent you from hearing the phone or other people since you're here to work first and foremost. That way, you could still listen to music." Parker knew the compromise would be unsatisfactory.

Mike looked at Parker and shook his head. "Is that *all* I need to do? Can I go now?"

"You're excused. Thank you for your cooperation, Mike."

"Yeah, sure." He shook his head and looked glaringly at his coworker.

"Is there anything else you wish to discuss, Chris?" Parker tried to offer him a neutral expression when he didn't move to stand.

"I guess things are just different here. Where I grew up, I never saw anyone drink or do drugs, and I never knew anyone with sexual, um, problems. It's just not normal...for me, I mean." He looked sincere and uncomfortable and completely oblivious to how inappropriate his comments were.

"Chris, I know you don't mean for your statements to be offensive, but you can't call someone's sexual orientation a 'problem' because it's not. You can believe whatever you want about someone who lives in a manner counter to your religion, but you *can't* let that manifest at work. You have to treat everyone the same whether they drink, smoke, go to a temple or a synagogue instead of a church, or marry someone of the same sex. Just like they have to do the same for you. Do you understand?" She sighed and wondered how long people would be so concerned about other people's lives even when it had no effect on them.

He shrugged. "So, you're saying that I can't even ask someone if they're homosexual or what their religion is?"

"Yes. It's highly inappropriate, Chris, because it's none of your business. Just like it would be inappropriate for someone to ask you a question about *your* sexuality or religion. Chris, you're here to do a job. The only thing you should be worried about is doing your job to the best of your abilities. Do you understand?"

He nodded and stood to leave. She wondered if he had

missed the numerous gay couples at the CTI party who had no reason to hide who they were while in the home she shared with Syd. He seemed to process his thoughts and forced himself to refrain from speaking them aloud. He turned and left her office without saying anything else.

Parker sighed loudly and dropped her head onto her desk, already exhausted at only 8:30 in the morning. She shoved notes into Chris Newkirk's file and packed up the day's work to head home. She caught movement out of the corner of her eye and watched Jen and Sydney head toward her office.

"What's happening? Is something wrong?" Parker's pulse raced at the sight of them, and she moved from behind her desk.

"Why would anything be wrong?" Jenny smiled teasingly at her.

"Um, because my girlfriend brought you into the office where you had no plans to be and a small child is missing and..."

"I had a last-minute meeting with payroll over the errors, and rather than have another car here, Syd brought me in, and I'll just drive your car home. Betty and Nicole are entertaining Olivia until you're ready to go, if that's okay."

"Of course, it's okay. I just got scared for a moment." Parker blew out a loud breath. "It's just been a stupid morning already."

"Yeah, we ran into Frank and crew in the parking lot. Chris looked like he just woke up from a very faraway place, and as usual, Ben said nothing to anyone. Frank just looks at the ground now. I think Syd scares him." Jenny chuckled at the strange dynamic.

"It's no wonder after their little show at the party." She pointed at Syd, thinking about her and Mack's interaction with poor Frank. "Remind me to tell you about my meeting later. You'll love it." She gathered her bag and hoisted a stack of multicolored folders into Syd's arms.

"Will do. Thanks for watching Olivia. I owe you."

"Hardly. I love that little girl. I think she might remind me why I shouldn't walk into traffic after a day in this zoo. Well, her and a particularly handsome woman in the hallway." Her stage whisper was exaggerated for Sydney's benefit. "Ready?"

"At your service, Ms. Duncan." Sydney headed toward the elevator and waited for Parker to catch up.

"Got everything?" She moved the files to the opposite arm and pushed a strand of hair away from Parker's eye.

"Pretty sure I left my sanity back there, but I've managed without it this long…"

"Let's go home, baby. I'll spike your tea and rub your feet."

Syd's disarming smile centered Parker and reminded her that this was just a job. The most important part of her life stood with an armful of her work.

Parker walked into the data processing office where Betty was playing hide-and-seek with Olivia, who was crawling around Nicole's ankles.

"Ready to go, Olivia?" Syd called, causing the toddler to hurtle in her direction.

"Sy-ee up!" She stared up in the same pudgy-armed pose she had offered during the breakfast ritual.

Parker took the files and nodded at Olivia's favorite non-parent. "She wants you, love. Take it while you can."

Syd crouched down, staring into Olivia's huge black eyes, and felt the child grab at her neck. With one arm firmly around her, she lifted her over her shoulder and blew loudly into her round belly. Delighted squeals echoed over the office, irritating more than one person not enchanted with a shrieking child in the workplace, Parker was sure, since she had once been one of them. She walked quickly to open the door of the car and strapped Olivia into her seat. She suddenly longed for the quiet their home promised.

By four that afternoon, Parker chucked the last file onto the coffee table and watched Olivia sleep soundly on the sofa next to her. Syd worked intently in the loft, her hard features locked in concentration while she recreated a Maclean murder scene for the DA's office. Jenny pushed through the door, looking uncommonly unnerved.

Jenny's entrance caught Sydney's attention, and Jenny motioned for her to come downstairs.

"What's wrong? You look like you've seen a ghost. Or worse, an accounting department who can't get their shit together," Parker joked.

"What's up?" Sydney clearly sensed it wasn't a moment for joking.

Parker watched nervously as Jen unloaded her bags.

She opened her phone and handed a photo of the now familiar white envelope and square of paper to Sydney. "Mack sent a unit to retrieve the original when I told her."

"Where was it?" Parker asked before her girlfriend could.

"On your car. Under the wiper on the driver's side. Nothing on the outside this time, but I could tell it was the same as the others, so I took a picture of the message."

Syd turned the phone around so she could read the words.

You built your life on Satan's lies
The kind of life that all despise
You whore your soul to the evil dyke
You know inside it's me you like

Your persistent gaze, it burns my skin
I'll do my best to ignore your sin
Regret must fill your mind at night
Her fingers groping you aren't right

"Tell me who you saw today and what was said." Sydney sounded angry and accusatory.

Parker reflexively took a step back and stared at her before she tried to formulate an answer. Syd didn't scare her, but the intensity paired with the circumstances was reminiscent of their first few months together. She tried to ignore the anger that wasn't directed at her. "I had a meeting with Chris Newkirk and Mike Reynolds about the argument over the radio. I had to explain to Chris that he couldn't ask people about their personal lives, including calling sexual orientation a sexual problem. Quint came by with Terry Carver to touch base and told me the city released the CTI project starting Monday and then you guys. That's it."

"What do we know about this Newkirk kid? He was here for the party, right?" Sydney paced away and then back again, her fists clenched at her sides.

"Yes, he was, but he doesn't even seem like he likes me much. He considers gay people something to avoid, from what I gathered today. He also isn't very assertive, and this just doesn't sound like him." Parker wanted Syd to see it the way she did.

"Please, tell me you'll both be here all day tomorrow." Sydney swept her eyes between them.

Parker nodded and walked to the bedroom. She sat quietly on the bed and scanned through emails on her phone. She sent Quint a message informing him that she would be working from home another day and fought the feeling of being held captive by a nameless bully. Tears of resignation coursed down her cheeks. She didn't deserve this; they didn't deserve this. She was angry. Not afraid, purely angry.

Sydney shut the bedroom door. "Can I say something, or are you too mad right now?"

"Go ahead." Parker shrugged and stared at her hands, not looking at her. She didn't want Syd to see how upset she was, as it would add to the burden she felt Syd was carrying already.

"I'm always apologizing, I know, but I *am* sorry I spoke like that. It wasn't at you. I just got upset, and Jenny tells me I go to the 'scary place,' and I didn't mean to. I can't stop what I can't see, and I got a little crazy."

"I know, love. I'm just as pissed about this as you are." New tears fell as she pulled her knees to her face, hoping to shield it from Sydney.

Sydney slid onto the bed beside her and pulled Parker into her arms. "We'll find whoever this is and stop them, okay? I won't let anyone hurt you again."

Parker knew that Sydney would always have irrational guilt about Becky, and it drove her fierce desire to shield Parker from anything unpleasant. She accepted that, but having to manage her own feelings as well as Syd's reactions made her a little resentful sometimes.

Parker drew a deep breath, determined to shrug off the past few minutes. "I'm going to have Jenny pull the file on Chris just to be sure, but if you met this guy, he's just so wimpy; a religious zealot but timid nonetheless."

"I want to check on Carver and Frank even though you think it couldn't be them. Can you look at any other new people? Perhaps it could be someone from the party that you hadn't talked to yet or at least been around much? Hopefully, they can pull fingerprints from the notes, but he might be smart enough to wear gloves, who knows."

"Would he? He doesn't seem to be very smart. The notes are juvenile, in a way. Would he think of that?" She leaned against Sydney to capture a placid moment in her arms.

"I don't know, baby. We just have to look everywhere and be careful. Mack just texted that she'll be home early. This is no longer just an incident report; this is threatening and serious."

"Jenny doesn't need this either; she has enough going on with me out all the time." Parker despised feeling helpless, and this was wearing on her, she would admit. She adored Sydney's protective nature, but it was bordering on suffocation. She was starting to feel very alone in her protective custody. She didn't like the world thinking she was some delicate flower, either. She wondered how she could be perceived as a no-nonsense operations manager when people thought she was too fragile to leave the house?

❖

Syd shut her office door, and Mack sat heavily in the chair, looking at the images on the screen. "I talked to Major Charles on the way here. I don't have any active cases, so he'll let me work it until something else comes up. I can't promise miracles, Syd."

Syd knew she should be grateful that the small department would allow Mack to be involved at all, given that it was thankfully far from the violent crimes Mack normally worked.

"I'm not asking for any. Can you get Darcy to push getting the fingerprints?" Syd's ex-girlfriend had worked with them on a corruption case the year before and was good at her job as the crime lab manager for Silver Lake.

"She's more likely to do favors for you, isn't she?" Mack teased.

"Not since Taylor stole her heart. She has no time for idle fantasies of me anymore." Syd had been relieved when Darcy found something else to occupy her romantic focus.

Mack looked back to the notes. "Let's look at these in pieces. Some of the words don't matter, of course, but some may be key. When I interview, I can use them, gauge how comfortable *they* are with using them, you know?"

Syd nodded and projected the notes onto the wall screen. Mack began reading the lines out loud and analyzing the phrases.

"*To the exquisite hostess:* We assume that means he or she, probably he, was here that night, or he would have referred to her some other way." Mack tapped a pencil against her boot as she thought out loud.

"*A precious time, a lovely night, a gorgeous girl, a ray of light, thank you for your help and fun, all the world knows you're the one.* He's created a fantasy with her at the center of it.

"*I see your heart, in your blue eyes.* There are many people with blue eyes, but given what we know about him being here and her being a hostess, it's logical to assume the inference is Parker." Mack shook her head. "This absolutely narrows our suspect pool to someone who was in the house that night."

"*To feel you makes my pulse rate rise.* She's touched him, or he's touched her. Maybe by accident; maybe he made more out of a handshake, or he brushed against her somewhere." Sydney shuddered at the thought of some creep touching her girlfriend, even by accident.

"Until the time we touch again, and I reveal my thoughts without this pen. So, he wants to have a more intimate conversation with Parker and feels like there hasn't been an opportunity. That's why I am leaning away from this Terry guy. She's known him for years, and they talk all the time. This smells like someone who sees or talks to her only rarely and by chance.

"She can't feel you the way I do, her sick ways are not for you."

"Well, I think we can figure that one out." Sydney rolled her eyes. "He's clearly not marching in Pride parades."

"Maybe. Maybe not. It could be that it only affects him when it comes to her. That it could have been just as wrong in his eyes if she had a boyfriend or a husband. This just gives him a way to fight. Of course, he could be a giant homophobe, too, but we don't know." Mack continued reading. *"I'll feed your soul and set it free, you'd love your life, your place with me.* Again, he's just feeding the fantasy that she could, or should, want him."

"You built your life on Satan's lies, the kind of life that all despise. You don't believe he's a homophobe? Or a religious nut who thinks we're all evil?" Syd stared at her.

"It's definitely possible, but we also need to make sure he isn't just throwing us off intentionally." Mack read another line. *"You whore your soul to the evil dyke, you know inside it's me you'll like.* One has to wonder if you did something to be evil in his eyes, Syd, or just the fact that you exist triggers him. Regardless, he is angry about her not being with him. You're just a stumbling block. *Your persistent gaze, it burns my skin, I'll do my best to ignore your sin. Regret must fill your mind at night, her fingers groping you aren't right.* Here is where he's devolving a bit. He's had recent contact with her that has unnerved him. He's getting angrier and possibly becoming irrational."

"Irrational and dangerous, Mack. You have to talk to *everyone* before this gets worse." Syd paced the length of the long room and rubbed at the tense muscles in her neck.

"And we will, Syd. Talk through it with me about who it could be," Mack said.

"Fucking anyone who was in our fucking house!" Syd momentarily lost control of her emotions when she realized how many possibilities there were and how far they could be from stopping him before he hurt Parker.

Mack stood up and stepped into Sydney's path, her nose barely an inch from Sydney's. "Stop acting like an idiot, and help me work through this, Sydney. You want to protect her? Then stop losing it every time you think about it. It doesn't help anybody...and where Parker is concerned, it makes you *stupid*. I need you using your head. You know you're good at this stuff when your heart isn't in the way."

Mack was probably one of the few people Syd knew who could talk to her that way. She was right, and Sydney knew it. She folded into her chair with her elbows on her knees. She grazed her fingers roughly through her hair while she replayed the night of the party.

"I know. I'm fine. What do we need now?" Syd was more focused than enraged now.

"List of names so far. New people, strange people, off encounters." Mack sat poised to take notes.

"I know vaguely who they are, but the girls have the details. We need them." Syd looked at Mack, who smiled at her.

"Parker needs you, too. You got this?" Mack looked less pissed and a lot more understanding.

"Yeah, I got this." Syd nodded and jogged down the stairs with Mack behind her.

Parker sat with Olivia as they practiced rolling the ball to her smiling mother. "Ma-a go!" accompanied every roll assisted by Parker. Syd sat on the floor behind Parker, and Mack perched on the sofa behind Jen.

"Need us?" Parker asked.

"Every second of every day," Syd whispered huskily into Parker's thick hair.

"Careful how you use that voice, Hyatt; we have company." Parker leaned back into Syd, who gently massaged her neck. Mack held her arms out toward her daughter.

"Okay. We need names." Mack moved her child to bounce on her left knee and prepared to take notes with her right hand. "Anyone new, weird, strange, or all of the above."

Jenny shifted as she seemed to snap into work mode. "Ten new hires in the last month. Four temps, six permanent." Jenny stared at the ceiling as she recalled names from memory. "I don't have anything on the temps except names, since we pay the agency, and they pay their employees."

"We have no idea who would be considered new from CacheTech or PRG, but we can ask." Parker shifted so she was closer to Syd.

"I'll call Richard, and Syd can call Taylor." Mack looked at Sydney. "See if she can remember anybody odd: a new hire, contractor, anything like that. Park, you work with Jenny and see if we can get a list together of everyone who was here: employee, contractor, or the male guest of one. Then brainstorm any early encounters, odd introductions, or reprimands. Both of you think back to the party, and who might show up on both your lists."

Jenny grabbed her laptop and shifted to sit next to Parker. Within an hour, they had finalized an exhaustive list. Jenny called prior employers on all six new permanent hires. Two of them were women, so it seemed unlikely, but they had decided not to skip a step because of a perceived exclusion.

Taylor had reported to Syd that no new people had attended the party from CTI. She joked that everyone there was weird, but only two contractors seemed even remotely plausible, and they weren't invited that night. Sydney saw a potential only with the people *at* the party. The unwelcome missives seemed to reference other encounters with Parker, ones that CTI people would have been unlikely to have. To be sure, Syd confirmed that Parker and Jen knew neither of the contractors.

Richard hadn't been able to think of anyone new. Aside from Dayne and himself, only four other members of their staff attended the party, two of whom were gay men and the other two women who came alone—all of them had been with the firm more than two years. Parker and Jen had never even spoken to them outside of the party that night.

Jenny handed over their list. "This is everybody. I called prior references again, trying to make it sound like I had misplaced the file or something. I should get calls back by the end of the week or so."

"I summarized my meeting with Chris Newkirk and the incident with Terry even though he wasn't here. I also just wrote some impressions on the other new hires. Syd, you saw four of them at the office on their first day. I also wrote down names of any reprimands or write-ups over the last month. None of those people were at the party, so I doubt that's even relevant."

"What do you really feel about this Newkirk guy?" Mack scanned the paragraph she had written.

"I think he's sheltered and small-minded. I think he has limited experience dealing with anyone outside his family or his religion. I don't think he'll make it long in the company, but that's more because he can't get out of his own way than because he's some crazy stalker." Parker closed her laptop and felt the weight of the day, and now the night, settle over her.

Jenny pushed up from the floor. "Can we get everything tomorrow night, Park? We have that early staffing meeting in the morning, and Mack and I have to get Olivia to bed. I have to say I'm looking forward to my own bed tonight."

"Of course. Go. I can bring some of it with me in the morning, or we'll get it packed up for whenever you need it." Parker took Syd's hand and pulled her up to stand beside her. "Why don't you leave me your keys and drive home with Mack?

I'll drive your car to work, and you can just drop me back here after the meeting?"

"That's perfect. Okay with you, hon?" Jenny smiled wearily at Mack, who seemed to share her sleepy constitution.

"Yeah. I'll drop you at the office before I head to the lab." Mack steered her family into the hall. As she shut the door, silence fell over the loft.

"Wow, quiet," Parker whispered to Syd playfully.

"You didn't tell me you were going into work tomorrow." Syd tried to keep the tension from her voice, but she knew she failed.

"I forgot about the meeting, and I can't stay locked up here forever. I have to go to the jobsite on Monday, and this is the only day I will have. Who knows, I might run into someone who triggers for me. Someone I didn't think of. I won't be there all day, and I'll call you when I leave. I feel like a disobedient child who has to call in her every move."

Syd understood. She could see Parker's point of view, but she wouldn't, couldn't, acquiesce just for Parker's peace of mind. They had been here before. Syd could feel the same gut reaction she had a couple of years ago when she knew that Parker was a target. She in no way wanted Parker to feel caged, but she couldn't work out how to protect her from an invisible threat without keeping her close.

Syd struggled to swallow all those words and more. *I need you here. You are everything to me. I can't lose you. I won't let him have you. I finally found what home means.* Instead, she just nodded and managed, "Let's get some sleep."

❖

Syd dressed for the gym as Parker shoved the last of the files into her overstuffed briefcase. She knew that Sydney would indeed go to the gym after attempting a discreet tail to her office.

She was mildly amused that Sydney thought she could do discreet in a black Porsche convertible. She didn't bother being insulted that Syd expected her not to notice; she loved her more for caring. If it made her feel better, she would endure the scrutiny.

As Parker steered Jenny's car into the Davidson properties lot, Syd made a U-turn and really headed for the gym. A few minutes later, Parker sat down at her desk to plow through stacks of paperwork and uncharacteristically forgot to check the clock. By the time she looked up, she was already five minutes late. She ran down the hall to join the eight o'clock meeting. All six new employees were being introduced as she pushed open the door, knocking into the unsuspecting group and nearly losing her balance in the process. She excused herself as she brushed past the crowd and headed for her seat next to Jenny. Parker was suddenly consumed by anger. At herself for being late and more accurately, at whoever was derailing her orderly, ordinarily happy life. She drove a pen onto the blotter at her seat and quietly fumed.

"...anything, Parker?" Jenny's voice broke through.

"I'm sorry, what?" She forced herself to focus on the room and then on Jenny, who looked at her carefully.

"I just asked if you had anything for the new group." Jenny's voice sounded casual.

Parker looked at each face staring at her from around the room. She studied them as if one would suddenly step forward and identify themselves as the despicable lurker haunting her life. She filled the awkward silence when she realized she had been staring too long, "I'm sorry, no, I don't. Thanks."

Jenny excused the new employees and continued a discussion with the remaining staff about hiring needs and potential issues within the various departments. Parker heard little and said nothing. When the meeting ended, she marched back to her office and firmly shut the door. She stood at the window and stared blankly into the hazy morning where other people carried on a normal day. Parker thought how normally she was capable, efficient, and focused. She hated not being those things because she had allowed herself to become a victim of what was probably nothing more than a sick joke or misguided admirer.

Jenny opened her door without knocking and shut it again behind her. She stood beside Parker at the window.

"You don't need to explain what happened. I already know. This isn't your fault, and you are entitled to be...disturbed, I guess. If it's one of them, we'll figure it out. If it's not, we'll figure that out, too." Jenny nudged her with a gentle shoulder. "Give yourself a break, and stop trying to control the world."

Parker continued to stare through the glass as she spoke, almost monotone. "Syd followed me to work today, and although I told myself I'm good with it because it's just that she's worried, I'm not okay with it. I might as well be riding a guarded bus for wayward kids. I was late for a meeting for probably the first time in my life, and then I sat there and stared at all of them, trying to see if someone was looking at me strangely or acting off. I feel like I have no control over my own brain, and instead of being sad or scared, I'm just incredibly pissed."

Jenny stood still and let her talk through it. "I've known you long enough to know that you're harder on yourself than anyone else will ever be. Remember that." She squeezed her hand and walked to the door. "Don't leave without talking to me, okay?"

Parker nodded and stayed at the window. She scanned the lot, knowing she would find nothing, just as she expected. No creepy guy with binoculars, parchment paper, and an evil look in his eye. She stared at cars coming and going in the lot and wondered if they would ever know which one carried a disturbed man intent on destroying them.

Chapter Twelve

Syd left the gym and pulled blindly down her street, running scenarios through her mind, half expecting some elucidating thought to sail into her brain and solve the nagging questions that crouched in the shadows. Syd turned into her space and noticed Mia's truck still parked where it had been early in the morning. Syd knew Mia often worked early, but she never knew her to go in late, especially on a Friday. Syd could hear her TV from the hall and tapped on her door.

Mia moved the door aside. "Hey, you. Come in." Mia opened the door wider for Sydney.

"Sorry to bother you. You okay?" Syd felt the chill from the air-conditioning move over her perspiring skin and shivered involuntarily. "I just noticed your car was still here, and I thought you might be sick or something."

Mia rubbed her warm hands over Syd's arms. "Sorry. I left the air turned down. I'm not sick; the boss just gave me a free day off because I've been going in and doing a lot of early mornings for him. Are you all right? You look distracted." Mia pulled at Syd's hand and walked her into the kitchen. "Want some coffee?"

"Sure, that would be great. Thanks." Syd watched Mia prepare mugs. "Are *you* doing better? I mean, are you feeling better about things?"

"Yeah. Thanks for asking. I guess I'll always have some up

days and some down days. It's good to report fewer down than up now, which is a hell of an improvement from a few months ago. You guys have really helped. You especially." Mia looked appreciatively at Syd and handed over the hot mug. "You remind me of Sandy a lot. The way you're always looking after everyone. You're a good person, Sydney."

"That's nice of you to say, but it's nothing anyone else wouldn't do." Syd dismissed the compliment.

"Yes, it is." Mia seemed to fade away in her memory. "You're like her. Like Sandy in a lot of ways."

Sydney remembered Parker proudly showing her around the newly renovated space just after they had met. Syd tried not to focus on the turmoil swirling around them now.

She looked up at Mia just before Mia pushed her mouth onto Sydney's and leaned her body onto hers. Syd's mouth responded automatically. Mia's tongue moved against hers before the foreign lips fully registered. Her eyes flew open, and she saw Mia's flutter closed.

Syd put her hands on Mia's hips and pushed her solidly backward. She stared at her, unable to form the appropriate words for what felt like hours. "Mia, what are you doing? We can't...I'm not..." Parker's face flashed into Sydney's mind, and fear at the implication of the last seconds in Mia's embrace overwhelmed her.

Mia's eyes suddenly focused on her. "Oh my God. I'm sorry, Syd." Mia's tone was panicked and embarrassed. "I don't know what happened. I didn't mean to...shit." She folded her arms around her waist as if she was unexpectedly in pain.

Syd recovered enough to think clearly. "Did I do something to make you think..."

"No. Syd, no. I was just talking to you and thinking about Sandy, about how like her you are, and I just wasn't thinking. Oh God, Parker is going to hate me. We can't tell her. Please, Syd, don't tell her," Mia begged.

"I'll explain it to her. I don't keep things from her, Mia. She'll understand that you were just thinking about Sandy, not me." Syd hoped her words would convince Mia and eventually Parker.

"I wouldn't understand, Sydney." Mia sounded frightened as she stared into Sydney's eyes. "If someone hit on Sandy, I would have gone crazy. Parker is going to hate me. Jen and Mack are going to hate me."

"First of all, you didn't hit on me. I was just here. It was a mistake. No one else will even know. Please, don't worry. It'll be okay." Syd held Mia's arm where she normally would have hugged her reassuringly. All she wanted to do was go home and wait for Parker. Then again, she hoped for time to think. She couldn't fathom that conversation heaped on top of the rest of the draining events in their lives.

Mia followed her to the door, and Syd tried to send her a casual smile that she feared might look like anything but. At home, Sydney stood under a scalding spray in her shower and attempted to wash away the feeling that she had just betrayed Parker. She silently prayed that the love of her life would truly understand.

She dried and dressed quickly in dark jeans and a polo shirt. She caressed a thumb over Parker's picture and sent her a text:

Can I pick you up from work when you're done?

I would love that. I will be ready in an hour. She was happy to receive Parker's return text, but her mind raced when she thought about the conversation she was going to have. One she felt now forced to have. She pushed away the thought of Parker rejecting her explanation, not understanding what really happened. Parker knew her better than anyone, so she forced herself to trust that Parker would understand. If the roles were reversed, Syd thought, she doubted she would be the least bit reasonable.

❖

Parker was waiting just inside the lobby when Syd stopped in front of the heavy mahogany doors. She waved to the receptionist and heaved her bags into the tiny trunk. Sliding in beside Sydney, she smiled at the welcome embrace across the console.

"I'm glad you're here." Parker rested her head on Sydney's shoulder as she shoved the car into gear.

"Me, too, baby. I needed to see you." Syd took a ragged breath and headed into a tiny city park greenway just off the main road.

"Did something happen? Was there a new note?" Her voice rose, counter to the calm she showed just seconds before.

Syd jerked the brake up after she backed into a secluded parking space. "No, no more notes. I just have to tell you something...about Mia." Syd felt she had pushed herself off a cliff and suddenly had to figure out how to fly.

"Is she okay?" Parker's worried face stared into Syd's.

"She's fine. She was at home when I got back from the gym. I thought maybe she was sick, so I went in to check on her." Syd's fingers traced an abstract design over the surface of the steering wheel.

"Was she all right?" Parker was studying Syd's face; her pained expression made Syd's stomach clutch.

"Yeah. She was." Syd breathed heavily and forced herself to finish. "So, I'm in the kitchen, and she's talking about Sandy. And I'm thinking about the first time I came into the loft with you after we met, remember?"

Parker nodded and smiled briefly.

"Then Mia says that I remind her of Sandy or something like that, and then, I think she's really thinking about Sandy at that moment, and she gets kind of lost in that memory or something..." Syd realized she wasn't being eloquent. "Then she...uh..."

"What, Syd?" Parker folded her knees under her and turned in her seat, letting her shoes fall onto the floor mat. She reached over and brushed a thumb over Syd's cheek.

"She kissed me. Well, not really me. I think she was just lonely and thinking about Sandy, and she wasn't thinking. I pushed her away when I realized what was happening, and she started to panic and apologize. Park, it wasn't me, I swear. It was just a mistake. I'm so sorry."

Parker stared at her as if digesting the information. "Did you kiss her back?" Parker spoke softly.

"I think I did, just reflex, for a second, a half a second. I was thinking about you right before it, and it took my dumb ass a second to figure out what was happening. Please, don't be mad." Syd held both her hands tightly.

Parker smiled and shook her head. "I'm not mad, love. If you told me you suddenly had feelings for her and didn't bother to tell me, I would be mad. But I'm not angry at you...or her, for that matter; she's had a rough year, and I don't believe she would risk her relationship with all of us for a roll in the hay with you. Despite how irresistible you are."

Syd stared in awe as Parker lifted herself from her seat to straddle her. "Don't look so worried, love. Things happen." Parker smiled seductively and grazed her fingers through her coarse black hair. "Once, though. They just happen once." Her mouth melted over Sydney's, and she pulled Parker down and against her in response, returning the unexpectedly frantic kiss. It was followed by another longer, more desperate one. Syd felt pounding electricity fire down her spine as Parker's hips pulsed against her heated core. Syd slipped her hands under Parker's thin blouse, and Parker slid her fingers under Sydney's belt.

Sydney reclined the seat, and Parker leaned more heavily against her chest as a result. Her strong fingers drew anxious lines up Parker's smooth back, and Parker whimpered at the sensation.

Syd broke from the kiss just long enough to speak. "You're killing me."

Parker pushed Syd's shirt up to caress her and press Sydney's chest against her own. Parker found her hard nipples, pinching the pebbled flesh that pressed into her palms and causing Sydney to moan in response. Syd forced the skirt over Parker's hips and felt the heat of her against her stomach.

"I have to touch you." Syd kissed the words into her. Her breath was fast and shallow as her fingertips found Parker's burning flesh under thin fabric. Parker moved roughly against her hand.

"Yes. Syd, like that. Make me come for you. Please." Parker coursed her teeth under Sydney's ear, and her hips ground impatiently against her.

Sydney tore the final barrier away and found the saturated place that caused Parker to cry out for her. Syd pressed her fingers over the buried crests that she knew could push Parker over. Sydney drove hard against her, relishing each uneven gasp she could feel hotly delivered against her skin. She felt Parker grasp at her shoulders when Syd was finally inside her.

Moving her thick hair, Syd exposed Parker's neck and grazed her teeth over the long muscle, causing a guttural groan to rise in her throat. Parker rocked harder and faster against her, the pressure seemed to be building in layers, as Syd navigated and steered her to her tumbling release. The tiny compartment of the car was engulfed with the thick desire that had built between them. The frenzied charge of energy multiplied as they consumed each other's mouths.

"Now. Syd, now."

Syd felt Parker propel her body mercilessly against her. She drank in every maddening, sensuous stroke of Parker's hips. She felt the last driving rhythm leak from Parker's body as Sydney pressed her mouth hungrily over hers. She felt Parker's heart pound against her chest as she breathed raggedly, crushing her body onto Sydney's. She slid the thick belt open and stroked Sydney, who jerked involuntarily at the exquisite contact when she was already aroused to the point of hypersensitivity. Parker skidded her tongue over Syd's bottom lip and stroked her center gently at first. Syd pressed back into the seat, accepting Parker's mouth on hers. Sydney arched against her hand and then jerked violently before she allowed herself to let go.

"You are so amazing." Parker sank against her.

"I love touching you." Syd pressed Parker harder to her. "I feel like I can't get enough of you."

"You seriously made me feel like I was going to explode." Parker began to breathe more evenly.

"I'm glad." Syd still held Parker against her, stroking her body lovingly, not willing to lose the connection she found everywhere their skin touched.

"I love you so much." Parker sighed. She glanced around the small, dark space. "I honestly didn't think it was even possible to do that in this car."

"You and me both. But I can't imagine a better christening." Syd held Parker's face, memorizing every feature as if it were her last opportunity. "Anywhere we need to be right now?"

"Home, where I can thank you properly and for hours." Parker arched her eyebrow playfully as she flopped indelicately into the passenger seat and attempted to straighten her wrinkled clothes. The remnants of her black thong remained on the seat between Syd's legs. She snatched them before Parker could retrieve them. "Mine. Souvenir." Syd smiled, shoving the useless garment into her pocket. She had to stop herself from speeding out of the tiny park, amazed that no one had pulled in while they were lost in each other. Sydney certainly hadn't expected the outcome when she told Parker about kissing another woman. Parker amazed her. She was practical and reasonable, always. She knew Sydney didn't want anyone but her, and Sydney would always make sure she remembered that.

For the rest of the evening, Parker felt like a giddy teenager with a new crush as she repeatedly drove Syd to her surrender.

Sydney teased her and sated her, and they found the blissful place they could bask in together.

They tucked the cover of their solitude around them, grateful for the private place that cradled them again. Parker didn't think about the mistaken kiss by a grieving partner or misguided notes by a potentially disturbed and presumably lonely man. She thought only of the safe place she found in Sydney's arms.

Syd pulled Parker's body to lie back against hers as they flipped through magazine articles and fantasized about vacations they would take together and places they would visit. By midnight, Sydney had fallen deeply asleep.

Parker wrapped the comforter over Syd and skimmed a kiss over her cheek. She moved quietly off the bed and threw on a long T-shirt over loose shorts. She carried their empty glasses to the kitchen, stopping briefly to stare out into the dark to wonder if anyone was out there, possibly watching her at the same time, and cursed herself for obsessing. She carried in a fresh glass of water and placed it on the coaster on the nightstand. She got into bed and found Sydney awake again, poring over her files containing copies of the notes as she ran her fingers absently through Parker's hair.

"Sex machines have to sleep too, y'know," Parker mumbled from her pillow. "I might require your services tomorrow, and I don't want you to wear down too quickly." She squinted into the light shining brightly from Syd's side of the bed.

"Message received, gorgeous. I'm right behind you." She dropped the file into a drawer and reached over her pistol to turn the switch on the lamp. As soon as the room was dark, Parker turned to lie against Syd's warm body, sending her instantly to sleep.

❖

The shower of glass was lessened only slightly by the thin blinds that blew gently in the breeze of the air-conditioning.

Sydney instinctively rolled over Parker and pulled her to the floor, using the bedding and the mattress as a shield. The noise ended just in time for Sydney to hear the roar of a poorly mufflered engine fade into the distance. She threw herself across the pillow and retrieved her gun, her heart racing.

"Parker, get in the closet, and call 9-1-1, now."

"Syd, no, come with me." Parker grasped her arm, her hand trembling.

"Go. I'll be right back." She ran through the dark house and into the lobby. Taillights faded into the distance, and Sydney had no idea if they were related to the incident that shattered the only peace they had known in a week. If she had been alone, she would have driven through the dark streets searching, but she would never leave Parker by herself.

She checked the lot and the cars, finding all three of them untouched. She whipped back at the sound of footsteps, her gun leveled in front of her when she saw Parker outside, now wrapped in the blanket. Parker winced at the weapon aimed at her. Sydney dropped it quickly and rushed her back inside.

"Why were you out there?" Syd rubbed her arms briskly as if it were ten degrees outside.

"Same reason you were." Parker's deadpan delivery made Sydney laugh despite the weight of the situation.

"Fair enough." Syd closed the door behind them. "Did you call the police?"

"Mack's on the way." She took a shaky breath. "Something's on the floor. A rock or a piece of a brick wrapped in paper."

"Did you touch it?" Syd moved toward the dim lights of the kitchen.

"No, I've been around the caped crusaders long enough to know better. I just left it," Parker replied softly.

"Are you cut anywhere?"

Parker shook her head. "Why are they doing this?"

"I don't know, Park." She no longer felt capable of handling this on her own, a fact she would never admit to Parker.

Parker nodded and sat on a barstool.

Mack slid open the heavy barn door, not bothering to announce herself. Syd took in the frayed cargo shorts and dark collared shirt as she stepped into the loft. She was off duty, but this wasn't about an assignment. She laid her black portfolio on the counter, and Parker barely managed a nod.

"You okay?" She pulled Parker against her shoulder and rubbed her back.

"I'm fine."

Syd watched her lie but knew better than to call her on it.

"Jenny said to call her if you want her to come now; otherwise, she'll be here when Olivia wakes up."

"No need. I'm fine. Let the baby sleep."

To Syd, she sounded resigned and resentful, definitely not fine. And if Mack's expression was to be trusted, she didn't believe it either. She led Mack toward their former sanctuary.

Syd watched Mack examine the area where the object, a broken brick, had landed. A white square of paper lay in a limp roll next to the jagged chunk of masonry.

She handed Mack tweezers from the vanity, which Mack used to angle the paper so they could read the latest missive.

You touched her skin with your tainted hand
It's only mine to feel, on my command
You use their bodies to quench your lust
You take their love and betray her trust

Lustful bitch, you groped her breast
She'll watch your heart ripped from your chest
It's her I love and you I hate
Cheating dyke—you'll learn your fate

Mack pulled her phone from her pocket and requested a crime scene technician while she flipped open her notebook against her knee.

She hung up and stared at Sydney. "I need to tell you something else."

Syd looked at her expectantly, dreading what she was about to say.

"Jenny found another one on her car this afternoon. I didn't want to worry you with it until the morning, since up until now, they haven't been overtly threatening."

"Yeah, until now. What did it say?"

Mack opened an image of a plastic-covered note on her phone and handed it to Syd.

Need to talk, to make a plan
Map out your life with just one man
Its time you join me for our date
Be sure this time you are not late

I saw the way she abandoned you
Aroused by a whore, her something new
One day you'll cringe at that one's touch
Her betrayal of you said so much

"What the hell is this, Mack? This doesn't make sense. What is he thinking?" She paced the edge of the room, avoiding the knots of glass that would crunch into the floor.

"I wish I knew, but I don't. Do you have *any* insight into what made him so crazy that he wrote *two* notes?"

Syd closed her eyes and pulled her teeth hard over her bottom lip, cringing at the implication of what she was about to reveal. "I picked Parker up at the office this afternoon, and we were talking at the little park down the street. We were just sitting there, and we were kissing. We ended up, um, together, in the car. I guess he could have seen us; he must have been watching us."

"In *your* car?" Mack stared at her skeptically.

"Yes, asshole. My car." Syd managed a smirk. "And stop trying to picture it because I know you are."

Mack shook her head.

"The thing is, he would have seen Parker. How can I be cheating if I *am* with her?"

"He's obviously not dealing with reality." She motioned for Syd to follow her to the living room where they waited for the crime scene tech to show up. Syd saw Parker sip from a tall glass of orange juice, and she knew it wasn't just juice. She raised her eyebrows in question.

Parker straightened and shrugged. "What? Technically, the bars just closed, so one screwdriver before bed isn't a big deal."

"You're right, especially if you share." Syd took a long swallow and pulled Parker against her, grateful for the soothing strokes of Parker's fingers down her sides.

"I need to tell you that there are two notes from today. The one from tonight and one Jen found on her car this afternoon."

"Why Jenny's car?" Parker looked confused.

"I assume because you were driving it this morning," Mack said from where she sat.

"This is crazy." She shook her head and stared at the counter. "I want to read them."

Syd wanted to shield her from the threatening words and disturbing implications, but she knew Parker wouldn't welcome the gesture at this point any more than she would have.

Parker finished reading and returned Mack's phone to her. She stood and stepped toward Syd, speaking quietly. "It means someone was watching me, us—today in the park, Sydney." She wrapped her arms around her body as if to cover herself.

"I think that's what it looks like, too. I'm so sorry this is happening." Sydney rubbed her hands over Parker's back and pressed her lips softly against her temple as Parker leaned into Sydney's arms.

A knock jolted them out of the moment, and Mack slid the door open to admit Darcy Dean.

"I saw your address and your call number on the dispatch." She addressed Syd and then Mack. "What the hell is going on?"

"Right now, criminal damage to property, but likely stalking and communicating threats by the time we finish."

Darcy hugged Sydney and moved to put her arms around Parker. "You okay?"

"Sure, it's a laugh a minute around here, Darcy. Don't you miss us?" Her tone was sarcastic and angry.

"I took a bunch of pictures before you came. Log in to your computer, and I'll port them over while you're working back there." Syd pulled a transfer cable from the junk drawer under the counter.

"10-4, Sy-Fy." Darcy used the nickname she'd used with Syd more than a decade before. The inference was once a flirtation aimed at reconnecting with her old love; today, she clearly meant only to create a familiar moment despite a stressful encounter at two thirty in the morning. Though Syd could tell Parker wasn't paying much attention.

Darcy followed Mack to the bedroom as Sydney started the transfer onto her laptop. Parker slid off the stool and walked slowly to the window. She pushed the blinds up and stared into the street, a solo homage to the darkness.

Sydney fought the urge to lower the blinds but chose to turn the lights out in the living room instead. She stood behind Parker and waited for Parker to focus on her. "We'll figure this out."

"How? When he actually comes after us? Or hurts you?" Parker turned abruptly and fisted her hands into Syd's collar. "Do you understand that I need you? That I'm more terrified to live without you than you could ever be to live without me?"

"Not possible, Parker." Syd pulled her to the bench away from the window and knelt in front of her. "Park, you're my world, and I'll make sure this guy pays for what he's doing to us, okay? Please trust me."

"I do trust you, Syd. But you can't stop this any more than I can if we don't know where it's coming from. Mack can't stop it. I'm afraid to leave you because I don't know where you'll be when I get back. I'm scared to be at work because I'm afraid my life will have changed by the time I get home. That you won't be here." Parker clenched her fists tighter and pounded them weakly against Sydney's shoulders. "That someone will try to take you away from me again." The vodka seemed to have only weakened her resolve to stand up and fight against the faceless stranger trying to invade their lives, and tears streamed down her cheeks.

Sydney fought the pain associated with Parker's sobs now creating an agonizing sound in her chest. "We *will* figure this out. I won't lose you. Not ever."

"You don't know," Parker whispered, sounding defeated. She again turned to stare into the darkness when she heard Darcy and Mack headed toward them.

Darcy, stopping behind them, looked upset when she noticed Parker's tearstained cheeks.

"I've gotten all I can. We have one smudge on the last note but nothing I can print. I'm sorry." She held Parker's hand. "We have a company that'll come and board that up until you can get someone out here. You want me to call them?"

Syd knew that the offer was the contribution of a friend and not the typical service of a tiny police department. "Yeah, that would be good. We may not find anyone with the weekend." Syd disconnected her phone from Darcy's computer and handed it back to her.

"Consider it done. I'll see if there's anything else we can find in the meantime." She turned back to Parker. "I'll really try, Park."

"I know you will. Thanks, Darcy," Parker whispered and stared out at the street. "Mack, please tell Jen I'll call her later. She doesn't need to come over."

"Will do." Mack walked with Sydney toward the door. "I'll call you if we get anything."

"Thanks." Syd locked the door behind them and turned to Parker. "Will you come over to the couch with me and lie down?"

Parker followed without answer, but neither of them slept. Syd pretended to rest, but she was on high alert for every creak of the century-old building, and any shift of any branch outside their window brought her laser focus to study, analyze, and brace for a call to action. She would *not* fail Parker, whether Parker thought it was her job or not.

CHAPTER THIRTEEN

Mack had told Sydney everything she didn't want to hear. Response from the lab had confirmed that there were no useable prints or any smidgen of forensic data that might tell them who was torturing them. Mack told her she now had an entire accordion file dedicated to the case, which she'd hoped would never even have been called a case.

Syd saw Mack's car back into the space next to hers but continued to stare toward the front door of Davidson Properties. Mack jerked open the passenger door of the car and dropped heavily into the seat next to Syd, who never moved to look at her.

"First rule of surveillance is to be inconspicuous. Since you're driving a shiny black Porsche, let's go to number two... lock your doors."

Syd was monotone as she replied to Mack, not looking at her. "Do you not think I saw your *inconspicuous* city ride with the visor strobes? And I *unlocked* the doors because you're predictable." Syd continued her stare at the front of the office building.

"What do you think you'll see out here?" Mack stretched her legs out under the dash and scanned the confined space.

"Probably nothing. Maybe some guy with three heads pulling his monster truck out behind her. Why are you here?"

"I talked to Davidson. I told him I wanted to do a few interviews with the new guys and see who I could eliminate.

Maybe the three-headed guy will show up while I'm here and tap me on the shoulder."

"Good thought." Sydney stared ahead, cataloguing every movement. Cars coming and going, employees and visitors arriving and leaving. She knew if she looked away she might miss the crucial moment when she could stop all of this.

"How's she doing since this all happened?" Mack asked.

"Depends. One minute she's pissed and the next she wants to give up and not leave the house. If I didn't think she'd blame me later, I'd take her up on option two. I'm smart enough to know that it would bite me in the ass if this is ever over."

"So, your fallback position is close your business and tail her until he shows himself?"

"Got anything better?" Sydney asked, clenching and unclenching her fists around the steering wheel. "What would you do if it were Jenny?"

"Likely arrest her every morning on some bullshit charge so she had to ride in my police car for the rest of the day." Mack grinned, clearly hoping to break her friend's mood.

"And you accuse me of being irrational." Syd tried to smile but knew it fell flat.

"Want to do something completely against the rules?" Mack elbowed her.

"Almost always." Syd pulled her eyes away from the door briefly. "What did you have in mind?"

"Listen to these interviews and give me your gut? Remotely, of course."

"You mean listen from far away, so I don't snap someone's head off?" Syd smirked at Mack, whose SLPD cap was pulled low over her eyes, masking her expression.

"Precisely. See? This is why we work well together. You get me."

Mack smiled at her.

"Who are you doing first?" Syd suddenly had a reason to

focus and could feel valued as a city contractor instead of a crime target's helpless girlfriend.

"Probably the Chris guy and then Frank. I don't think he's good for it, but I don't want to skip him, either." She read from her notes.

"Do Frank first. He's nervous enough to spill his guts about everything before he knows it's even relevant. He might have a gut on his new guys without knowing it, too." Syd felt the fire in her return. Not being some helpless bystander was the only thing she thought might help alleviate the frustration of doing essentially nothing.

"Good call. I'll call you from the conference room in ten. Mute your phone, and don't move from your car unless your ass is on fire."

"Yessir, Lieutenant."

Mack turned to look back toward Sydney's car before disappearing through the heavy doors.

Syd answered Mack's conference app call the second it came through. To her delight, Mack had activated the video as well, placing the phone at the end of the table so Syd had a nice visual vantage point. Syd obediently muted her line and watched as Mack settled in and dialed the conference room speakerphone to request Frank Meyers meet her in the Sycamore Conference Room.

"Good morning, Frank." Mack stood as the small man entered the room. His eyes darted over the table and he took the seat she gestured to.

"Morning." Meyers's voice shook as he sat and cleared his throat as if to steady it.

"Frank, do you know why we're here?" Mack began without small talk and intentionally didn't reintroduce herself to him.

"No, ma'am. Am I in trouble? Did something happen?" His eyes darted around nervously.

"You tell me."

The technique rarely worked on the innocent. Guilty people usually redirected or made something up to try to steer the conversation. In Frank's case, Syd thought he might just black out.

"I really don't know what you're talking about."

"Fair enough. Let's move on." Syd saw Mack's hands move to cover her notebook. "If I asked you to identify someone at work that made you concerned or that you thought maybe wasn't stable, who would you name, Frank?"

He smiled for an instant and then looked unsure if he should smile. Syd watched him visibly censor the obvious flippant response he had considered and she'd heard a thousand versions of.

"I guess I don't know anyone. There are quite a few people that I don't know at all...you know, new people." He scanned the table as if looking for clues he couldn't find.

"Who are the new people?"

"Ben Barrett, Chris Newkirk...they work for me. Then there's Randy and another guy named Steve in accounting. They all started at the same time, but I don't work with them much."

"Describe them to me, Frank."

Syd knew Mack never asked a yes or no question in an interview if she could help it. She asked for descriptions or details because then the person had to say something or overtly refuse.

"Well, Ben is quiet, I mean *really* quiet. For a while I thought he just hated me or DPI, but then I realized he just doesn't talk to anybody. I took all the new guys out one night, and he just stood in the corner and watched people. He's great at his job, he just doesn't talk much. I think he's shy."

"Know anything about his personal life?" Mack rolled her pen between her fingers.

"Not a thing. He doesn't wear a ring, so I guess he's single. Someone said he has a girlfriend, but he hasn't ever said anything to me." Frank chuckled as he relaxed into a comfortable place where he got to talk about other people instead of himself.

"How about Chris?" Mack didn't let his mind wander too long.

"He's a mess. Pretty good at his job. Says he did scheduling work for his dad's company before this, but outside of that, all I know is there's a long list of things he doesn't do. Real religious, which is fine, but everything in his world is religion and perfection. He prays before every meal, irons his ties, and carries his own pencils to work. Part of me thinks he had them blessed or something." Frank smiled at his own joke.

"Tell me more about how everything in his world is religion? How does he bring it up?"

"Well, he had a fight with Mike on his second day 'cuz he was playing the radio, and Chris said he couldn't listen to it because it wasn't Christian music. And there was the party for the folks at CTI, which is a big project we're doing, and he got real quiet 'cuz everyone was drinking, and some of the people were gay."

Frank had obviously failed to recognize Mack from the party or as Jenny's wife, a fact that made Syd grin. It could be useful.

"What did he say about that?"

"He said he saw two girls holding hands and another guy was talking about his husband. He said that they had sexual problems, and they needed to find God to fix them because it wasn't natural."

"What did you say to him about that?" Mack wrote some key words on the tablet, and Syd scribbled notes of her own.

"I just told him that folks around here wouldn't like him talking about that. Especially those girls in HR. Around here they call it homo resources." He smirked and then looked immediately as if he wished he hadn't said it.

"And why is that, Frank?" Mack's expression was passive as she spoke.

"Well, because the two women that run that department are gay." He shrugged as if the officer had asked him an idiotic question.

"Do you know those women, Frank?"

"Yeah, I see them all the time. One of them is running some of my projects now. She's really good, and she has always been nice to me. Jenny, the other one, is my friend. We talk a lot about stuff, just shooting the crap, y'know?"

"Does anyone seem to have a problem with the people in human resources? Because they're gay, maybe?"

"Problem? No way. We joke sometimes about them being, y'know, queer because they're real girly and kind of cute, and we say stuff about them needing a real man to change them back. But it's just a joke; no one means anything by it." Frank spoke as if trying to convince the officer of his politically correct intentions.

Sydney itched to choke the unenlightened idiot, but she kept her promise to stay put.

"Have you ever had any fantasies about anyone at work, Frank? About being with them or hurting them?"

"God, no! What kind of a guy do you think I am? I mean, I might think some chick looks good or something, but I would never think anything sick about them. When I get married, I sure wouldn't want anyone thinking like that about my wife." His cheeks flushed as he tried to verbally distance himself from the implication.

"You mentioned the party you went to."

"Yeah. Somewhere downtown on Meridian, I think."

"Have you been back there since the party?" Mack stared at her notes, and Syd watched genuine confusion manifest on his face.

"No. For what?" He studied Mack.

"No reason. I just wondered." Mack spoke quickly and moved past the question. "Did Chris ever mention anything else to you about the people he thought might be homosexual that work here?"

"He asked me if Parker and Jenny were 'that way,' but I told him not to ask me stuff like that because I didn't want to get in trouble."

"Did he say why he wanted to know?" Mack offered an intrigued look.

"Just that he couldn't figure it out since they were pretty and stuff." He shrugged at Mack, who leaned a little closer and pushed her notes to the side.

"Do you think only ugly people are gay, Frank?"

"No! I don't, but I guess he does. At least the ones in his head maybe don't look like Jenny and Parker."

"Who else does he talk to around here?"

"No one. Everybody steers clear of him because they're afraid they'll get reported for something." Frank shook his head solemnly. "Kind of sad, if you ask me."

"Did he ever mention anything about wanting to date anyone or liking anyone?"

"Nope. In fact, he said he would never be around a female alone unless he met them at church. He said his daddy would find him a nice virgin from their church, and then they would teach him about sex so they could have babies. Can you imagine? Having your father pick your wife? Sometimes, I think people spend too much time in other people's business, and churches seem to be the worst."

"Some churches can be good and helpful places, don't you think?"

"True, it just doesn't sound like he goes to a very nice one. Real judgmental. I told him he needed to keep a lid on that stuff while he was here, or he would get in trouble."

"What did he say?" She picked up her pen again.

"That he would just pray for the sinner, and God would do the rest." He rolled his eyes.

"Did he ever mention Satan or use the words 'whore' or 'dyke'?" She issued that statement quickly and with the same intonation as the other questions.

"Hell, no. I mean, someone said 'damn' in the office, and I thought he was going to have to bless himself just for hearing it. The worst he has ever said around me was 'golly,' and I haven't heard that since the fifth grade." He looked genuinely perplexed.

"What about you? Do you use those words?"

"Well, yeah, I have, but not like every day or anything." He looked as if he was going to be issued some official sanction for admitting it, but Mack ignored him.

"When was the last time you've written poetry, Frank?"

Syd wrote the word "poetry" and underlined it before she looked back at the screen.

"Um. That's easy...never. I don't get into that stuff. I don't write much of anything. I have really atrocious handwriting, so I usually type everything."

"Frank, when was the last time you sent someone flowers?" She flipped to another page in her notebook.

"Never have. My mom always told my dad that spending money on flowers was a waste because he was really just bringing home things that were going to die in a few days. She said if he wanted to spend fifty bucks he should just hand her the money and let her go get her hair done."

Mack took a moment to respond. "If you had to buy flowers, maybe for a girl, what kind would you buy?"

"I don't know. Roses, I guess. I don't know any other kind you would buy for a girl."

What kind of car does he drive? Syd scratched in her notebook.

"What kind of car do you have, Frank?"

Syd chuckled to herself as she realized how well she knew Mack's general strategy.

"I just got a Prius. I drive so much for work; the gas was killing me. It's a great car, but sometimes it's a little scary because you can't hear the damn thing running." Frank seemed desperate to secure some rapport.

"Thank you, Frank." She smiled at him. "Can I ask a favor?"

"Okay."

"Would you keep our conversation confidential for right now?"

"Sure. Is there something I need to know about people around here?" He tapped his fingers on the table distractedly.

"Not yet. I just know you're one of the top guys around here, and people look up to you. I don't want anyone getting the wrong impression." She flattered him in order to get his buy-in.

"Me either. And I'll think on it a little bit. If I get any lightbulbs about anyone else, I'll let you know." He was suddenly an eager puppy with a task, and he clearly liked it.

"Thanks. My number is on the card." He took her business card and slid it into his pocket without studying it. He left the room, issuing an awkward wave as he went.

Syd unmuted the line when she saw the phone move. "Too simple, doesn't know when to quit talking," she said immediately. "He could never run a covert stalking op. Hell, I'm not sure he can go to the bathroom without telling twelve people."

"Agreed," Mack said. "But I'm really intrigued to talk to our new friend, Chris."

"Me, too. And by the way, there is entirely too much discussion about the women in HR for me. I'd prefer not to think about Parker as the subject of anyone's fantasies but my own."

"Trust me, I know." Mack agreed and whispered, "Incoming."

After a brief knock, Chris Newkirk stepped into the conference room. His khaki pants were perfectly pressed, and his ironed short-sleeved button-up was tucked in flawlessly at his waist. Syd thought she detected a military crease at each hip.

"Hi, Chris. I'm Lieutenant Foster, SLPD, have a seat."

Mack stayed seated, and Syd knew Mack was establishing her power position.

He watched her cautiously and sat across from her at the table. "What's this about?" His tone was irritated and sullen.

"You seem like you're already angry about something, Chris, and we haven't even started talking." Mack reclined comfortably in the chair, and Syd watched her let the young man be compromised by his own reactions.

"I just don't know why the cops would want to talk to *me*. I haven't broken a law in my life, ever."

Syd thought that was a lie since it *always* was.

"Good, then you shouldn't be worried about talking to me, right?" She gave him a wan smile.

"Okay." He shifted uncomfortably in the chair and pushed it back slightly from the table, increasing the distance between them, perhaps unconsciously.

"What do you do here, Chris? Is it Christopher?" She moved her notebook in front of her, poised to take notes.

"Christian. Christian Joseph Newkirk," he said proudly. Mack made an obvious effort not to smirk at him as she wrote it down.

"What do you do here, Christian?" Although any skilled investigator like Mack would already know the answers, she would use baseline questions to gauge the veracity of future responses.

"I'm a scheduler II, which means I help plan out all the jobs that we do." He seemed very impressed with his title.

"Do you like it here?" Mack was still writing.

"It's okay. I miss my hometown." Chris looked faraway as if recalling fond memories.

"Young guys like you usually want to go sow their wild oats, meet girls, go clubbing. None of that for you this close to DC? No wild flings with loose women?"

Chris's expression immediately hardened. "I was raised in the church. My parents raised me to behave as God expects me to. To do God's work, not succumb to the sins of the flesh. I believe if you do that kind of stuff, participate in that type of behavior, you're going to go to hell." The response was rehearsed and familiar.

"Wow, that's a serious consequence for partying when you're in your twenties. I used to party every night before I got married."

Syd watched him form questions, the expression on his face easy to read.

"Wasn't your husband disgusted by your behavior?"

Syd thought they were getting somewhere now. "Actually, my *wife* and I met at a party."

Syd watched Chris's expression change. He looked as if he had suddenly tasted something revolting.

"Two girls can't be married." His disgust was audible.

"The state of Massachusetts said we could, and now the United States Supreme Court says we can, for that matter. We got married in Boston. In a church there."

"I'm a Christian." Chris dropped the statement as if it answered all past and future questions.

"Me, *too*." Mack was clearly enjoying this.

"God says that marriage is between a man and a woman. Like Adam and Eve. A real church wouldn't have done that; it's against God." His fury was mounting, and his eyes darted back and forth as if looking for the thing that would change what Mack had said.

"Hmm. I guess we must have a different God." They only had to wait for a second before Christian Joseph Newkirk exploded.

"There is only one God!" His face was beet red, and his fists dragged angrily along his thighs.

Mack waited a long time before she spoke. "Okay. Then how about we agree to disagree and move on?" Mack didn't wait for an answer. "Do you like working here at Davidson Properties, Chris?" She had unnerved him on purpose. People were much more likely to slip up when they were pissed.

"It's okay. Different." He spoke quickly and breathed rapidly, as if he had just scaled a flight of stairs.

"Different how, Chris?" She was conciliatory in her delivery now.

"I'm not used to being around people who are not…God-fearing." Chris spoke quietly now, almost weary.

"What does that mean to you?" Syd wanted that answer most of all.

"Go to church on Sundays and Christian days of observance, and respect the Lord always. Don't drink or smoke or defile your body in any way. You know, do what it tells you in the Bible." Chris had practiced that speech or been made to practice it many times. It seemed to somehow calm him.

"What about sexual orientation? You seem to have a strong opinion on that." Mack pushed just a little but still spoke evenly.

"It's a sin to have relations outside of marriage. And I already told you what the definition of marriage is." His look was bordering on pitying, as if he were explaining the alphabet to a slow child.

"When people do that, what should happen to them?" She poised to write this answer down word for word, and Syd was doing the same from her car.

"They should repent for their sins." His delivery was measured, and his tone was again suspicious.

"Should they be punished?" Mack leaned a little farther over the table, which drove him farther backward into his chair.

"Of course! God will punish them. Sinners are punished." The answers were repeated from memory, not from original thought.

Syd wondered when Chris had last had an original thought.

"Does anyone deserve to be punished by someone else? Maybe someone doing God's work?"

"Maybe the preacher could talk to them and get them to mend their ways before God got to them." He seemed to relax into his answers since they were indisputable in his world.

Syd wondered what kind of God "got to" people.

"What ways would *you* think of to fix them?" Mack pushed, lobbing the conversational ball gently.

"I wouldn't." Simple as that.

"Would you ever go on a date with someone who maybe had dated another girl a long time ago?"

"No, ma'am! I am only interested in courting a girl who is pure. They must have walked the path of righteousness, and then our parents decide if we are right for each other."

Syd knew Mack couldn't follow the current line of questioning without him shutting down.

"Do you ever talk about Satan, Chris?"

"Of course. Every Sunday in church. He is the devil that makes people do the wrong things. We are taught about how to stop from getting sucked in by the devil."

"Do you think women who don't walk the right path are whores?"

Syd watched him wince at the word.

He breathed as if preparing to defend himself from an assault. "I do not have the right to use such language. If they are cast out by the Lord, then *he* makes the judgments on their souls, not me."

Mack pushed. "Have you ever called anyone a dyke or a bitch, Chris?"

"It is a sin to use such language, Miss Foster." He looked indignant.

"It's *Lieutenant* Foster, and you didn't answer my question." Her voice was hard.

"No, I would be cast down in the eyes of my church and my God for using such language." He was so sure and so pious.

Syd again wondered if he had *ever* had an idea that hadn't been hammered into him by someone else.

"Do you believe that there is anyone here that would make a good prospect for your wife?"

Syd thought Mack was no longer interviewing a potential stalker; she was looking at the textbook definition of mind-control in its purest form.

"No. I am to marry a virgin bride selected for me from my church."

Mack saw a glimmer of sadness cracking through the armor of doctrine.

"Have you ever sent a woman flowers, Chris?" Mack pulled her notebook onto her lap when he seemed too interested in what she was writing.

"No. I've picked flowers for my mother, but I'm not courting a woman at the moment. Such gestures should be reserved for courting."

"Have you had any difficulties since you have been working here?" Mack was beginning to sound weary.

"It's just that I'm still getting used to working with people who aren't Christians, and sometimes, that's hard. The lady in HR told me I have to be better about keeping my religion and my beliefs to myself, but the Bible says that I should spread the word." He looked genuinely bewildered by the concept that not everyone should believe as he did.

"What do you think of the lady in HR? Ms. Duncan, right?" Mack acted as if she was simply a name she was reading from a page in her book.

Chris nodded. "She's nice, I guess, but I don't think she's a Christian."

"Why not?"

"Because I asked her, and she said it wasn't appropriate to ask that stuff in the office. And that she would choose who to tell about what she believed." The evidence was obviously sufficient in his mind.

"Did that make you mad?"

"No, I just feel sorry for her, I guess. She's real pretty, but she isn't married, so maybe she's lonely. My dad says that some women try to act like men at work by being the boss, and then no man wants to marry them."

Mack stared at him. "Do you think something is wrong with her because she isn't married?"

"I don't know. She just seems sad and tired, and I feel sorry for her." The sentiment was genuine and, for once, not practiced.

Sydney felt responsible that her girlfriend could be seen as sad. She yearned to relieve the burden of their present nightmare.

"Would you ever want to be with someone like that, Chris? Like Ms. Duncan?"

"No, ma'am. I told you that they have to go to my church. Can I ask why you're asking me all of these questions?" He suddenly looked at her as if the totality of the conversation had just dawned on him.

"We've just found out that someone might be giving some other people here unwanted attention, and we need to make sure that they stop."

"If I saw anything like that, I would tell my boss. It says in Leviticus: Do not stand idly by when your neighbor's life is threatened."

Syd thought he seemed to give himself an internal point for pulling that out of his impossibly tight ass.

"Good rule to live by. By the way, what kind of car do you have?" She asked quickly so he couldn't think about his answer.

"I have a Ford F-150 truck, beige."

Syd wondered if he knew that his whole life was varying tones of beige.

"If you think of anything that might be helpful, you can give me a call." Mack slid a card across the desk, and he scanned it quickly.

"Yes, ma'am. I'll do that." His former stoic nature returned.

"Chris, not everyone is as, well, honorable as you, shall we say. Can I ask you to keep this conversation between us?"

"Proverbs says 'A gossip betrays a confidence, but a trustworthy person keeps a secret.'" Chris turned and closed the door behind him.

Mack spoke into the speaker after a few seconds of reflection. "And what do you think of that bundle of fun? Have you met anyone more frustrating in your life?" Mack asked Sydney.

"You have no idea how much I want it to be him just so we can break his holier-than-thou persona. I just don't think there's much chance." Syd rubbed her temples, frustrated they were hitting dead ends.

"I agree. Just from watching his face and his body language, you can see he's too timid. His ideology is too ingrained for the modern world he has to live in with the rest of us, but I doubt he would dare step over a line…any line, at least not on purpose."

"Our guy is angry. He's got a problem with any woman who doesn't want to sleep with him or who rejects him. He expects her to return his affections even if he hasn't made them known. Mr. Newkirk can't even imagine a first date not sanctioned by Daddy."

"Very true. I think our guy is impotent or just got dumped on by enough chicks that it's manifesting like this." Mack was writing her thoughts as she spoke to Syd.

"I think he definitely got dumped on somehow, except my gut says it's *one* chick, Mack. One that maybe reminds him of Parker or vice versa."

"Yeah, he mentions cheating in the last note when he talked about you. Maybe she stepped out on him or left him for someone else…even a female someone else. He definitely has a significant history with one woman." Mack flipped through her notes. "Frank is like a dog in heat, chasing any woman who'll look at him, but he doesn't have the maturity to keep one of any substance, not for any length of time anyway. And he's not a misogynist, and I think on some level, our guy is. And the Newkirk kid might pass out if he even touched a girl. He's incredibly frustrating, but I don't think he's the one. I certainly can't picture him lurking outside your car for the free sex show. The good news is we can cross two off the list."

"Great. Our odds of figuring this out either went way up or way down." Syd felt defeated.

"I'm going to bank on 'way up' because *one* of us has to

be an optimist." She spoke quietly. "I believe contestant number three has arrived."

Syd muted her line as Randy Miller walked into the conference room talking rapidly on his cell. He held his finger up to indicate that she should wait. She stared at him until he got the message and hung up.

"Sorry. Accounting in this place still runs on ledger paper and hope. I found out they needed me way more than I needed them, but I guess everything works out. What can I do for you?"

From his appearance, Syd had expected the nerdy forty-two-year-old to be quiet and reserved. Instead, he was a classic narcissist in bad clothes.

"Randy, I'm Lieutenant Foster with the SLPD. I'm looking into some incidents, and I wanted to see if you can help me."

Syd had seen guys like Randy Miller many times in her career. She knew direct was the only way to go.

"No problem." He looped an arm over the back of his chair and spun his phone like a top on the shiny surface of the conference table as if he was waiting for a waitress to show up and take his beer order.

"How long have you been at DPI, Randy?"

As Mack spoke, Syd watched incredulously as he flipped the phone over to achieve a better spin.

"A few weeks."

"How do you like it?" He was intently watching the table and his toy. Syd thought his aloof act was as practiced as it was obnoxious.

"Seems okay, so far. They have a lot of catching up to do from a technology perspective, but I like it well enough."

"How about the people? Any issues with the people, Randy?" She spoke louder in the hope of bringing his attention to her.

"Every place has its weirdoes and its assholes, but nothing I can't handle." He continued to spin his phone until Mack slammed her hand over his and slid the device out of his reach.

"Any people in particular you can think of?"

Syd knew Mack loathed having to spend her time coaxing simple information from asses like Randy Miller.

Miller gave her a cautious look before answering, clearly rattled by the passing moment.

"Well, I've been in the accounting field for a long time, and those people are *always* weird, so I don't pay much attention to them. Tess is the new lady in Davidson's office, and she's kind of stuck up, but I guess that's because she works for the man." He offered air quotes around "the man."

"Anyone else?" She was taking notes on her lap again.

"That Jesus freak in Frank's office. He won't talk about anything except religion, so I just avoid that dude. I don't want to talk about that stuff." His sideways smile followed a dismissive shake of his head.

"What would *you* rather talk about Randy?"

"I dunno. Sports, chicks, world events, something else besides religion. I hear enough of that religion shit from my old lady."

"Meaning your wife?" Mack visibly bristled at the dismissive and chauvinistic term.

"Yeah, my wife. Married twenty-one years in March. She got religion, so I go to church and stuff, but not like this guy."

"Who do you talk about chicks with? I'm assuming not your wife."

He laughed and tried a wink. "You got that right. Frank's cool. Ben's nice but a little conservative, you know?"

"So, you talk about chicks with Frank but not Ben."

"Well, he hangs out with us at lunch sometimes, but he has a girlfriend or a fiancée or something, I think, and he acts like it's cheating on her to talk about other women."

"You ever talk about the women you work with?"

"Sure. There are some hotties in this place. It doesn't hurt to look, right?" He slid a glance in her direction, as if they were old friends swapping stories.

"Yeah? Who are the hotties?"

Syd wished there was a criminal charge for being a witless asshole. She knew Mack would cheerfully have made sure he was indicted on about fifteen counts.

"Nicole in data; she's smoking hot, but she's engaged, too, so all she wants to do is talk about the wedding plans...blah. Tess would be hot if she wasn't such a *beeotch*, if you know what I mean. Then there are the two babes in HR, but they play for the other team, so I hear." Randy smirked, obviously proud that he was able to gather so much intel in so little time.

"They don't date men, you mean?" Mack leaned back in her chair and tapped her pen absently against her shoulder as if this was just casual conversation between acquaintances.

"Right, still hot, though, especially the little blonde—I could picture that body—I don't want to offend you or anything." He reduced his voice to a whisper as if he was dying to talk but had to get the cop to give him permission.

"Randy, I've been doing this job for fifteen years, it would take a *long* time to offend me, and even then, you'd have to work at it."

Syd watched Mack dig her nails into her thigh to keep from smacking him while he spoke about her wife as if she was a show cow.

"I got ya. You know, guys think that's totally hot...two chicks together. I told my wife that's what I wanted for my fortieth birthday, but I got golf clubs instead."

Mack rubbed the heels of her hands over her eyes and resumed looking at the Neanderthal sitting across the table. "Do you have anything against gay people, you know, other than the sex being 'totally hot' and stuff?" She practically sneered when she spoke to him.

"Hell, no. I think it's awesome. Like I said, I told my wife she can become a lesbo any day, and I'd be a happy man." He looked pleased with himself as he spoke and spun his chair back and forth with one foot, rolling from side to side to maintain the motion.

Syd watched the corners of Mack's mouth pull as she seemed to fight the urge to laugh in his face. Giving his wife permission? Syd wanted to smack him.

"Do you ever feel angry at anyone at work, Randy?"

"Nah, what's the point in that? I go home, get a beer, and take it out on my Nintendo. Then I'm good."

Syd thought he was smug and more than a little dim.

"Sounds like the perfect plan," Mack lied casually.

"Works like a charm." He gave her the thumbs-up as if he had solved one of the world's great problems and had just let her in on his secret.

"Anyone else you can think of that seems to be angry or disturbed at work, Randy?"

"Not a one, but I'll think on it for ya. Got a card?"

Mack pulled one out from her folder as she stood, indicating that their chat was now over. "Here you go, and thanks. Mind keeping this conversation between us?"

Randy nodded and snatched up his phone. The door bounced loudly against the frame as he exited. When it finally settled into the latch Mack jerked up the phone. "Kill me now. I honestly kept looking for the scars where his knuckles had been dragging the ground."

"I can't believe you didn't tell him the 'little blonde' was yours." Syd laughed.

"Believe me, it took everything I had not to choke him. But I figured my being here would get around faster if I said something."

"So, it seems when you get a job at this place, they tell you where the break room is and then say, 'Hey, two babes in HR, they date chicks, but we figure they just need the right guy.'"

"It certainly seems that way. I plan to warn Jenny to stay away from Mr. Miller and his disturbing mental images that I luckily didn't get any details on."

"Are you going to do any more today?" Syd folded back the page of her notebook to reveal a clean sheet.

"Nope, I'm going to go tell Jenny that I'm leaving. Does Park know you're here?"

Syd hadn't discussed the fact that she was camped out in the parking lot with Parker, and Mack likely already knew that. "I really don't know. She isn't talking much lately, so I wasn't sure how to bring it up. I don't want to remind her about it all the time, so we just talk around it." Syd returned to her earlier funk.

"Don't let it fester, Syd. You're crazy about each other. Don't give some random creep the power to screw that up." Mack sounded exasperated.

"I know." She tried to change the subject. "When can we do this little tag team again?"

"I want to meet with Ben Barrett and Steve Akeroyd tomorrow. I'm going to head to the CTI jobsite to cross Terry Carver off my list and no, you aren't coming. You already have a problem with that guy." Mack sounded like a stern parent.

"Call me and tell me if anything smells bad?" Syd couldn't stand not being in the middle of the action.

"You know I will. Now, go make nice with Parker. She needs you, and she needs to trust you; otherwise, you'll both miss something important."

"Yeah, I'm on my way." Syd shut the car door and headed across the parking lot. She knew Mack was right, and they had risked letting this come between them.

Parker was leaning over her credenza marking up plans with her back to the door when Syd walked in and shut it solidly behind her.

"Please, don't say there are more issues today, Jenny, I'm too tired to care who's fighting with whom." She was exhausted and edgy.

Syd walked behind her and pulled her from the chair, eliciting a startled gasp. She tilted Parker's chin to hers and kissed her slowly and deeply. Parker seemed to take a second to focus on the sensation before stroking her hands over Sydney's broad shoulders. She allowed herself to melt into her, relishing the warmth of the embrace. She suddenly grabbed against her more strongly and buried her forehead against Sydney's chest.

"I missed you." Parker exhaled into her.

"I've missed you. I'm sorry things have felt so screwed up."

"It's my fault for being so angry. You didn't do it, and I shouldn't take it out on you." Parker focused on Syd's face.

"I love you. The fact that you're in my life is all that matters."

Parker looked suddenly grounded again. She leaned back against Syd's encircling arms and smiled. "So, other than checking on me, what are you doing here?" She smiled knowingly.

Syd knew her car would have stood out in the lot. "I just wanted to see you. Are you going to CTI today?" Syd hoped that the answer would be no.

"Nope. Too much to finish here. I'm still catching up from last week. If I promise to call when I leave, will you stop babysitting me and go do some of your own work?"

"Not babysitting, sweetheart, just adoring you from a little closer than usual." She winked at Parker, and relief washed over her for a moment.

"And I adore you for that, love, but it's not necessary. It's been a week since the window thing, and there hasn't been anything else. Maybe he found someone else to play with." She didn't look as if she believed it, but it felt good to stand in the land of denial with her, if for only a moment. "How about you invite Mia to dinner? We haven't seen her since the, um, incident, and I don't want it to get weird between us, okay? We can do homemade pizzas. I'll stop for the stuff on the way home." Parker relaxed as she welcomed the prospect of their old normal.

"How about I stop, and *you* invite her? That way you'll be home sooner, and I may have time to ravish you in our boarded-up bedroom."

"Always an ulterior sex motive, Hyatt." Parker shook her head.

"Are you complaining?" Syd spoke softly in her ear, delivering the hot words against her skin. Parker always told her that her unwavering confidence in that area was intoxicating. Syd used it to her advantage.

"Oh, hell no." She shivered. "In fact, I just decided to leave early." Parker stroked her fingers over Syd's sculpted features.

"Are we okay?" Syd asked quietly as she locked eyes with Parker.

"Always okay, as long as you love me."

Syd left the DPI offices feeling lighter than she had in days. She called to check on the progress with the window order and arrived home with the groceries just in time for Parker to walk in beside her.

"The window's still being fabricated, so they'll put it in just before the floors are redone. I'll talk to Mack about staying there for a few days so we don't have to live with the smell."

"Sounds good. We'll be sleeping in the bed I loaned them from my loft, you know. It would be nice to sleep in my old bed again. Like when you used to sneak over and seduce me," Parker teased her.

"I couldn't help it. You're my kryptonite, baby, what can I say?" Syd winked at her playfully.

"Why don't you say that we have an hour before Mia gets here and remind me a couple of times how you seduced me?" Parker walked backward toward the bedroom, and Syd watched her eyes darken. She slid Parker's body on to the bed and under her own, claiming her hungrily.

❖

"Hi, Mia. I'm glad you're here." Parker pulled their nervous neighbor in for a genuine hug. "What would you like to drink?"

"I'm thinking a little cold regret over a thick blend of remorse and humiliation." Mia spoke apprehensively as she looked down at Parker and acted as if she didn't see Sydney watching her.

"Wow. Heavy cocktail. I was just going to share a little red wine." Parker smiled at her and clasped hands on her shoulders. "Mia, stop, seriously. Not a big deal. Do you know how many lips I had to scrub off her when we first met?" Parker earnestly worked to relieve Mia of the awkward feelings she knew she felt the weight of. Sydney laughed, obviously okay if the joke made at her expense caused Mia to relax.

"How can you not want to kill me?" Mia groaned and dropped her head onto Parker's shoulder.

"Sweetie, there are so many more viable options in line ahead of you. You aren't even in the last heat." Parker kissed her friend on the cheek.

"Sydney, if you ever screw this up, you are a colossal idiot." She laughed and pointed to Parker.

"Trust me. You won't be the last to tell me that." Sydney looked over at Parker before returning her focus to Mia. "Wine okay?"

"Yeah, great." Mia sighed. "You guys okay? I haven't seen you, and Mr. Kessler said someone broke your window the other night." She took a sip of wine and exhaled loudly.

"Yeah, so we should probably let you know what's happening in case you notice anything." Syd stood behind Parker and kissed her shoulder softly before dusting a finger over the bruise that Parker knew had faded substantially.

Parker began. "It seems I have a fan, probably someone who was here at the party. He started with a nice note, and now he's angry and a little mean…a lot mean, in fact. So, if you see anyone creeping around, call the police, okay? He doesn't seem to be dangerous to anyone but Sydney because, according to him, she is an evil dyke." Parker thumbed over her shoulder at Sydney and tried to smile in the face of the renewed vitriol she felt toward a faceless stranger.

"Crap. Not good. Any idea who it might be?" Mia looked between the two of them as if she could recall a feeling she profoundly missed.

"Not yet, but we're working on it. We'll keep you posted, but just let us know if you see anything, okay?" Syd met Mia's gaze, and Mia looked quickly away.

"Are you really okay, Mia?" Parker looked concerned when Mia refused to look up. "Look, it was a mistake. I don't believe you have designs on the evil dyke." Parker seemed to be trying to make a joke to force a mood switch. Syd swatted at her playfully.

Mia dropped her head on the counter. "I just feel like an idiot. I got lost in her memory, and all I saw was Sandy…"

Parker stepped off her stool and put a comforting arm around her shoulder. "I think you have done amazingly well at coping with all this. No one but us will ever know, and it will be something we can laugh about one day. Hell, we're laughing about it now. Mia, give yourself a break."

Mia lifted her head and threw her arms around Parker's shoulders. "Thank you. I don't know that I would be that generous."

"Sure, you would." She spun Mia's stool toward a bowl of chips. "Let's eat bad food and watch junk TV." Parker couldn't help recalling the moments after Mia had lost Sandy. She had watched gut-wrenching anguish cripple Mia, and now it seemed too close, too real. She couldn't fathom losing Syd, and the prospect of it made the acid rise in her throat. She swallowed against the fear of threats unexplained.

CHAPTER FOURTEEN

Syd pulled into DPI by ten a.m. and backed into what was now her customary spot. She knew many of the players now, what they drove, when they arrived, and who was always late.

Within thirty minutes, Mack had backed her city-issue in beside her and motioned for Syd to move to her car.

"Take a look." Mack handed her a stack of printouts. "Unofficially, of course, while I'm looking the other way." Mack smiled and pretended to be lost in paperwork while Sydney perused official police files on the new employees at DPI along with those on Terry Carver.

"Well I'll be damned." Syd made a tsking sound at the information in her hand. "Our little pastor-in-the-making was caught for lewd and lascivious at the Rainbow Tavern. Who would have ever thought? So much for his finding a perfect wife at church."

"Poor woman; whoever he ends up with is going to be marrying a gay man. No wonder he keeps talking about it. He doth protest too much." Mack shook her head as she returned her stare to the blank page in her notebook. "Why don't people just live their lives instead of trying so hard to be what they aren't?"

"Because everyone's afraid of rejection on some level, I guess." Syd continued to scan down the pages. "How was

Parker's little hero, Terry, yesterday? Anything pop for you?" Syd stopped on his page and found only two bar brawls from ten years before which had been knocked down to disturbing the peace citations.

"Not a thing. I got him to talk about Parker and meeting you. He admitted to being shocked only because it never occurred to him that she wasn't straight. He was just stunned and didn't handle it well. He loves working with Parker, but he doesn't think of her in any way other than a friendly one. He has a new girlfriend, who he proudly showed me a picture of. Oh, and his sister's gay, so he doesn't have an issue with it anyway."

"Good. She has to work with him more regularly, so I'm glad we can cross him off." Syd shifted the page to the back and continued reading on the next.

"Public intoxication for your little blonde's biggest fan? I can't imagine that, unless he just couldn't win on his Nintendo that day."

"Right? His wife was probably happy to have him out of the house, even if it was to stand in line for his mug shot." Mack shook her head in disgust. "What a tool. I can just hear him giving his wife permission to become a 'lesbo.'"

"Or he's full of shit and just likes to hear his own line of bull." Syd had come across plenty of guys like him, and they were often more talk than action.

"It's definitely possible. Either way, he's a tool."

"You'll get no argument from me. You showed a hell of a lot more restraint than I would have."

"I know. That's why *you* were cooling it in your personal sex machine." Mack offered Syd a knowing smirk.

"You just can't get over it, can you?" Syd shook her head at her de facto partner.

"No, I can't. I was *in* that passenger seat yesterday. I'm not even as tall as you, and *I* barely fit." Mack's incredulous tone made Sydney laugh.

Syd returned to look intently at the paperwork and murmured, "Driver's side."

Mack whipped her head up to look at her. "Now I know you're lying. There's no way."

"Oh, there's a way, believe me. I have a bruise from the emergency brake to prove it." Syd tapped her fingers along her right hip and chuckled at her friend still staring at her from under her black SLPD cap. "I'd lend you the car for a date with Jen to prove it, but I don't want you to taint my ride." Syd tensed right before a punch hit her left bicep.

"Maybe someone should give *you* a ticket for lewd and lascivious, Hyatt."

"I would take that citation willingly," Syd said proudly and returned to the stack in her lap. "So, other than an accounting guy with a lead foot and quiet Ben with a penchant for parking in the wrong place, no one floats to the top."

"That's what I saw, too. Or rather, didn't see. Let's get these over with so we can focus on what's next. I'll call you in ten."

"I'm getting back in mine; the velour upholstery in here gives me a rash." Syd grinned as she unfolded from the car.

"Liar. You just have better flashbacks in that one." Mack pointed at the sports car.

"Very true, my friend, very true."

Mack rolled her eyes and strode to the building, activating the video app as she walked. She turned and tapped her breast pocket as she dropped the phone inside. She exited the elevator and Syd watched her head for her wife's office. Suddenly, angry voices came through.

"...total fucking idiot, Newkirk. My calendar is *not* offensive. It's a goddam charity calendar from the Humane Society! The girl just happens to have big boobs. Give me a break!"

"It's not proper for a woman to display herself that way. You have to respect my beliefs; Ms. Duncan told you."

Frank and Ben stood nearby, watching the circus unfold.

Parker stood next to Jenny with her hand on Mike's shoulder, trying to move him away.

"You are a total idiot, Newkirk. Get over yourself. The world doesn't work like that. Go back to where you came from!"

"You are a heathen, and you're going to hell," he said just before Mike wrestled easily out of Parker's light grip. Chris suddenly launched at Mike, who stumbled back and into Jenny, flattening her under Mike's flailing body.

Mack broke into a run, the camera bouncing wildly, and arrived just in time to pull Mike roughly up and away from her wife. Parker helped Jenny to her feet before Mack shoved both battling men into Jenny's office.

Jenny quickly mouthed, "I'm fine," and stepped out of the way of the closing door that Syd was more than grateful to be behind, albeit only virtually.

Mack launched at both of them. "Have you both lost your minds? This is the shit that ten-year-olds argue about."

Mike was still visibly steaming at being toppled by the irritating new employee, and Chris looked as if he had won some moral battle no one had asked him to fight.

"You are supposed to be professionals; instead, you'll both be charged with assault. That should look good in the church bulletin, huh, Chris?"

Syd knew Mack wouldn't waste her time unless one of them pressed the issue, but she was making her point.

Chris began to cry. Mike started to make fun of him before Mack wheeled on him with a look that made him rethink his next move.

"You open your stupid mouth for even one word, I will parade you out of here in handcuffs, am I clear?"

He nodded, and his shoulders slumped.

"Where are you supposed to be right now?" She addressed Mike, who suddenly looked frightened instead of smug.

"Working at my desk, ma'am."

"I suggest you go do that unless you have something else to say. I'll come find you later, how's that?"

"Yes, ma'am." He walked out quickly.

Mack closed the door and pivoted in Chris's direction. Syd nearly felt sorry for the sniveling moron. "Do you need your job here, Chris?" Mack placed her hands on either arm of the chair, effectively boxing him in and bringing Syd's point of view to somewhere near his left eye. He looked thoroughly uncomfortable at the proximity. Syd was unsure if it was because she was a cop or a woman or a lesbian. The combination, of course, might be more than he could take.

"Yes, I do." He leaned away from her as far as the stiff chair would allow.

"Then why are you trying so hard to piss everyone off?"

"I'm not, but people are supposed to respect my religious beliefs."

Even she was tired of the argument, so she couldn't imagine what his coworkers thought.

"And you're also supposed to be an adult. If you start a confrontation every time you see a picture of a woman in a bikini in a store window or an ad on a bus shelter, you are going to have a very long, tedious life. You're entitled to your beliefs, but you don't get to act crazy. If he had a naked picture on his wall, that would be one thing, but you are taking this too far. You understand that you could be arrested...*again*...right?"

He started to protest when she fingered the handcuffs on her belt.

"Yes. I understand. I won't say anything about the pictures again. Please, don't arrest me; my dad would kill me. Literally."

Syd thought he looked terrified, though less of being arrested than of his father, which seemed incredibly sad.

"I have no control over what happens to you at work, but I *will* charge you next time. That means prior convictions could also come out, got it?"

He nodded apprehensively, clearly understanding the

thinly veiled warning. He began to stand, looking to Mack for permission.

She straightened and pointed at the door. "Go."

The hallway in front of the offices had cleared when Mack found Jenny and Parker shut inside Parker's office. "You okay, sweetheart?" Mack slid an arm around her wife and stroked a hand through her long hair.

Syd waited, unsure if she should speak to Parker or keep her promise to remain silent. She decided silence was better. The less her involvement was known, the better.

"I'm fine. Those two are just crazy." Jenny shook her head at Parker, who was already typing up disciplinary actions on the computer.

"Sure you're okay?"

Jenny nodded.

"I used to think you had a safe job, and now it just looks like you're running an asylum." Mack pushed a loose strand of hair behind her shoulder and looked into her pale eyes. Parker looked angry. "And you're okay, Park? A certain someone would be really pissed if I didn't ask."

Syd strained to examine every nuance of the woman she loved slamming the keys into submission on her computer.

"Yes. You can tell her I'm fine. And I think we *are* running an asylum sometimes. They're both getting finals because I am so done with this crap at work." She continued to pound on the keyboard as she spoke, and Syd knew that no one should ever want to be on the wrong side of Parker when she was pissed.

"I hate to ask, but can I have the remaining two employees for a few minutes?"

"Sure." Parker waved her hand. "It's not like anyone's working around here."

Jenny squeezed against Mack one more time. "I'll walk you to the conference room."

"No, you try and put your day back together. I remember where it is. Oh, and try not to get in any more full-contact sports while I'm gone. I like everything right where it is." Mack tapped a quick kiss over her lips.

"Funny, Mack," Jenny called to her as she walked out.

❖

Syd unmuted the phone when Mack shut the door behind her and laid her folder on the conference room table.

"What the hell? Are you sure everyone's okay? Parker looked…"

"Down, tiger. She's fine. It's handled. Truth be told, I think he tripped."

"I truly wanted you to deck him." Syd vibrated with the desire to do it herself.

"No, as you saw, the threat to arrest him might have been worse. Did you see him start to cry?"

"I did. Is Jenny really okay?" Sydney was much more concerned about her friend than the whiny choirboy.

"Yeah, fine. This guy is going to have a very hard life if he gets into fights over every woman wearing a tight shirt in a calendar."

"It seems like we should get him a male calendar or two," Syd joked.

"He might pass out. Gotta go, incoming."

Syd saw her view change as she put the phone back on yesterday's perch, and Syd muted her end.

"Ben Barrett? Have a seat."

He nodded and shifted nervously on his heels when Mack gestured again for him to sit. "Is this about what happened today?"

"Well, I would like to get your take on it, sure. Why don't you tell me about it?"

"Well, we were all in the offices, and I saw Chris get up and head toward Mike's desk. I didn't hear the radio, so I didn't think anything about it. The next thing I hear is them yelling about some woman on a calendar, and Frank tells them to take it to HR, and well, you saw the rest."

"Did you see the calendar?"

"Well, sure, I went and looked after that. I didn't see anything wrong with it. Chris just seems to get bent every time *anything* happens." Ben shook his head.

"What do you think about Chris?" Mack took the opening while it was there.

"I think he's sheltered, and he's scared of everything, and he doesn't know when to shut up."

Mack seemed to think that was a reasonable summation. "Aside from Chris, can you think of anyone who seems to be having a hard time adjusting to working here? Or who has a problem with anyone?"

"Nope."

Mack thought of Jenny's warning that he was very reluctant to engage. "What about women? Do you know anyone that has a problem with any of the women here? Maybe a crush?"

"No. But then again, I wouldn't notice, I'm not looking. I have a fiancée, so I'm always trying to be respectful of our relationship." Ben spoke emphatically.

"That's good. Important."

Syd saw Mack make sure she was visibly impressed for Mr. Barrett's benefit. Mack had always been good at subtle rapport building.

"When are you getting married?"

"Sometime next year, I guess; we don't want to rush it." Barrett rubbed at the skin of his ring finger as if imagining one there.

"How long have you been together?"

"Eight years. We met right after high school. I saw her and knew she was the one." He displayed a faraway smile.

"You worked for the family business before this, right? What made you go work for someone else?" Mack probed.

"Lillian. I want to be where Lillian wanted to be, and she likes living near here." He stared at his hands.

"Where did you meet?" Mack waited. They needed him to tell her as much as he was willing.

"At school and then we went to a party together," he answered quickly.

"That's how I met my wife, at a party." Mack scribbled notes on the paper.

"Your *wife*?"

If he was trying not to sound surprised, Syd thought he was failing.

"Yup. We've been married for nine years now."

"Uh-huh." He was obviously distracted.

"Does that bother you, Ben?" Mack tried to look genuinely interested, not judgmental.

"Uh...nope. I mean, obviously, I don't get it. I just think people, especially kids, can get hurt in all of this."

"Why is that?" Mack looked intense, as though there was a scab to be picked.

"They don't understand adults' personal lives, and then parents separate and try to win them over, and they get confused." He was briefly emotional.

Mack looked puzzled, "Did your parents get divorced and fight over you?"

"Yup. Didn't see my dad for ten years. If it wasn't for my mom, that wouldn't have happened."

"I see. Do you blame your mom?" Mack had repeatedly said she felt more like a counselor than a cop, but it was during those times she got the most answers.

"Sure, *she* did it. Mothers shouldn't take fathers away from their kids." He managed to school any further reaction born of a bruising childhood, but Syd could see him struggle.

"I agree. Kids need all the love they can get."

Syd watched Ben nod in emphatic agreement.

"Has that affected how you interact with people, do you think?"

"No. Used to, I guess, but now I just keep to myself." Ben rubbed his fingers together before dropping his hands back into his lap.

"Why do you think you do that? Keep to yourself, I mean."

"I guess I'm just careful who's around. I want to make my wife happy when we get married, and I don't want to make her suspicious or jealous, like I would expect her to do for me." The statement sounded certain and final.

"That makes sense, Ben. Is there anyone here that you feel attracted to that she might be jealous of?"

Ben looked horrified by the question. "Of course not. Lillian is everything to me." The faraway look returned.

"Ben, do you use words like 'whore' or 'dyke' in your everyday language?"

Ben's head snapped up. "A person would have to be pretty angry to say those things. I don't like that language. I want my kid growing up knowing that she should be respected."

"Good enough." Mack paused briefly as if she were consulting her notes. "What kind of car do you drive, Ben?"

"Pathfinder, why?"

"We've just been looking into some things at work, and we want to make sure there aren't any strange cars hanging around the parking lot." She dismissed it easily.

"Haven't noticed." He stared at her now, clearly intrigued.

"You think of anything that doesn't seem right, will you call me?" Mack smiled quickly.

"Sure, I guess." He shrugged and took the card she held over to him. He looked at the table as if he was stalling and then simply walked stiffly to the door.

"Well, that was like eating a bread sandwich," Mack grumbled.

"I can't imagine what this Lillian chick is like, but she can't have met another human being before she got engaged to that guy."

"To each his own, or her own, in this case."

"Anything I missed not being in the room?" Syd asked.

"Up-close boredom? Trust me, he was as vanilla as he seemed."

"So, Steve, the speed demon is our last great hope?"

"Seems so. Talk to you in a few." Mack shuffled her previous notes into her folder.

Steve Akeroyd sauntered in wearing high-water chinos and a DPI polo. Syd noted his loafers had seen better days, but he offered a genuine smile and a firm handshake.

"Feeling better, Steve? I heard you were under the weather yesterday."

"Yes, ma'am. Bitch of a migraine."

Syd guessed that answered the question about whether he ever used *that* word.

"Sorry to hear that. I'm Lieutenant Foster with SLPD. I just wanted to take a couple of minutes to talk to you. I know you're new here, right?" Mack set the baseline tone for a friendly exchange.

"Sure." He shrugged.

"Have you noticed anyone behaving strangely? Perhaps someone who concerns you?"

"Not really. I mean Jesus-Chris Newkirk is a total whack job. You would think he had never been out of his house before he came here. But he doesn't concern me like in a going-to-bring-an-Uzi-to-work kind of way."

"Anyone else?" Mack looked him in the eye. She was skilled at catching any microexpressions and deception indicators.

He took a moment as if to search his mind. "Not that I can think of."

"Have you made friends here?" The question was casual.

"I talk to people, but it's a new gig, so those things take

time. I have a lot of friends outside of work that I usually do stuff with." His reply was casual and direct.

"What kind of stuff?"

"Car rallies, boat shows, sports. Guy stuff, I guess." Steve shrugged at her.

"Do you have feelings for anyone or a relationship with someone here that might be more than friends?"

"Like want-to-date-them kind of feelings?"

Mack nodded.

"Hell, no. I just broke up with my girlfriend, and no offense, but I've had enough of women for a while. I told her that I wanted out, and she took all my money and most of my stuff. I'll pass on riding the babe train for a while."

"I've never heard it put that way before now, but I get that." Mack doodled on the page as she listened to him and continued to watch his body language. "Ever use the terms 'dyke' or 'whore'?"

"Well, sure, I guess. I mean, not like every day or anything. Why, is that a crime?"

"No, just a question. When was the last time you sent flowers to anyone, Steve?"

"Easy, to my mom for Mother's Day. She gets all bent if I don't send them, so I do. I think she likes to show off for the other women in her office about how much her son cares, etcetera. So, I do it."

"That makes you a good son," Mack offered genuinely.

"Actually, it makes me her only son. My sister and my mom don't get along, so it falls on me a lot. But whatever, she's my mom." He gave a silly grin and a shrug.

"What kind of car do you drive?" Mack obviously didn't want him to get too comfortable even though nothing rang for Syd about this particular interviewee.

"Well, I drive a Dodge Magnum to work and I have an old '72 Beetle that I restored. My ex didn't bother to take that, so I usually drive it on the weekends and to VW meet-up groups when they have them." He stopped and looked at her curiously. "Can I ask what all this is about?"

"I'm just trying to track down some information about some incidents at the office. Make sure no one at the office has anyone to worry about."

"Fine with me. While you're at it, maybe you can get Reverend Newkirk a big plastic bubble in a padded cell downtown. He might be happier there."

"You never know." Mack chuckled, and Syd was surprised how much she was actually amused by Mr. Akeroyd. "If you think of anything, will you give me a call?" She handed him the last card in her folder.

He read the card. "You got it...Lieutenant Foster." He looked thoughtful. "Hey! You're related to that Jenny lady in HR, right?"

Mack simply put her finger to her lips. "Let's keep this chat between us, okay?"

"Yes, ma'am." He returned the gesture, placing his finger to his lips and headed out.

"That was humorous. He certainly has a history with one woman," Syd said.

"I actually found him entertaining. He does have a history, but it seems they ended on his terms, so I'm not as impressed by that. Any chance you heard a VW that night?"

"No way. They're loud, but they have that really distinctive, air-cooled engine whistle I would have recognized right away."

"That's what I thought. I'll catch you up if I get anything new. Go home and do some work now, will you? Someone's got to make the payments on your sex machine, right?"

"True. I'm out. Watch out for my girl, okay, Mack?"

"I got it. Go."

"Just letting you know I was leaving." Parker looked up to find Mack leaning into her office doorway.

"Jenny will be mad she missed you. She is delivering write-up papers on your friends from earlier." Parker swiveled her chair away from her computer in order to look directly at Mack.

"No worries. I'll see her at home." Mack stepped in a little farther and spoke quietly, "I know I don't have to tell you to be careful, but I sent my unofficial partner and your unofficial bodyguard home. She would be mad if I didn't at least say it."

"Thanks, Mack, and I will. I owe you for getting her out of her damn car." Parker hated to think of her sitting there idly for hours. She hated being the reason she was doing it.

"No problem. I understand, though. She loves you more than anything. If it was Jenny? I would be crazier than she is, but don't tell her that, okay?"

"It's our secret. Thanks, Mack. See you." Pretending. Secrets. She wondered how many people around her were keeping them. She had caught herself more than once staring at random acquaintances in the elevator or the parking lot. After years of keeping who she really was a secret, this all felt like a bad remake of an unpleasant story. She drove the sharp tip of a felt pen into her blotter, leaving a black stain over today's date.

Having to fear what might be lurking in every shadowy corner and forcing her girlfriend to disconnect from her own job made Parker stop to fantasize about catching him and making him feel the same fear. She caught herself being uncharacteristically pleased with the thought of inflicting just a little pain on the creepy coward.

CHAPTER FIFTEEN

Syd had managed to use up the afternoon on mundane tasks she should have taken care of over the last week but had ignored. She pulled the Porsche into the warehouse lot where Charlie Kessler's Cadillac sat alone outside his office, the unit just next to Syd's. She wondered if she should talk to him about the window incident. For all he knew, the boarded-up window was simply vandalism, so there wasn't any reason to make more of it, Syd supposed.

The white envelope was tucked inside the handle of the lobby door. She saw it before she reached to punch in the code. She turned around as if someone would actually be waiting there to further taunt her or take responsibility. She dialed 9-1-1 and slid her finger under the flap since she was certain he wouldn't have left any evidence behind. Again.

> *You told your dyke to look for me?*
> *She's too close to even see*
> *I'll lay you down and make her view*
> *As I crawl on top and slide into you*
>
> *She thinks now she runs the show?*
> *One night with me and then she'll know*
> *It's close, my dear, the bitch will pay,*
> *You crave my love, you will obey*

Syd fisted the note and cringed at the thought of the revolting pervert touching her girlfriend's body. She took a photo of the vile missive and sent it to Mack.

Are you still at DPI?

Mack responded quickly. *No, at station. A patrol unit is on the way to pick that up. Want her to ride to our house with Jenny?*

Sydney was already waiting outside when the marked police car headed in from Meridian Street.

Syd replied, *I'll go get her.*

She stood in front of Parker's office door fifteen minutes later and stared at her empty desk. Assuming she was down the hall or speaking with another employee, she waited.

After ten more minutes, Syd checked in Jenny's office and saw her rushing back down the hall.

"Hi, Syd. I thought you went home?" The question in her voice made Syd feel as if she should defend her overprotective reputation.

"I did. I just needed to talk to her. I have some things I need to tell her about."

"That doesn't seem very productive, Syd. What's going on?" Jenny sat on the edge of her desk in front of Sydney.

She sighed heavily. "There was another note when I got home."

"Bad?" Jenny asked nervously.

"They're all bad, but yeah, I think he's escalating." She didn't want to talk about it at the office any more than she had to.

"We were talking about you guys coming to stay with us tonight, and she got a call about some emergency on the Ellison office project in Maclean. She was stopping by the architect's office and then going out there."

"That's over an hour away, Jenny." Syd was dumbfounded. How could Parker leave without telling her? Why would she take such a risk?

"Yes, Sydney. That's her job, remember? She hasn't been out there in over a month, and they needed her. They had no one at the party, and they aren't linked to the notes. Give her some air, Sydney. Just call her on the phone and don't be crazy."

Syd nodded and walked out of Jenny's office. She pulled her phone from her pocket and dialed Parker. The phone sounded from Parker's office where it sat alone on her credenza. Syd stared at the device making its noisy walk across the surface, spurred by the vibration. She clicked off and grabbed Parker's phone, squeezing it in frustration and dread.

"Jenny, she left her phone." Sydney tried to stay calm, but it took every bit of control she could manage.

"Well, you take it home with you, and I'll try to call the stops she was making to let her know you have it, okay? I'll leave a message for her to call one of us. I'll be home by four, and you can meet me there then. Why don't you go pack and bring your stuff over? Leave a note or something in case she goes back there, but she'll call me first." Jenny was clearly trying to give Sydney enough busywork to keep her occupied.

"Please, call me as soon as you hear from her." Syd didn't mean it as a question. She fought her instinct to rush out on a mission to find her, but she forced herself to respect Parker's space. Chasing after her would make Parker feel like a child once again.

Jenny picked up her desk phone and dialed the architect as Sydney walked out. "Hi, Aaron, it's Jenny Foster at Davidson Properties. Parker Duncan was supposed to come down there for a meeting this afternoon; have you seen her yet?" She waited and listened to the reply. "Oh, okay. No worries. I'll call the Ellison jobsite and track her down that way. If she comes back by for some reason, could you give her a message to call me? Thank you."

Jenny gave her a bored look. "Already been there but may be back. I'll try the jobsite if you promise to leave now. You can hang out with me all day, but you won't be packing to get her out of the house by hovering here. Could you please go and be productive?" She smiled to soften her words.

Sydney managed to relax a tiny bit, knowing that at least Parker was far away from the danger that seemed to lurk at the office and their home for the moment.

"I'll go, but I'm not happy." Sydney grimaced.

"Yes, you are. You're just miffed that she's out of your grasp for the moment. Most of that is sweet, a small part is suffocating. She won't tell you that, but I will."

Syd recognized that Jenny had stopped pulling any punches with her. She stared at Jenny for a moment, weighing her words against her emotions. "I'll see you this afternoon." Sydney managed not to beg Jenny to give her the address of her destination.

She walked to the elevator and fought the urge to search through Parker's phone. She knew what she would probably find. Business calls, texts to her and Jenny, and an email folder full of blueprints and other business correspondence. She might have been overprotective, but she couldn't bear the thought of losing Parker. She shoved the phone in her back pocket and marched to her car. Parker had to know that she was vulnerable and that, despite her job responsibilities, she owed Syd some consideration. She couldn't help but feel angry that Parker wasn't just a little conscious of her feelings.

❖

Parker took the shortcut via County Line Road headed into Maclean. The early afternoon traffic would have been heavy on the main highway, and she enjoyed the scenic route and the tiny towns that usually consisted of a bar, a multipurpose store with gas, and some kind of antique shop or craft boutique.

She was mentally calculating another thirty miles in the car when a loud clunk sounded just before her steering wheel jerked to the right. She slowed to a crawl, hoping to make it just a little closer to the next town only a mile away. The smell of burning rubber and the uneven slope of the ride told her that this was as close as she could get on what she surmised was a blown tire. She dug in her purse for her phone to call the auto club but couldn't find it. Pulling onto the soft shoulder, she jammed the car into park. She searched clumsily through the bag, failing still to locate her phone. She overturned the bag onto the seat. She could suddenly picture the phone on her credenza at the office and let out a frustrated growl. She cursed and stared down at the skirt and heels she had worn to the office, not anticipating a hike through a construction site, let alone a lonely trek down a deserted highway in ninety degrees.

Parker hoisted herself from the car and fished through her trunk. She came up with scuffed ballet flats from a bag earmarked for Goodwill. She dropped them onto the asphalt and stepped into the shoes that had just enough cracks in the soles to make her wonder if she might as well go barefoot. She walked around to inspect the offending tire. A large nail protruded from the sagging tread, and she briefly contemplated changing the tire herself. She reconsidered when she saw the steep drop into a muddy creek and couldn't fathom keeping her balance, let alone a sufficient place to brace her ill-clad feet, when tightening the lug nuts. She wished she'd been able to drive a bit farther.

She strapped her purse diagonally across her body as she was nearly toppled by the wind of a speeding truck. She waffled between grateful that he had kept driving and a little pissed that he hadn't stopped to see if she needed help. She looked ahead and began the mile-long trek to whatever small town was next.

A few cars passed her, but no one slowed. People must assume everyone had a cell phone, so walkers were there by choice. Her choice would have involved a different outfit, of course, but she only had a few thousand more steps to go. She attempted to peel the damp strand of hair sticking to her neck, and she searched through her bag for a hair band. She managed an improvised knot and began to walk faster when a black SUV slowed as if to stop. When they didn't, she was at once resentful and somehow grateful. Goose bumps skimmed down her arms despite the oppressive heat. She realized how vulnerable she was, alone on a relatively deserted highway.

At the sign promising a quarter of a mile to the town of Woodview, a loud black Ford Mustang pulled to a stop a few yards in front of her. Tint wasn't uncommon in Virginia, but she thought it was too dark to even be remotely legal. She couldn't see the driver and stopped short of passing the vehicle now parked on the grassy slope of the shoulder.

The driver's door opened, and a wiry blonde pushed out. Parker's gaydar went off, but she thought she shouldn't trust anything on an isolated county road. Besides, being a lesbian didn't necessarily preclude you from being an axe murderer.

"Should I assume that the Audi back there is yours?" The woman with nearly shaved blond hair smiled at her.

Parker nodded and stood quite still, unsure how to react.

The driver made no move to approach, and Parker was grateful. It must have been very clear that she was wary. There was no indication that her stalker was anything other than what they assumed: simple, deranged, and male, but she wouldn't take any chances.

"My name's Charlie. I own a tavern up the road in Woodview, which is, I assume, where you're headed since this ain't exactly Vegas, and there aren't many other choices." She chuckled and seemed to wait for Parker to decide whether or not to trust her. Charlie dug her wallet from her back pocket and produced a small card from a slot inside. She extended the item in Parker's direction. "Here's my business card so you know I'm legit. You can call the number and hear the message if you like—it's my voice. I just figured you could use a lift to town before you melted."

Parker relaxed a tiny bit. "I just need to call the auto club, and I apparently walked out of the office without my phone, like an idiot." Parker thought she had just tipped her hand to the potential axe murderer. She'd confessed to not having a backup plan. She smiled and took a few steps closer and decided to assume she was a Good Samaritan instead of a psychopath.

"Yeah, I figured you weren't priming tobacco in that outfit." Charlie gestured toward Parker's skirt and matching jacket, now draped over her arm.

Parker stared down at herself and laughed. "You mean this isn't what we're all supposed to wear on our first day?" She threw up her hands in mock exasperation. "Now I'm going to look out of place." She stepped closer and reached for the card.

"Come on, I'll drive you to the bar, and you can wait for the auto club to come find you."

Parker warred with her brain that recalled all the childhood admonitions about getting into cars with strangers. Looking down, she read from the simple white business card, "Charlie's Tavern. I'm going to assume, since I'm batting a thousand today, that you own the place?"

"Guilty as charged. Do you want to continue this inside the car? Even I'm sweating to death out here."

Parker finally nodded and walked to the passenger side of the car, trying to see inside. She briefly imagined herself telling Sydney how she got into a car with a strange woman on a deserted road. Then she thought she should come up with something less crazy. Charlie spun the temperature dial until it sat firmly on the snowflake symbol and turned the fan to high. Parker quelled her urge to lift up her skirt in the direction of the vent to cool her sweating thighs. She mused that she would one day convince car makers to include a crotch vent that would forever be known as the Duncan Cooler or something like that. She forced her brain back to the situation at hand. Leap of faith—or at least a step of faith. She had to make a choice between a lonely road and whomever stopped next or a fairly-well-presented possible Good Samaritan.

"Oh my God, thank you. I think I was about to melt." Parker

was more appreciative as the air hit her collar and pushed the wisps of hair from her skin.

"Don't worry. We'll be there in two minutes, and you can have a drink while you wait, on the house, of course."

Parker appraised the woman and decided she didn't look much like a criminal, but the tattoo of interlocking female symbols behind her right ear made her family.

"Why a bar out here? Are you from here?" Parker couldn't help but dig for the center of other people's stories.

"I used to own a women's bar under the same name in DC until my dad got sick. So, I had to come back to Woodview, and I opened this place."

Parker found life interesting, and she found people even more interesting. "Would you mind if I asked you a question?"

"Shoot." Charlie pushed the muscle car over the hill, and Parker could see store signs and buildings a few blocks ahead.

"How do you manage to live here and run a business when you're used to DC?" Parker was genuinely curious.

"You mean, how does an obviously out lesbian manage to not go crazy serving drinks to straight farmers and desperate housewives?" Charlie smiled as she turned into the packed gravel lot in front of the one-story brick tavern.

"That wasn't meant as an insult." Parker rushed to correct whatever error she had made.

"Don't worry; it wasn't taken as one. It's a fair question." She slammed her car door and waited for Parker to join her as she unlocked the steel grate covering the front entrance. She rotated it until it sat flush against the brick.

"I hated it when I first came back here. I was glad to get out the first time and would have bet you I would never spend another night in Woodview, Virginia. At first, I thought I would have to be in the closet again, which made warring factions in my brain very unhappy. Then I decided that I refused to live my life in reverse. Either they accept me for who I am, or they have to drive twenty more minutes to buy a drink in Peter's Station." Charlie pushed the wooden front door open and slapped her hand over the light fixtures, revealing a small room with twenty mismatched tables and a long, lacquered bar.

"That's a great way to look at it. Congratulations on making it work." Parker remarked as Charlie retrieved her phone and laptop from behind the bar and signed in. She flipped the screen until it faced the barstool she pulled out for Parker.

"The problem is convincing a woman that I'm worth the move to this burg. I haven't had a date in a year." She spoke with resignation as she started stocking clean glasses onto the shelves behind her. "You can call whoever you need to. Your car is on mile marker 24 just west of the turn-off for Pebble Creek on State Road 17."

"Thank you. You're a regular GPS." Parker brought up the auto club homepage before she dialed the emergency number. After she gave them the information, she handed the phone to Charlie. "Do you mind giving them a call-back number and an address?"

Charlie delivered the information and clicked the off button on the phone. "Sorry to tell you this, but they said ninety minutes before they can come out. I guess you'll have to watch me set up. You can pick your poison." Charlie swept an arm over the mirrored bar shelves packed with bottles and held up a tall glass.

"A ginger ale over ice would be great. Thank you." Parker thought she would have accepted a drink if she hadn't still been so hot. It had been a hell of a day, and it was only two in the afternoon.

"Need to call anyone else? Office? Girlfriend?" Charlie held the phone toward her.

"What makes you think I have a girlfriend instead of a boyfriend or husband?" Parker was genuinely intrigued since people rarely pegged her as a lesbian.

"I'm no detective, but the 'my girlfriend loves me' keychain might have given it away." Charlie chuckled as Parker felt the blushing heat rise in her cheeks.

"Yeah, well, it was that or a tattoo that said Property of Hyatt on my forehead." Parker scrubbed her thumb over the metal square and thought how much she was missing Sydney at that moment.

"I don't blame her. If I had a girlfriend, I'd probably do worse things to keep the public on notice." Charlie resumed her stocking duties after placing a glass of ginger ale in front of her. "Feel free to call her if you want."

"Well, it's only the middle of the afternoon, so I think I'll wait. We've been going through some scary stuff lately, so the less I can worry her during what's left of her workday, the better. She isn't expecting me until five thirty or so anyway. I should be back in plenty of time to recount my lunchtime ordeal." Parker guiltily thought she was enjoying the relative solitude for just a moment. She could be assured that no one would deliver a scary note to a random bar in the middle of nowhere.

"You never told me your name." Charlie's voice pulled her out of her thoughts.

"Oh. Sorry! It's Parker Duncan." She held out her hand as if they were meeting for the first time.

Charlie smirked and took the proffered handshake across the bar. "Charlie Harris. It's a pleasure."

"Thank you for everything, really. You may have saved me from being found in a ditch suffering from heat exhaustion."

"For a while there, I thought I was going to have to drive you back tied to the trunk. I didn't think you were going to accept the ride." Charlie kept busy as she spoke.

"Well, considering I was in the middle of nowhere without even a phone to beat you over the head with, I felt pretty vulnerable, and I don't do that very well." Parker was honest about a revelation she normally wouldn't put into words. Certainly not to someone she'd met only moments before.

"Understood." Charlie stopped and watched Parker shred the wet cocktail napkin and roll it into rice-sized pieces. "What kind of scary stuff has been happening lately, if you don't mind my asking? The best bar confessions I get around here involve Betty Jean getting it on with Stan Truman's wife in the back of their tack barn."

"Sounds fascinating," Parker said, honestly intrigued.

Charlie shook her head. "Small-town gossip like that swirls around here nightly. I honestly doubt any of it is even remotely factual."

"We might have to come hang out here sometime. I think it would be fun." Parker raised her eyebrows at the thought of the potential entertainment value.

"Trust me, you would get bored. I live for a chance to spice up my life at someone else's expense."

Parker started to give the highlights of their life over the past few weeks, and the recount to a stranger felt strangely unburdening.

Parker watched Charlie reach under the bar and was intrigued by the stranger that had successfully convinced her to come back to her deserted bar. She was amused by how she would frame the story for Syd. A loud crack punctured the silence of the small tavern, and Parker felt her body topple from the stool.

❖

Syd threw socks and underwear into her large canvas duffel before tucking jeans, T-shirts, and a few pairs of shorts on top of the stacks. She left a few collared shirts on hangers near the suits she was bringing for Parker. She neatly folded similar items for her into a small, hard-sided roller bag and placed in the shoes she had seen her wear with the suit selections.

She put on gym clothes and forced herself into a cursory workout in the spare room. It was a legitimate attempt to quell her compulsion to go search for Parker, who was in another town without a phone and with a stalker at large. She knew that Parker was more than capable of taking care of herself, but Sydney didn't do helpless well at all.

She pushed extra weight and forced herself to focus on her burning muscles instead of the sense of unrest that stole any hope for serenity. She should have been working like she told Parker she would. A few projects needed her attention, but she was far ahead of schedule, and her mood wouldn't allow her to be very productive on this particular afternoon.

After an hour of sweating off the buzz she attributed to her being a control freak, Syd racked the bar and wandered toward the shower. She spun the hot tap hard and tried to quell her disappointment when she found no notice of missed calls on either her phone or Parker's. A twenty-minute shower made her body feel better, but her mind still raced. She reached for her phone again.

Jenny picked up the phone quickly. "Yes, Sydney?"

"Have you heard anything?" Sydney tried to sound casual.

"Syd, she has only been gone a couple of hours."

Syd could almost hear Jenny biting back a lecture, but she knew Jenny was concerned as well. "But you left messages, you said, right?"

"Yes, but for all I know, she met them at the site, not in the job trailer. If we haven't heard from her by five, I'll go look for her myself, okay?"

"Yeah, okay. Just tell her to call me when you hear from her."

"I will. Try to relax, okay? We'll hear from her soon." The tone of Jenny's voice told Syd that Jenny was worried, too.

Syd put their clothes into the car and laid the hanging garments flat over the top of the bags. As she locked the trunk, she heard Mia's truck pull in next to her.

"Wow, you're home early," Syd said as Mia stepped out of the vehicle.

"Don't be too impressed. I have to go back at eight tonight for a teleconference briefing on the West Coast. You would think working for a lawyer, we would at least have regular business hours *sometimes*." Mia headed toward the door with Syd close behind her.

"What's the case, if you can tell me?" Syd was grateful for any distraction that didn't involve her missing girlfriend, deranged stalkers, or relationship discord. She forced herself to focus on Mia and not the turmoil.

"You're welcome to come in and have a beer, if you...um, feel safe with me in my apartment." Mia crinkled her nose, her expression apologetic.

"I believe I can manage." Syd winked at her and followed her into the loft, avoiding the end of the bar. Mia slid an amber IPA in front of Sydney, who took an appreciative draw from the glass bottle.

Mia began to review the case she had been working on for weeks. A civil suit involving a shady strip-club owner in Modesto, California, who was being sued by their client in Silver Lake. The client had reported a harrowing experience, five years ago on a blind date, when she claimed to have been raped.

"Did you know that there is no statute of limitations on rape in the Commonwealth of Virginia?" Mia asked Sydney, who was listening carefully.

"No. I wouldn't have guessed there was anywhere like that. A rape that long ago would be hard to prove, though, wouldn't you think?" Syd nursed the beer.

"Yeah, but this is a civil case for us now. And the burden is substantially lower, as you know. She waited for the criminal justice system to take action but gave up when it was pretty clear that it wasn't going to happen. She has pictures of bruises and a pretty disturbing 9-1-1 tape. The cops filed charges three years ago but failed to be granted extradition since the case was so circumstantial. So, unless he comes back to Virginia, he'll never be arrested. That's why he's responding to the civil case by video conference. He *could* be compelled to appear in person if the civil case goes to trial."

"Which is good for your client since he'll be more apt to settle from the safety of California." Syd finished the thought.

"Exactly. Unfortunately, any settlement would likely require her to drop any pursuit of future criminal action, so she kind of has to weigh it. I guess she's kind of making a deal with the devil." Mia shrugged and poured herself a glass of white wine from an open bottle in the fridge.

"You mean possibly putting a rapist back on the street to do it again." Syd made designs on the napkin with the condensation from her bottle. She felt the affront on behalf of every victim of violence, but sexual violence was something else entirely. She quietly raged at the entitled scum that exercised their privilege over another person. She knew the helplessness she was feeling in her own life at the moment fueled her fury.

"That's the way I think about it, too, but the reverse is that he won't answer the charges in Virginia anyway, unless he's a total idiot, so he's walking free regardless. He has deep enough pockets to continue to fight if the courts try to get him here."

Sydney brooded about the justice system that regularly forced victims to accept the lesser of numerous evils rather than grant them anything resembling absolute justice. "I guess we take what we can get. Hit him in the wallet. It's often what bothers them the most anyway. Rapists are violent and narcissistic. Rich rapists aren't any different, but the money hurts them more than anything because that's how they qualify their worth." Sydney tried not to fume at a battle that wasn't hers to fight. Violence, especially sexual violence, was a particularly hard fact of society for her to accept.

"Agreed. I don't think you could sit on the calls with this smug guy without wanting to rip his face off." Mia gave Syd a small smile. "Everyone knows you have a habit of stepping into battle. I saw it myself when you and Mack went after the guy who shot Sandy."

"I guarantee you, I couldn't be on those calls." Syd shook her head, trying to drive the images from her mind. "One of the first cases I worked on for the DA involved a serial rapist and murderer who would lure teenage girls from parties he threw. Because the parties involved drinking, the girls often made up stories about staying over with friends. Parents didn't start to question their whereabouts until much later, too late to save them from that monster. He raped them repeatedly before choking them to death." Syd had questioned her ability to look past the depravity and do the job she had been hired to do. "I almost quit. That is, until the juror who cast the swing vote attributed the guilty verdict to the video I made."

When Sydney refocused on the present, Mia was staring at her.

"Where did you go?"

"Sorry, I was just thinking. There are a few cases that never leave you, I guess." Syd shook her head, hoping to reset her memories.

"Things always haunt you from somewhere." Mia's voice faded.

"Are things any better for you?" Syd watched Mia's expression transform from haunted to smiling.

"Actually, yes." Mia brightened. "An attorney from an affiliate firm actually asked me out the other day. I told her no, of course, but for the first time, I didn't feel like I was cheating on Sandy when I considered it." Mia looked relieved.

"Then why did you tell her no?"

"Because she looked like a swimsuit model, and I don't need anyone who takes longer to get ready to go out than I do." Mia chuckled at Syd, who nodded knowingly.

"Understood." Syd wanted to be fully into the conversation, but her instinct that something was wrong was hammering at her, making it hard to focus.

"What else is happening with you? You aren't over here with me in the middle of the afternoon because you have nothing better to do with your day. What's up?" Mia waited with her arms folded on the bar top.

"We're still dealing with the creeper. I found another note today on the front door, and it was pretty bad. I think he's accelerating. To make matters worse, when I went to pick Parker up at the office, she'd gone to a jobsite and left her phone. So, I have no way to get hold of her, and I don't know where she is. It's making me crazy."

"Ah." Mia nodded knowingly. "Superman has lost Lois and can't function without her?"

"Of course I can *function*. I just prefer not to." Syd caught herself smiling at Mia and felt suddenly ridiculous. "We just don't know anything about the guy who is doing this. We don't know what his goal is or even have a clue who he is. I just need her to be safe."

"And she needs her brand of normal, Syd. Don't strip her of that because you need to be her bodyguard. She's aware of the danger, and everything you know about Parker should tell you that she's very careful. We're all worried, but it can't stop us from going on with our lives." Mia held Sydney's gaze. "You know, when we first got together, Sandy used to call me every other hour while she was on patrol to 'see how I was doing'...aka check on me to see if I was still breathing since the world is full of terrible things and dangerous people. You've seen the worst of the worst, like Sandy and Mack, but you can't make Parker live that life, or she'll fold under the weight of it."

"Why are women always telling me to back off and stop smothering her?" Syd rubbed the tension from her shoulders.

"Because they see it. Trust me, there is nothing sexier than being with a protective, accomplished, and confident woman—right up until you force her to become the child you have to manage through a cup of cocoa because she's suddenly incapable of drinking it on her own."

Syd processed Mia's words and let them settle over her.

Mia continued. "Women don't find themselves in

relationships with women like you because they want a shrinking violet who requires their every need be tended to. They want someone to be the yin to their yang, excuse the cliché. Why did you fall for her in the first place?" Mia's question was obviously rhetorical as she didn't stop for an answer. "You told me that you liked the fact that she was a strong person who could make it on her own, but someone who would let you be who you were naturally. That hasn't changed, Syd. She's still okay if you want to be a little stronger or tougher than her sometimes; just don't achieve that by forcing her to be weaker."

Sydney stood up and walked to Mia. "I think you might be one of the smarter people I know." She hugged Mia tightly and kissed her happily on the cheek.

"I'm counting on the universe discovering this one day," Mia said grandly as she followed Syd to the door. They both seemed to be grateful to be past the awkward legacy of the notorious kiss. "Be good."

"I will." Sydney slipped into their home and grabbed the last of the belongings she would take to Mack and Jenny's. She heard the warnings and considered them all. Parker deserved to be treated as an equal. Syd could do that better than she had, certainly, but she wouldn't be convinced to stop hunting this bastard interfering in their lives. She sped out of the drive to find Parker.

As soon as she walked through the door of her friends' little blue bungalow, Jenny greeted her. "Don't go crazy, Syd, but Parker called the jobsite and told them she had a flat tire. She said she was waiting for the auto club and would likely miss the appointment."

Syd fought the urge to react and instead forced herself to speak calmly. "Okay, I'm sure she'll be here shortly. She's more than capable of finding a way to call the auto club even without her phone. Of course, I wish she had called me, too, but I know she can handle a flat tire."

Jenny peered at her as if she was a science experiment. "Excuse me, I need to go find my friend Sydney, who you apparently hit with your car on the way up the drive."

Syd managed a wry grin. "No, I'm right here, and I'm fine. She would normally be home by five or five thirty, so there's no reason to panic. I'd like to take a ride out that way just in case she's sweating alone by the side of the road, and you're more than welcome to accompany me."

"I really think I should, since you appear to be in no condition to be by yourself." Jenny reached for Sydney's forehead.

"Funny girl. Mack should watch *you* in case the comedy scouts come calling."

"Yeah, well, you'll need me to show you her shortcut anyway. She never goes on the main roads." Jenny looped her purse over her shoulder and palmed her keys.

Sydney took an exaggerated breath. "See? My girlfriend, the target of a stalker, is lost on some isolated road in the middle of nowhere with a flat tire, and I haven't killed anyone yet. I think that's major progress, don't you?"

"I do indeed. I am, of course, afraid that your head is going to blow off at any minute. We'll take mine in case we need more than two seats. I'll even let you drive." She dangled the keys in front of Syd, who walked quickly to Jenny's car, fighting the pangs of fear and regret that she hadn't started her search earlier. Righteous justification was nice, but it didn't put Parker any closer to her.

❖

Charlie dropped the soda gun and grabbed on to Parker's arm, trying to break her fall to the dusty floor of her bar. "I'm really sorry about the stool. Preston Sinclair usually sits on that one, and he's not a small guy. I guess it was only a matter of time before the cheap wood gave in for an easier life in the fire pit."

Parker laughed at herself and graciously accepted the help to her feet. "At least no one can blame it on alcohol consumption. I'm really embarrassed."

"Why? I should be embarrassed." Charlie dragged over a more sturdy-looking replacement and took the newly minted kindling to the back room. "I guess your drinks are free if you ever come back again."

"Careful. Syd only drinks single malt scotch; you might go broke."

"Don't worry; one taste of the swill I carry, and she'll do anything for a beer." Charlie's eyes shifted as a burly man pushed through the door.

"I'm here for a Parker Dugan?"

"It's Duncan, but yes. You're from the auto club?"

"Yes, ma'am. I would have passed right by where they said you were waiting, so I thought I would see if you needed a ride to your car."

Charlie approached him, obviously reading his name from the patch on his shirt. "How long to switch out the tire, Tom?"

"Give me about twenty minutes or so?" he answered casually, and Parker began to collect her wallet and shove it back into her purse.

"How about we give you the keys, and I'll bring her down in just a few?" Charlie suggested. She held her hand out for Parker's keys with a questioning look, and Parker handed them to her.

"Sounds good; see you in a few." He took the keys and headed back to his truck.

"Hope that was okay with you. I just figured you'd rather not stand by the road any longer than you had to."

"Fine with me, thanks. I'm certainly not missing the heat."

Twenty minutes later, Charlie opened the passenger door for

Parker, who looked a little uncomfortable. "Sorry, ma'am. Force of habit. I promise I'm not flirting."

"Oh no! I didn't think that. I'm just surprised there's more than one of you left in the world."

Charlie chuckled good-naturedly as she closed Parker in the hot car and jogged to the driver's side. "Sorry, I shouldn't have shut the door. A black car with black interior tends to heat up like a sauna in the middle of the desert, but I guess you already know that, huh?"

"Definitely. Sometimes I have to let the AC run for a while before I get in because the steering wheel's too hot to touch."

Charlie guided the car to the shoulder so it faced the grill of the Audi. The mechanic was just rolling her sad-looking tire to the back and had liberated the small spare from her cluttered trunk.

Parker exited and walked to the rear of her car to begin collecting her belongings from the grass. Charlie took the keys from the mechanic and leaned in to start the car and the air-conditioning.

"You just want everything in the backseat?" Charlie asked Parker, who carried blueprint rolls in her direction.

"Yes, please," Parker said as she thrust the bundle into Charlie's arms. Charlie deposited the load and followed Parker to the trunk. A blue sedan pulled to a quick stop behind them. Charlie turned to look back and Parker saw Sydney appraise the woman helping her on the side of the road. She straightened, suddenly feeling guilty for something she hadn't done. She prepared herself for the inevitable conflict.

"Hey, baby." Syd stepped from Jen's car wearing jeans and black sunglasses.

Parker smiled and walked happily into Sydney's arms despite the expected awkwardness.

"Hi, love. It's a long story, but I'm almost fixed up thanks to Tom over there. I guess there was an accident on the highway, which would have made it a good thing I was back here if it hadn't been for the flat, of course. How did you know I was here?" She was babbling, but she was also relieved that Syd was there. She finally had to admit to herself that with whomever was tormenting them, breaking down on a lonely country road had been just a little terrifying.

"I have spies everywhere; I told you this." Syd leaned down and pressed a kiss over Parker's mouth.

"I believe it now." Parker replied to her uncharacteristically calm girlfriend and gave Jenny a side hug. "Come meet Charlie; she found me walking to call the tow truck, and it turns out she owns the bar just up the road." Charlie had heaved the last armload of stuff from Parker's trunk into the back seat and closed the door on the struggling air-conditioning.

"You must be Sydney. I've heard a lot about you over the past hour or so." Charlie sauntered confidently toward Sydney.

"All good stuff, I hope. Thank you for taking care of my girl." Syd's expression said that she hadn't intended for it to sound possessive, but she knew it had.

"Not a problem. I wouldn't want anyone to leave someone I cared about out here in the heat." She held out her hand. "Charlie Harris."

Sydney shook her hand. "Sydney Hyatt. This is Jenny Foster, who was acting as my navigator on this little back-road search excursion."

"Nice to meet you. I know it seems like we're in the middle of nowhere, but we're only thirty minutes from Maclean one way and Silver Lake the other. I have to remind myself of that when I start to choke on the tobacco fields in this town." Charlie offered a friendly smile "I guess my job here is done. I have a bar to open. If my regulars don't get their brew by four thirty, I'll have hell to pay."

Parker stepped toward Charlie and offered a casual hug. "Thank you for everything. I owe you."

"Nah, just bring me some city life up here every now and

then. Good luck with the tire." Charlie headed back to her car and roared down the abandoned road just as the mechanic rounded the car holding a lug wrench and a clipboard.

"Sign here?" Tom thrust the papers at Parker and tapped the space where she should sign.

Parker took the pen and scribbled her name on the line. "Thank you so much for coming out."

"Yes, ma'am. Get that tire fixed as soon as you can; that spare won't do you much good for long."

"We'll take care of it," Sydney said as she wrapped her arm around Parker's waist and squeezed.

"Have a good day, then." He tipped his hat and walked back to the heavy, diesel tow truck idling loudly on the other side of the road.

Parker watched him go and got lost for a moment in what could have been.

Jenny took her keys from Sydney's fingers and headed back to her car. "I'll see you at home then, okay? Glad you're all right, Park."

Parker nodded and walked to the passenger side of her car where Sydney opened the door for her. She smiled at the recent exchange with Charlie and waited as Syd slid the seat all the way back and climbed in to drive.

Syd didn't say anything as she turned Parker's car around slowly, favoring the mini wheel on the passenger side.

"So," Sydney began, pulling Parker's hand onto her thigh. "Should I worry that I found some muscle-car-driving butch with you on the side of the road?" She smiled, relief evident in her voice.

"No. We decided that a relationship born on a dusty road, in the middle of the country, would only end in disaster." Parker leaned over onto Sydney's shoulder and closed her eyes.

"Did you also explain that she would have been in grave danger when I found out?" Syd grazed her palm over Parker's cheek.

"I might have mentioned it. She was willing to take the risk, but I told her my heart belonged to you." Parker smiled and began recounting the details of her day in earnest.

When she finished, Sydney only had one question. "Why didn't you call me from the bar?"

"Because you had only just gotten to do an hour's worth of your own work and I figured you would have never known I was even gone. By the way, how *did* you know?"

"I went to pick you up from work, and your office was empty. I saw your phone, and then Jenny left a message with the construction foreman. So, when you called to say you were going to miss the meeting, he called Jenny."

"Okay. That explains why you came here but not why you came to get me at the office in the first place, especially since you had left just before I did. Nor does it explain why you aren't acting like a crazy person."

"I keep hearing about my alternate personality today." Syd shook her head. "I just wanted to pick you up." Her muscles tightened as she gripped the steering wheel.

Parker could see otherwise tense replies being packaged into pleasant answers. "Love, it was only the middle of the afternoon. I wasn't planning on leaving work then anyway." Parker searched Sydney's face, seeming to look for some clue to her sudden mood shift.

Syd sighed. "No matter what other people think, we're faced with a very real threat. You need to know that when I got home, I found another note. It wasn't very nice, and I thought you would be safer with me."

"Of course we would be safer together, but I don't want to hide from this bastard, Sydney." She clenched her teeth and was uncharacteristically defiant as she sat up in her seat, no longer in physical contact with her. If she was being honest, she was taking out her building fear on the very person trying to save her from it. But working that out would make her admit how scared she was, and she wasn't ready for that yet.

"Well, I would rather hide you *from* him than hand you *to* him. This is not the time to handle things by yourself." Syd reached to grip her hand tightly. She was tired of having to defend protecting Parker from a faceless criminal.

"I want to see it." Parker held out her hand, and Sydney saw it tremble, but her eyes never left Syd's face. Parker's eyes betrayed her true feelings with a look Syd had only seen only twice before. When she had saved Parker from Becky's knife and when she nearly perished with Mack in her car. In this case, it the fear loomed large in their lives, and Syd would readily defend every step she now took.

"There's a picture on my phone. Can we please wait until we get to Mack and Jen's?" Syd didn't leave Parker much room for further discussion. She was silent as Syd drove them back. A solemn Parker was at least a safe Parker. She moved her hand that had been resting on the gearshift and wrapped it firmly around Parker's. To her surprise, Parker curved against her. Syd knew that meant she was truly frightened, and maybe now they could work together.

Before the door was even shut behind them, Jenny pushed a glass of wine at Parker. "You might need this after the day you've had."

"Thanks." Parker took a sip and turned to see Syd bringing in their bags in from her car. "Let me read it, please."

To Syd, her voice had lost some of its fire and defiance. She didn't consider it progress. She pulled her phone from her back pocket and handed it over.

You told your dyke to look for me?
She's too close to even see
I'll lay you down and make her view
As I crawl on top and slide into you

She thinks now she runs the show?
One night with me and then she'll know

It's close, my dear, the bitch will pay,
You crave my love, you will obey

She shuddered and handed the missive to Jenny. "He's sick, Sydney. We have to find him."

"I know, and we will. Until then, we have to make sure you're safe." Sydney spoke slowly and stiffly.

"Of course. Why don't I just quit my job? I can stay home and clean your house and make your dinner, Sydney. You can sell my car since I won't be going out alone anymore. The whole fucking world is unsafe for fragile me now." She stared out the window before she spun back to Sydney and Jenny. "Well, I'm not fragile, and I hate being a victim." She spoke angrily, and her eyes fired at Syd. "The only person he wants to hurt is you, and *you're* worried about me." Parker walked to Sydney and slammed herself against her before wrapping her arms around her tightly. "I'm sorry."

Syd hung on to her, desperate to stop the torment invading their lives. "I know. I'm sorry. We *will* find him and stop him. I won't let him hurt you."

"He wants to hurt *you*! You make this just about me, and it's about both of us. Most importantly, him taking you away from me. I can't believe we're debating who some deranged person views as his target."

"How about we agree he's not safe for either of us, okay?" Syd dragged her thumb along Parker's tense jaw as Mack walked in.

Mack dropped her keys on the counter and reread the note from Syd's phone.

"He's accelerating. He's going to show his hand, but I need everyone where they're safe, and it's not at the office, and it's not at your house," Mack said firmly.

Parker moved away from Sydney and picked up her briefcase. "Fine. I'll call Quint. I have a meeting at CTI, but I assume you'd like me to try and take it by phone?" The hint of a smile crossed her face.

"You assume correctly." Sydney felt calmer when Parker offered tacit cooperation.

Parker crossed to Jenny, who was leaning against Mack. "I'm sorry this is affecting you as well. Sorry you had to come find me today."

"Parker, you're my best friend. You would do, and have done, way more than that for me. You don't ever need to thank us because that's what friends do. Olivia is next door for the evening, so let's have some wine and try to relax, okay?"

"Let's have lasagna from Amici's. I'll go pick up whatever we want," Mack said.

"Only you would turn this into a frat party." Parker leaned over to kiss Mack's cheek. She wasn't really hungry. The constant gnawing sensations in her stomach weren't pangs of hunger; they were very much a toxic stew of dread, fury, and terror. The room seemed darker, and every step she took now felt as if her legs were mired in quicksand. Sydney obviously saw it. Shadows of concern clouded her expression as she led Parker to their temporary bedroom.

Parker gritted her teeth and looked past Syd to keep the tears from falling. She lost the battle, giving in to exhaustion, anger, and the dread of what the next moments might bring.

"I can't do this." Parker could barely manage a whisper.

"Yes, you can. Together, we can do anything."

CHAPTER SIXTEEN

Parker watched Olivia manipulate wooden blocks into a bucket with her name painted on this side. She was optimistic when the quiet day had been free of notes and turmoil, and she decided to take that as a sign. She refused to dwell on the fact that stalkers didn't just leave and find new playmates, but today, for just a few hours, she wanted to feel normal.

Parker listened to the casual banter between Syd and Mack from the backyard and glanced at the clock. Jenny should be home soon, and her ringing phone jolted Parker from her thoughts.

"Red or white?" Parker's answer took the place of a customary hello when Jenny's contact photo filled the screen. She angled the microphone away from Olivia's delightful baby blather.

"Park? Red or white what?" Jen's words sounded rushed.

"Wine, silly. Which one?

"Um red. But listen, are Mack and Syd with you?"

"Yeah, she's outside with Mack fixing the bouncy swing thingy. What's up?"

"Okay, thank God," Jenny exhaled heavily into the phone.

"What? Are you okay?" Parker held the phone closer to her ear and tried to listen more carefully to Jenny's voice over that of the exuberant toddler.

"I'm fine. I have something, and I need everyone to stay put. I'll be home in just a few minutes. Love you, Park. And tell my wife to answer her damn phone from now on."

Parker heard the line go silent and scooped Olivia from her spot on the couch. Her blissful moment of peace was gone. She found Syd with a ratchet in her hand and a frustrated look on her face as Mack held the metal frame steady.

"Sorry to break up the fun, but that was Jenny. Mack, do you have your phone on? She said you didn't answer." She bounced Olivia on her hip.

Mack fished the phone from her pocket and grimaced. "Damn, I left it on silent from my afternoon meeting. Is she okay?"

"She just said that she had tried to call and wanted us to all be here when she got home. She said she had something, that's all." She shrugged and watched the duo reassembling the swing.

"Well, I don't think we're going anywhere for a while." Mack pointed at the collection of screws and bolts scattered around the aluminum frame.

"How about I go buy a new one, and you let me run this one over with your car?" Syd smacked at a stubborn fastener with a wrench. They all turned as Jenny rushed through the door and onto the deck.

"Come inside. I need you to listen to this." Jenny stopped to dust a kiss over Olivia's fat cheek, but she was clearly on a mission.

Obediently, the assembly followed her to the living room. "So, I was running around today and didn't have a chance to check voice mail until just before five. I think we can finally put a name to our problem." She almost sounded triumphant, but the threat still loomed, and Parker was very aware of it.

"Yes? And?" Sydney looked intense.

"Right, okay. So, I was checking voice mail this afternoon, and this lady leaves me a message about one of *my* messages. She doesn't tell me who she is because it's an off-the-record thing. She doesn't actually say who she's calling about, either; I'm sure she assumed I was inquiring about just one employee. Listen to this." Jenny dialed her phone and laid it on the ottoman. An unfamiliar voice spoke through the speaker.

"Hi, Ms. Foster. I received a message from your office about a reference on our former employee. I am, of course, not making an official call because our company forbids it. However, I am going to step out on a limb here. I hope you will respect that I am doing this anonymously as I would be fired if you pursued it.

"I wanted you to know that we were forced to terminate the employee because he was harassing his girlfriend, well, his ex-girlfriend. Police kept visiting him at work, serving him court documents and causing a constant disruption in the workplace. Then he would be gone repeatedly for mediation appearances.

"The company finally had to let him go. When we cleaned out his desk, we found stacks of notes that he had written to her; some of them were pretty violent and disturbing. The company felt as if they had an obligation to warn her. We contacted the woman and told her that we believed she was in danger. Her name is Leanne Mason. Ms. Foster, I met Ms. Mason when I gave her the notes. She is a sweet girl, and I am concerned about her and her family if he is at it again. Please contact the Maclean Police if she is still a target.

"Out of professional courtesy, I'm begging you to keep this message confidential. "

Jenny quickly copied down the number left for Leanne Mason and saved the message. She pulled pending files from her bag and held them up when the call ended. Parker stared at the phone and tried to brace herself for what Jenny had to say next.

"I only lacked responses on two employees, Ben Barrett and Steve Akeroyd. Ben had listed a family business in Fairfax as his last employer, but Steve *had* listed a privately held company in Maclean, and I remember Mack saying he mentioned an ex-girlfriend."

Mack motioned for her to go faster.

"Anyway, she says that our employee in common had to be termed for harassing his ex-girlfriend, right? It had to be serious. Technically, employers aren't covered under duty to warn as far as I know, so it must have been bad enough that they felt they had to tell her."

Jenny retrieved a sticky note with the summary of information and handed it over to Mack. Mack reviewed it and passed the paper over to Syd, who began tapping away on her phone.

"So, I went back on the only two remaining files, Ben Barrett and Steve Akeroyd. Ben worked in Fairfax according to his application and has a fiancée of eight years, you said, yeah? But *Steve* has a former employer in Maclean and an *ex*-girlfriend, right?"

Mack nodded and looked back at Syd who shook her head. "Nothing on a Leanne Mason anywhere in Maclean, at least not on social media or who's under the age of fifty-five. Are you sure that's how you spell her name?"

Jenny issued her a withering look. "Really? I can listen and write stuff down, Syd." She smiled when Sydney looked uncomfortable. "Yeah, that was the name."

Mack stood up and glanced at Sydney. "Why don't we go try to call her?" Mack kissed Jenny. "You did good, sweetheart."

"Don't go anywhere, you two," Syd warned. The sense of urgency flooded her voice as she followed Mack into her home office.

"I really hate that I believed this guy, even liked him."

"I did, too. I would have bet he was on the level." Syd stared at the name on the sticky note.

"Me, too." Mack dialed the number and left a message when it clicked over to a generic prerecorded voice.

"I want to finish this, Mack."

"We're going to. If I don't get a return call, we'll go there first thing. Shall I assume you want to ride along?" Mack asked the ludicrous question.

"Please. Like you could leave without me." Syd rolled her eyes.

"We'll get my car from service in the morning. This may be the last piece we need."

❖

After a restless night, Syd found Mack in the kitchen pulling mugs from the rack over the sink. "Did you sleep?" she asked.

"Not much, you?"

"I just kept replaying the interview with Akeroyd. I can't see where I missed it, and it makes me crazy."

"You didn't miss anything. I heard the whole thing, remember? It wasn't there." Syd spoke reassuringly, though she had spent the night scanning her memory for the moment *she* had missed. He was a typically jerky guy coming off a breakup. He hadn't sounded particularly angry or vengeful.

"Did Parker sleep?" Mack asked, obviously trying to shake off the nagging disquiet she felt.

"She fell asleep on my shoulder, but I tossed a lot, so I probably kept waking her up."

"You didn't do it, love."

Syd heard Parker's voice from the hallway. Syd noted it lacked its customary strength, a reminder that the toll this was taking threatened to change who they were.

"Don't worry; I was restless myself." Parker slipped her arms around Syd's waist. "Not such a great night for you either, huh?"

Before Syd finished refilling coffee, a distinct click of high heels echoed in the hallway. Jenny rounded the corner in her trademark plum shoes.

"Good morning, peoples," she cheerily greeted the crowd in her kitchen.

"The deadly heels twice in one month?" Parker motioned at Jen's pumps with one hand while gripping her mug with the other.

Syd watched Parker grin. She didn't think it was more than a function of her mouth. The look in her eyes was tired and cautious.

"Yeah, I figured I would be tall today." She crossed to her wife and snaked her arms easily around Mack's neck. "I can actually almost look Mack in the eye." She laughed and took a hot cup of coffee from her. "Besides, I can use them as a weapon if Steve comes by."

"Wrong answer, wife. Keep your door closed, and stay away from that guy until we figure out what's happening, please." Mack was deadly serious. "Maybe you should reconsider even going into work."

"No, Lieutenant. Besides, I won't be long anyway. Don't worry." She whirled back to Parker. "You sure you want to keep Olivia? I can take her next door if you want." Their retired neighbor relished being Olivia's caregiver.

"Hey, I'm a shut-in, right? I can manage an adorable little girl for one day."

"Okay, then, I'm off to slay payroll!" She gestured grandly and slid her bag over her shoulder.

Syd knew Parker felt guilty that she wasn't going to be there. She stepped in to reassure her. "You taking Olivia today will keep your mind occupied and allow us to go make him a nonissue, you know."

"Trying to placate me, Syd?" Parker locked her hands behind Syd's neck.

Syd was thoroughly thankful for the connection. It meant they were still a team, and all this would be a story from their past one day, not the thing that ripped them apart. Being without

Parker would always terrify Syd much more than any criminal. "You promise, no field trips today?" Getting her to agree to cancel the CTI meeting was a huge step, and to Syd, that meant she was worried as well.

"I have no place to be. Besides, no one even knows I'm here." She smiled up at Syd.

"Call me if anything happens *at all*, okay? I love you."

"And I love you. Now go, both of you. I know you're dying to talk to that poor woman in Maclean. Let me know what happens, please."

Parker clearly hated being on the outside, and Syd understood. She longed for the moment this chaos was behind them.

❖

Syd parked the Porsche in the SLPD lot while Mack picked up her car from the service bay.

"We'd get there faster in mine." Syd fell into the aging Taurus.

"You know how I feel about your car now, and besides, I don't think reluctant witnesses are going to think much of us pulling up in the batmobile."

"I think I liked 'sex machine' better," Syd grumbled.

"I'm sure you do." Mack pulled onto the busy on-ramp and sped into the left lane.

"How are we planning to find this Leanne Mason woman if she won't return your call?" Syd had come up with a million questions and scenarios in the night, but she would defer to Mack's official channels first.

"I guess I'm hoping I can get a little interagency cooperation." Mack shrugged. "Otherwise, we ask around and hope we get lucky."

"Why don't I try something while you drive? I have some friends in low places at a couple of cell companies. I might be able to get a billing address if it's not a prepaid line." Syd began tapping away at her phone.

Mack frowned. "I see nothing; I hear nothing. It's like I'm in the car by myself."

Syd knew that she had to toe every line when she built a case. Syd was under no such obligation.

Fifty minutes later, Mack pulled the Taurus into the gravel drive of a rural tract home on the east side of Maclean, the address of which happened to come in a text to Sydney's phone from a restricted number.

The yard was tidy and plain, and the house had recently been painted a muted green. Syd noticed a small plastic tricycle in the unfenced backyard surrounded by other scattered children's toys. They walked up onto the porch, and Syd knocked on the screen door before stepping back down the stairs.

A frilly white curtain moved from the window in the door, and Mack pressed her badge to the glass. "Silver Lake Police. I called you yesterday." The curtain fell back into place, and the house was silent.

"Ms. Mason." Mack spoke louder through the door. "Your ex-boyfriend may be putting some people in danger. We just want to talk to you for a few minutes and understand what happened to you, so maybe we can stop him."

Syd heard a noise behind the house and followed the sounds, leaving Mack to continue to knock. A short, androgynous woman with a shapeless brunette hairstyle stepped off the back deck and began throwing toys into a pink plastic barrel.

"Hey," Syd called.

"This is private property. You have no right to be here." The woman pointed a toy bat at her and shook it vigorously.

Sydney raised her hands and stopped where she was. "Look, I know you don't want to deal with whatever this is, but you're my only hope." She tried to appeal to the woman, though she'd already turned her back.

She turned around again, her hands on her hips. "If he found her, it would all start again, but this time, I think it would be worse. I believe this time, he would kill her."

"You need to know that I'm trying to protect my family, too," Syd blurted out without much forethought. "He has fixated on my girlfriend and has threatened to do some pretty disgusting things. He wants to kill me to get me out of the way." She hoped her words would sufficiently jolt the woman into some form of acquiescence.

She stared as if she felt swayed by the statement for just a moment. Then she stalked to Syd, who was standing in the center of the lawn.

"If that's not some bullshit story you just fed me, then you would understand how I feel. The only way we can have a decent life is if we don't have to relive this every time we turn around." She was nearly touching Sydney as she spoke.

Syd had eight inches and fifty pounds on the younger woman, but Sydney bet she wouldn't think twice about taking on the world to protect her family, and Syd could appreciate that.

"I do understand. Look, we don't want to bother you or make you live through whatever it is again, but you're the only shot I have of catching this guy. Please." Syd held up her phone and showed her a picture of Parker, the phone's wallpaper. "This is the only woman I have ever truly loved in my life. If I can't make this stop, I could lose her, and I can't risk that. Please, help me, and you can forget we ever met." Syd slipped the phone back into her pocket and waited.

"Wait here." The woman jerked open the screen door and disappeared into the house. Syd saw Mack, who had obviously watched the exchange from behind her.

"Any progress, or are you just pissing people off like always?" Mack scanned the back of the house.

"Sometimes, Foster, you just have to stick with your strengths. Now I'm praying she's not in there loading a shotgun."

"Well, there's a nice Friday morning mantra." Mack

instinctively backed out of the path of the window and watched as Sydney, unfazed, continued her vigil in the yard.

Five minutes later, the thankfully unarmed woman returned and motioned them into the house. Mack pushed her shirttail out of the way of her weapon before stepping into the unfamiliar territory.

The door moved partially open, and a petite blonde with nearly translucent skin and delicate features peered at her. "Could I please see your badge again?" Her voice was as small as she was.

Mack held up her ID. "I'm Lieutenant Foster; I called yesterday." The visit was clearly still not a welcome one.

She nodded when Sydney stepped up and introduced herself as well. The angrier of the women moved the door wider, and the waifish blonde stepped out of their path.

Syd heard locks engage on the door behind them.

"I'm Leanne Mason. This is my wife, KC. Can I get you a drink? I just made some coffee." She looked as if she needed something to do with her hands as she wrung them repeatedly in the now crowded kitchen of the small house.

"No, ma'am. We're fine. We'll try not to take up too much of your time. Thank you for seeing us." Mack looked at both of them as the brunette was stroking her fingers over her wife's arm.

KC encircled Leanne's wrist, and she spoke soothingly. "Angel, you don't have to talk to them. We can ask them to leave right now."

"I know, sweetie, but what if he tries to hurt someone else, like she said?" She looked into KC's wary eyes.

"Then it's something the police can handle without you having to go through it all again. I can't pretend this didn't nearly tear us apart last time. You want to risk him coming after Georgie again?"

"We have papers that say he can't." She shifted in the bright yellow kitchen to face her.

Mack looked uncomfortably at Sydney, who felt as if they

were eavesdropping on a private conversation they had no right to hear.

"That doesn't mean he won't." KC paced the small room and rubbed at the back of her neck.

"Can we just hear them out? I would rather know what's going on than be blindsided if he finds us again." She stared at the muddy brown tiles on the floor and shook her head.

Syd wondered if she was shaking out unpleasant memories.

"Fine. Sit down so you can go sooner." KC moved with Leanne, leading them into the modest living room, which boasted a large tan microfiber sectional sofa with baby blankets spilling from a laundry basket on one end.

Mack sat near the two women, and Syd stood against the wall as if attempting to fade into the background.

"I'm sorry. I know this is an inconvenience, but it seems like your ex-boyfriend may be harassing another woman at his new place of employment, and we hoped you might be able to tell us a little about him."

KC spoke first. "All you need to know is this guy's a total freak. He needs to be locked up. No one did anything about it before, so we have no reason to believe this time will be different. My wife could have been seriously hurt, and so could Georgie." She backed into the corner of the sofa and pulled Leanne against her.

Mack looked up from her notebook. "I'm sorry, who is Georgie?"

Leanne spoke first. "Georgia, we call her Georgie, is our daughter. It might be easier if I start from the beginning."

"That would be helpful." Mack usually asked the questions her way, but Syd thought it very likely they would be tossed out by the angry woman hovering over her wife if she asked one the wrong way. Since the entire interview was technically just a giant favor, she knew Mack stayed quiet to let them proceed their way.

"We met at City College in Fairfax. Right after high school, I was taking a computer course so I could maybe work in an office and save up for a four-year school. He sat next to me, and we became friends. I guess I always knew he had feelings for me, and I guess I just sort of got used to having him around.

"After about six months of him asking me repeatedly, I agreed to go out with him. I didn't have any family around to speak of, and I suppose I was a little lonely. We went to a party for some friends at school. After a while, we were just always together, and I met his family who were really nice to me and kind of became my family.

"See, my dad left when I was little, and my mom died right after I turned eighteen. My mom's boyfriend owned the house we were living in, and it wasn't a good place for me to be. I figured he would never be the great love of my life, but he was stable, and his dad had a construction business where I could work in the office answering phones and stuff while he worked on the jobs with his dad. It was great for a while and…"

"What happened that changed that?" Mack's tone was cautious as KC leveled a heavy stare at them both.

"Well, nothing, really, for a while, but then he started getting really jealous of everyone I talked to and everything I did. I wanted to take more classes, and he would freak every time I mentioned it. I sat at the front desk in the office, and every time a guy came in and was friendly, he would make a scene. Even his dad started to get pissed because it was affecting the business, you know?" Mack nodded, and Leanne glanced over at Sydney before continuing.

"I took that for about two years, and it just started making me crazy. I knew I wasn't in love with him, but I thought I could settle. Well, then KC started working for our blueprint company, and she came in to pick stuff up or drop off plans. We became friends, and we would talk when no one was around." She wrapped her arm over her wife's knee and smiled at the recall of a seemingly fond memory.

KC picked up the story without prompt. "So, I would bring her a coffee or a muffin or something like that when I made the run to her office. I knew I was starting to have feelings for her. I knew she was having feelings for me, but she had never been with a woman before, so it was weird for her, you know?"

Mack nodded. Syd watched the two hold on to each other, obviously comforted by the closeness.

"I brought her a cupcake on her birthday, and he walked in behind me. I thought he was going to hit me; he just got so unbelievably pissed. I got out of there as soon as I could, mostly so it would be less of a problem for her."

"And I knew I was attracted to her, too, but it was so complicated. I didn't want her to have to be involved with all the drama. He was becoming angrier and threatening me a lot. He started pushing me and getting really rough. He had hit me a couple of times before, but nothing too bad. It wasn't like I hadn't been around that before." Leanne words were intentionally vague.

"Anyway, one night he held a knife up from the kitchen and asked me if I knew what he could do to me with it. The next morning after he went to work, I found a note on my car. It said that if I talked to KC again, he would kill her. I started to believe that he was really dangerous. Then when I got to work, there were flowers and candy on my desk like it was our anniversary or something. I didn't know what to think." Her voice became weak and strained.

"That night he, um, forced himself on me and told me that a dyke couldn't give me what I needed." Leanne stopped to catch her breath while KC openly fumed.

"He said he would show me all the ways he could...um... satisfy me that she couldn't. It went on for hours and hours." Her voice faded. She fought a sob and leaned back into KC.

KC tucked Leanne's face against her before she managed to find her voice. "He raped her. I don't care whether they were living together or not; he raped her." KC practically spat the words.

Mack nodded. "Any nonconsensual sex is considered an assault. Did you report it?"

Leanne nodded before regaining her composure. "But I knew no one would believe me. The sheriff was his daddy's best friend. So then, I just wanted out. When my mom's boyfriend lived with us, I tried to tell her about things happening with him, and she didn't believe me either. I knew what was right and wrong. I just got used to men, y'know, doing what they wanted, I guess."

Syd walked to the window, fighting the rage she felt on the woman's behalf. She could only imagine what KC must have felt at the time.

"Anyway, I waited until he was out on a job, and I called KC. I told her what happened and that I needed to get out. I didn't have a car anymore. He sold it and told me it was a waste of money since we worked and lived in the same place. I told the other lady in the office that I was going out for a walk, so KC picked me up around the corner. I went home, and we packed all my stuff in trash bags and pillowcases, whatever we could find. I didn't take any furniture or other things, just my clothes and personal stuff. I didn't really have much to start with. I was so scared the whole time we were there, I couldn't breathe, you know? I knew if I left him, I was going to have to give up my job, so I would have no money. Everything had just changed, but I knew I wanted to be with her." KC leaned up and wrapped her hands over Leanne's thin arms. She was trembling from the memories of the story she had just told.

"I didn't care what she had. I was in love with her, and I just wanted her away from that maniac. I wanted to take care of her. And I wanted to kill him; I fantasized about it. When he found out that she had moved out, he started calling her. He called a hundred times a day. Literally, *a hundred times*." KC was obviously furious, and Leanne tipped her face against KC's in an apparent effort to calm her.

"I asked him to stop, and it just made it worse if I talked to him. His mom called me once and begged me to come to my senses. I told her what happened, and she said that no son of hers would ever do anything like that.

"He bought me gifts and left them on our porch. Really creepy gifts like a framed picture of me and him together, except it was at different times in the past, and he just taped them together in the frame. He followed me to the store or anyplace he could, and I would have to wait until someone could walk out with me to the car. Once, he um…"

KC kissed her cheek and took over the conversation. "He freakin' watched through our window one night while we were on the couch together, y'know, *together*."

Mack turned as Sydney shifted closer to the sofa, knowing the similarities had just cemented their suspicions. She found a side chair and perched on it, staring at the couple and trying to imagine what that kind of hell it must have felt like.

A tiny version of Leanne ran into the living room and threw herself into KC's arms.

"Georgie, it's not time for your nap to be over," KC whispered to her.

"Mama, I need water." KC rolled her eyes toward Leanne, who whispered something in her daughter's ear. "Yes, Mommy." KC scooped the child into her arms and headed for the kitchen.

Leanne continued when KC left the room. She spoke more quietly. "It was really scary. He called me the next day and said he saw my dyke lover's hands on me, and that he would make her pay. He said he would make me watch as punishment for being a whore." It was obvious that she had recounted the words many times. "I called the police before KC got home because I was so scared of him. The police said they couldn't help me because he hadn't made any specific threats, so there was nothing they could do. We tried to get a restraining order on him, but his family has money and friends in high places. His lawyer would fight it every time, and the judge listened to them instead of us. KC says it was because we were together, but I just think justice is only blind when she isn't wearing expensive glasses, if you know what I mean. I think I cried for three weeks straight, but she still stayed with me." She took a deep breath and gave them a small smile when Georgie could be heard laughing from the kitchen. Her hands were wrapped tightly in a blanket as she continued her story.

"Then KC said we should move again, out of Fairfax, and then she asked me to marry her. Of course, I said yes." Leanne stared down at a simple silver band nestled against a small diamond on her left hand. "The first thing I did was go to the court to get my name changed. I figured maybe he wouldn't be able to find me as easily. I thought maybe he would just give up, but he didn't. It got worse. He followed me home from the grocery store to our new place without me knowing. The next day, he drove behind me when I was picking up a prescription. He got out of the car next to me and started yelling. Then he saw my engagement ring, and he went ballistic. Some people walking by called the police because he was acting so crazy, but the police just told him to go home. I waited in the drugstore for two hours until I was sure he was gone."

KC returned to the living room and settled behind her wife again. "She's back down. She really wanted water, go figure."

KC continued where she heard Leanne leave off. "He started harassing us again, leaving notes and flowers and candy until we felt like prisoners in our own home. Somehow, we never caught him doing it, but we knew it was him. We both always wanted a baby, and we wanted to start our lives together. We couldn't let him control everything.

"We found a volunteer donor, and she got pregnant right away." KC absently rubbed over her wife's now flat stomach before she continued. "We decided to go to the fair with some of my old friends. We were just wandering around, eating junk food and enjoying being together before Georgie was born, y'know? All of a sudden, he was there. I don't know if he followed us or if it was an accident, but he saw us together and then he saw her belly. Anyway, he went crazy again and started yelling that it was his baby and that he was going to take it away before we corrupted it. Bizarre shit like that."

Syd looked at the couple and took the chance of asking a question for the first time, "Did he really think he was the father?"

Leanne answered quickly. "He would have to have known, logically, that he couldn't have been. The last time was a year and a half by then. I think he just wanted any part of 'us' he could get or the fantasy he had made up of us. At that point, we were afraid to be anywhere near him. As soon as the baby was born, we moved again. We had DNA tests done to prove once and for all she wasn't his, but he wouldn't let it go." Leanne scraped her fingers under her eyes when she started to cry quietly. KC turned on Mack.

"You need to go. We just got to the point that we feel safe, and you come here and bring it all up again. You have no idea what we went through."

"I'm sure we don't, Ms. Mason, but if we can stop this from happening to someone else, then we'll have taken him off the streets for a while. Does Steve know what your new name is?" Mack asked, trying to manage the tension in the room.

"Who's Steve?" Leanne looked confused.

"That man we're talking about isn't Steve Akeroyd?" Mack shot a look to Syd.

"No, it's Ben Barrett." Leanne looked as if she couldn't make sense of the past conversation possibly being a misunderstanding.

Syd rocked forward and stared at them. "I'm sorry, we thought Steve was your ex-boyfriend. Ben works at the same company. He says he has a fiancée named Lillian."

"That's me. Lillian Zimmer. At least it used to be. I changed it to Leanne Mason when we moved the last time."

"Were you ever engaged to Ben?" Mack asked.

Syd stood quietly, hoping that they wouldn't be thrown out at this critical juncture.

"No. We never even talked about it. Although I guess he talked about it with other people like we already were. He told KC that when she started coming to the office. Apparently, he knew before we did that she and I had feelings for each other."

"Wait, so Barrett *isn't* doing this?" KC looked incredulous.

"No, he is. We just had two names, and we assumed the wrong one. It's a long story. Sorry for the confusion," Mack said.

Syd started to walk back and forth again in front of the window. She briefly fantasized about what her hands around his neck might feel like. To punish him for everything he had done to her life. To Parker's. She refocused on the information Mack was continuing to gather.

"You mentioned he sent you flowers and gifts. When he sent you flowers, were they lilies?" Mack asked.

"Yeah, for my name, I guess. They just became the flowers he always sent. They aren't even my favorite." She rubbed her hands over the skin on her upper arms.

"Do you have any of the notes he would write to you?" Syd held her breath for the answer.

"Most of them I threw away, but that lady from the company he started working for when he followed us to Maclean gave me the ones they found in his desk. I don't know if she was supposed to or not, but I kept them in case."

"Would you let us see them?" Syd was cautious and checked Mack's reaction out of the corner of her eye.

KC abruptly stood and walked to a chest sitting under the window and retrieved a white plastic shopping bag that was taped closed. As soon as she removed the contents, Sydney's heart clutched. The same white parchment stationery was tucked into numerous white envelopes. The handwriting was unmistakable.

Mack walked over and took the bag. "Would you let me have those for a while? I promise you can have them back; it will just help our case if we can compare the two sets of them."

"You can have 'em." Leanne suddenly spoke from where she was now curled up on the couch. "I'm sick of living with his ghost and the memories. Just take them, please." She looked pleadingly at KC, who handed them over.

KC stared intently at Mack and then Syd, suddenly less anger and more concern in her voice. "Listen to me. If it *is* him, he won't get the message. He still doesn't get it. He's dangerous. He is crazy, and I don't want him anywhere near our family. How do we know this whole thing isn't going to bite us because you were here?" KC demanded.

"It won't because I say it won't." Mack rewrapped the package and tucked the bag under her arm.

"Look, I appreciate what you're doing." Leanne suddenly sounded strong and a little pissed. "KC is just scared he'll come after us again. Now we have Georgie, we can't risk it."

"I understand. My wife and I have a daughter a little younger than Georgie. I would feel the same way." Mack held out her hand to KC, and she shook it before turning to Sydney.

KC's voice softened. "I really hope you can stop him before he hurts her."

Syd bristled. "I won't let him touch her. You've really helped, and I appreciate it more than you know." She wanted to get back, make sure Parker was safe, and let Mack deal with Barrett.

Once they were out of the house, Syd watched Leanne offer a sad wave. Mack jammed the car in reverse and headed for Silver Lake.

Syd texted Parker. *Don't leave the house, please. It's Ben, not Steve.*

Mack dialed Jenny's office line from the speakerphone as she drove. Syd knew she was offering silent prayers until she answered.

"Jenny Foster, may I help you?" She sounded official and busy.

"Sweetheart, it's me. Are you alone?"

"Yes, did you want to talk dirty to me?" Jenny laughed, and Mack was visibly relieved that all was okay for the moment.

"No, but I'll hold you to that later. Listen, it's not Steve. It's

Ben Barrett. Can you steer clear of him until I can get warrants sorted?"

"That'll be easy; he called in sick today." Jenny sounded uneasy. "I just can't believe it's him. He seems so quiet and normal."

"Well, trust me, he's not. Hopefully, I can pull him in before the weekend is over, but you still need to be watching for him, okay?"

"Sure, sweetie. I'm cutting out fairly soon anyway. So much for Friday being a work-at-home day." Jenny still sounded distracted.

"Okay, I'll see you as soon as I can. Maybe I can take you out for dinner tonight if I'm not tied up on this? Syd and Park could probably survive without us."

"Richard and Allen are picking up Olivia for his niece's birthday party at four, so it would be a great night, as it turns out."

"I love you, Mrs. Foster." Mack smiled.

"Love you, Lieutenant. Be good." They heard Jenny hang up the phone.

Sydney looked at Mack. "Was that a setup so Park and I can deal with our stuff?"

"I thought you already dealt with your stuff. Besides, I just thought it would be more comfortable than your car, Casanova."

Syd punched her arm as they pulled past the Silver Lake city limits sign.

"I hope you know that's battery, Hyatt."

"Why don't you find the real criminal, and I'll let you cite me later."

Mack became serious. "It was all there, you know? When I was talking to Ben, and he got all bent about the kid thing. I should have pushed harder. He said his *kid*. It was a red flag, and I ignored it."

"You didn't ignore it; it just didn't jump out. It didn't flag for me, either. I just need to get to Parker until you can move him to a very tiny cell." Sydney read through the notes that the Masons had provided. "The wording is even the same on these. It's like he just made Parker the stand-in for Leanne even though they're nothing alike."

"I know. He needs some serious help. I'll spend the next six hours of this shift doing everything I can to put him where we can watch him. Trust me, my next interview will be very different."

Syd thought of nothing but getting to Parker. She could breathe then. She could imagine the relief she would feel to tell her that Ben Barrett was in custody. A few more hours that felt like a millennium was all it would take.

Chapter Seventeen

Richard and Allen waved to Sydney as she passed them on the little residential street leading to Mack and Jenny's home. Sydney could see Olivia perched in the car seat behind them, her black hair pulled into a waterfall of a ponytail on top of her head.

Jenny's car was already next to the Audi in the drive, and Syd felt relieved that Parker wasn't waiting alone. Parker was still hard at work on the sofa when she walked in and locked the door behind her.

"Hey." Syd leaned over the back of her seat and kissed her neck.

"Hi, my love." She reached up and skimmed her fingers absently through Syd's hair as she saved her work with the other hand. "I guess it was fairly productive in Maclean?"

"If you call scary as shit productive, then yes. Ben Barrett is a psychopath and an abuser, Park." Syd moved around to sit next to her and looked into her eyes. "Until he is away for good, you can't take any chances, promise me."

"I'll promise if you will." She kissed Syd's cheek as if to reassure her. "At least we know who's behind it now. It's almost over."

Jenny tapped into the kitchen in a pale-green-print halter dress and tall wedged sandals. Her hair tumbled loosely around her shoulders, and she was applying fresh lipstick.

Syd whistled at her from the living room. "Aw, you don't have to dress up just for me, Jen, but I do appreciate the gesture. You look gorgeous."

"Don't get excited, Hyatt. I like to look nice for Parker. After all, I need to keep our secret affair fresh and sexy before she leaves me for someone tall, dark, and brooding." She beamed at Sydney over a small mirror and applied mascara around her blue eyes.

Parker laughed loudly. "Don't let Randy Miller hear you joke about that; from what I understand, he's already picturing it anyway."

"I always knew I should keep an eye on you two." Syd winked at Parker and skimmed a kiss behind her ear.

"Ah, who am I kidding? Park's too frilly for me. I like 'em armed and dangerous. Which is why I am meeting a certain lieutenant for a picnic in Summers Park." She sounded thrilled by the prospect.

"She must have delegated the Ben Barrett case as soon as she walked in. A picnic, huh? Look who's trying for romance points. Remind me to tease her about that." Syd chuckled.

"Don't you dare; this is serious progress. She even left me a note tucked in my door on one of her business cards like she used to when we she was trying to win me over. At this rate, we'll be home very late and may do very bad things in a public place." Jenny beamed at them.

"I'm impressed. Barrett's investigation is a big deal. I suppose there's progress when Mack can turn it all over for a night with her wife. Just remind her of the citation she threatened me with the other day." Syd was delighted Mack could put such a smile on Jenny's face after the month they had all had been through. Happier still, it meant that warrants had dropped quickly, and Ben might already be in custody. Jenny blew a kiss from the back door and stepped out only to return in seconds.

"Crap. Park, can I drive yours? I just remembered I'm out of gas, and I don't want to be late."

"Of course. Have a great time; love you." Parker called back to her.

"Love you both, bye," she called as she slammed the door hurriedly behind her.

"I hope the very bad things don't happen in your car," Syd mumbled to Parker, who nudged her playfully.

"So, Ms. Hyatt, where are you taking *me* this evening? Everyone seems to have plans but us."

Syd would never settle for being outdone by her friends, and Parker knew it.

"Ah. Not true. We're headed to Sandstone Café for dinner and then for drinks and dessert on the patio at the Segue." Sydney was pleased with herself and knew Parker was just happy to be far away from this nightmare for a night.

"Very fancy. I'm impressed. I hope I have time to change first." She looked down at her jeans and flip-flops.

"Of course. You're perfect regardless, but we have time, and I just want to hold on to you a bit longer."

After twenty minutes of lounging together, Parker tapped Sydney's arm to release her. "I should go change so we don't miss our evening."

"How about I go put gas in Jenny's car so it will be done before the morning?" Syd pulled Parker to her feet and walked into the kitchen.

"Incredibly thoughtful and ridiculously gorgeous; how did I get so lucky?" Parker closed her eyes and rested her head against her shoulder.

"I love you, Park." Syd turned her in the direction of the bedrooms before stepping out to Jenny's car after checking twice that the door was locked behind her.

Syd yelled for Parker in a way that made her run back down the hall. Syd saw the panicked look on Parker's face, but she couldn't stop to soothe her now.

"What happened, Syd?" Parker gasped when she saw the envelope in Syd's hand and took it from her. The paper was folded to conceal a long poem on the now very familiar stationery. She obviously didn't care that it was evidence she shouldn't be handling.

"Have you read it yet?"

Sydney shook her head. "It means he knows we're here, Park." Fear tore at them both. Parker pressed open the page on the counter.

I see her always, but you don't see me
You stained her soul, but I'll set it free
Your filthy fingers stroked her skin
But with me is where her life begins

The day when she ignored my voice
Your ending move left me no choice
She stayed with you, but not in her heart
It's my last move ... it's time to start

We'll be alone in the empty park
It's there I'll have her in the dark
She'll be good and decent, I will approve
I'll lay her down and make my move

She will be ashamed of those purple shoes
The perfume she wore, not subtle cues
Stand behind, this man will lead
You'll feel my knife as I make her bleed

Parker looked at her, horrified. "Oh my God, Syd, it's Jenny, not me."

Syd grabbed her keys, and Parker rushed out behind her. Sydney drove as fast as she reasonably could through the residential streets before hitting the main road doing eighty. Mack's phone went immediately to voice mail both times, and Sydney gave up and dialed Chief Cash's personal cell phone, the number of which she had acquired when he worked with them to expose the previous corrupt police administration.

"Chief, it's Sydney Hyatt." He started to issue customary pleasantries before she cut him off. "Chief, I can't get Mack on her phone. I think Jenny's at Summers Park with a man named Ben Barrett who is a stalker and a rapist. I'm on my way, but I believe at this point he's unraveling. He's desperate and dangerous. I believe he will hurt her—if he hasn't already."

"Hank Lu is the sergeant on right now. You know him?"

"Yeah. I've worked with him before."

"He and his team will be en route. Give me a second. And, Syd? Wait for him. Please." He disconnected to try to raise Mack on the radio, and Parker sent a text to Mack from Sydney's phone. *9-1-1.*

She took out her own and sent a text to Jenny. If Jenny was safe, she'd respond right away. *We are headed out for dinner. Is there anything you need before we meet you at the restaurant later?*

She hit Send and stared blindly out the window.

Sydney reached to hold her hand. "We'll get there. It will be okay. Five minutes." Syd was doing double the speed limit when she blew past two unmarked police cars parked at the side of the road. She wouldn't have stopped if they had pulled out behind her, but the fact that they didn't meant that Cash was making the world move for Mack and Jenny. She silently prayed they weren't too late.

Syd pulled in behind Parker's car, which sat vigil next to a dingy green Pathfinder. A closer inspection revealed a rusty muffler that hung from tired wire beneath the frame.

Parker grabbed her chiming phone and read the text from Jenny. "Syd, he's with her. She just wrote 'Lillian and Ben,' and the word 'Help.'"

Parker's phone then vibrated in her hand. "How is she able to call me?" She moved to answer it when Syd pulled the speaker away from Parker and motioned for her to say nothing. The open line told them everything they needed to know. Syd pressed the button to mute the microphone.

"Ben, um, where did you come up with this idea for a picnic? Everything looks so nice. The wine and the cheese…"

"Don't be stupid, Lillian, we always have a picnic on our anniversary. Apparently, letting a woman use your body has affected your brain." Ben's voice was dismissive and condescending.

Jenny said nothing. Syd stared over the expanse of lawn separating her from their view. Syd noted the sign indicating that the park gates would close at sunset. She was happy that no one should be coming or going at this hour. The park was deserted now, but Jenny was alone with a maniac who didn't know her name. She began formulating her next move, one that Chief Cash had warned her against and one that would make Parker furious.

She imagined how Jenny must have felt when she saw him standing there instead of Mack. When he walked to her, she must have known then that those notes had all been meant for her. They had been wrong; he wasn't stupid. He was clever and calculated and fixated. Because of the time they spent at each other's homes and driving each other's cars, he'd clearly mistaken Parker's for Jenny's. Hopefully, it wouldn't cost Jenny her life.

Ben's voice came clearly through the phone mic. "Take off your shoes, Lillian, or you'll make the blanket dirty. I don't know why you insist on wearing those shoes when I've told you that you look like a whore."

Syd understood that he very much believed her name was Lillian. Since they were now face-to-face, his delusion must be all consuming.

"You never used to dress like that, you know. You were respectable before she defiled you. I *will* deal with her."

"I…I'm sorry, Ben. It won't happen again." Jenny sounded bewildered, as if she had no idea how to interact with him; agreeing to everything was a good play.

"Of course it won't. When we move back to Fairfax with

the baby, you'll be raising her at home. There will be no need to have those things. You will be a proper wife, and you will stop this behavior."

They heard a cork being removed from a bottle and the sound of liquid being poured into plastic cups. Syd was texting information to Sergeant Lu and fantasized about Jenny being able to use the bottle as a weapon. Syd imagined the satisfactory *thunk* as the heavy glass cracked across his skull.

"Sit!" he suddenly yelled, and Jenny made a startled noise.

Syd started at the sound, her fingers curved tightly on the door handle, poised to sprint after them. She forced herself to wait. She needed to know just a bit more about Ben Barrett's current mind-set.

"Here! Take this. I'm not going to hold your glass for you. In fact, you should be serving me."

"You're right. Sorry." Jenny seemed determined to play his game or at least make him think she was.

"I got your favorite wine. Remember when we bought it on our first date? You said you had never had wine before, but that you would remember it forever."

Jenny mumbled in the affirmative. Syd could hear the thickness of unshed tears in her voice. She hoped Ben wouldn't ask specifics of his and Lillian's history together. In Jenny's current state, Syd worried how far she could manage the charade.

Parker looked horrified as the scene unfolded before them, and Syd whispered, "This is good. I just need to know where his head is. She's doing great, Park."

Ben's voice sounded calm and matter-of-fact now. "So, before we discuss your disappointing behavior, let's have a toast. Eight years ago today, I saw you at a desk in computer class, and we fell in love that moment. From now on we will be together and raise our daughter the way a good family should. Now, I know you didn't get all the chances in life that I did, Lillian, but we can change that. My family will forgive you and take you back like I have."

He was evidently satisfied with his proclamations, Syd thought. He clearly couldn't conceive of the ludicrous irony of his statements. "Arrogant fuck." Syd seethed at the man and at the fact that she should have dug deeper, found it sooner.

"Thank you, Ben." Jenny's voice trembled.

"First, you are going to have to explain some things. I saw you with her, that woman you lived with at the loft. Sydney, is it? You were walking our daughter. I saw her kiss you in *public*. How could you humiliate yourself with her? Did you move in with that cop woman when she cheated on you? I followed you there. You didn't even notice. But I used to follow you in Fairfax, too. I was trying to protect you from these people, but you didn't appreciate me.

"You know, I saw her with the other woman in the car. Do you even understand how disgusting it was for me to watch them the whole time?" He spat the words and sounded increasingly angry.

Syd wondered how he could have gotten things so confused. He seemed to know other people but insisted on calling her Lillian. The events were jumbled, peppered with only a sprinkling of any reality.

"I guess I made a mistake, Ben. It won't happen again."

Syd saw Parker jump as a rustling near the phone caused the sound to muffle. His voice got louder as he obviously moved closer to the phone. Syd glanced in the mirror and wondered when the SLPD contingent would arrive. She wouldn't wait any longer. Parker's closest friend would *not* be harmed while she sat vigil in the car, waiting for the cavalry.

"I know it won't happen again. I told you before what I could do to you with a knife like this. If you contact her again, I will cut her heart out while you watch her die. Is that understood?" He spoke as if he was explaining basic math to her.

Syd unlatched the door and braced a foot on the gravel. Parker clung to her arm in a fierce grip Syd allowed to stop her movement for the moment. She listened carefully to every breath, every nuance in his words. She would use it all.

"I watched you at that party, when you were caressing me. Then you spoke to the dyke about 'our bedroom.' In front of people! I was so ashamed of you. People acted like it was normal to be like that. I know they didn't believe it. It's disgusting, isn't it, Lillian?"

There was a pause when Jenny didn't reply.

"Well?" He sounded annoyed. "Say it! Say that you will never let that woman touch you again."

"I will never let her touch me again," Jenny managed to say with an audibly shaky breath.

The sound of plastic wrapping and packages being opened gave Syd a moment of relief. Her answer must have placated him for the moment.

"A lily for my Lillian. Your favorite. I would have brought you a dozen, but you haven't earned my generosity yet. It seems you have become accustomed to many things with your pathetic excuse for a woman. She tries to behave like a man, but she isn't. She never could be. I showed you what a real man was, didn't I? I will show you again, Lillian. You won't forget this time."

"Of course not. Should I call and let people know not to expect me home?"

Gripping the wheel, Syd hissed, "No, no. Your home is with him. Let him think that." She squeezed the phone harder and again waited for an explosion. Parker covered her mouth and seemed to hold her breath until Ben spoke again.

"Who would be at our house, Lillian? It's no one's business where we are. Certainly not those horrible people you've been around. Surely you aren't referring to them."

"Of course not. I told you I wouldn't associate with them anymore."

"No, I told *you*! You remember who is in control here."

It was all about control. Sexually violent predators were

driven by control, something Syd knew too well. The longer Jenny was alone with him, the more dangerous the situation became. She began to formulate the next steps in her mind.

Ben's breathing became louder. Syd feared if they could hear him, it meant he was closer to the phone and in turn, closer to Jenny.

"Your skin is very soft, Lillian. I always think of that. Maybe we should be reacquainted before we eat."

Syd had heard enough. She pressed the phone in Parker's hand and pointed to the approaching police cars stopping behind them.

"Go let them listen; tell them what's happened so far. You need to brief them on everything."

"Where the hell do you think you're going?" Parker looked furious and adamantly gripped Syd's arm.

"Listen to me. I won't be in danger. We just need him to see me and want to go after me, so they can get Jenny away." She jerked her head behind her, indicating the assembling law enforcement contingent barely a hundred feet away. She was running out of time before they would stop her.

"Oh, and that's your idea of not being in danger?" Parker stared, clearly too angry to continue.

Sydney watched tears well in Parker's eyes and held her shoulders. "Look at me. Jenny needs this. I'll be safe, I promise. I need to know you'll tell them everything so they can get him. Please, stay with them until I get back."

Parker shook her head. "Sydney, what if he has a gun?"

"I don't think he does. This guy has a history with knives. The reports say he has used a knife. Leanne told us he threatened her with a knife; the notes talk about knives. I promise I'll come back without a scratch since I don't plan on getting that close to him. I have an idea how to get him to walk away from Jenny, but you have to trust me and go fill them in. I'll be right back."

Parker shook her head. "Why does the universe keep

reminding me that I could lose you in a second?" Parker repeated Sydney's own words from not so long ago.

"Touché." She tapped a kiss briefly on her mouth. "I love you more than anything. Go. Please."

"I love you." Parker stared as if willing herself to trust Syd's words.

"Be right back, Park." She kissed Parker more soundly and walked between the cars, shielding her movement. She heard her cue when Parker called out.

"Sergeant, you need to listen to this."

Syd crouched around the gate and followed a wood line. The park consisted of a field surrounded by trees, and they would be easy to spot, assuming she could get there undetected by Ben Barrett and by the cops who would never have let her in.

Syd jogged through the thicket of pines skirting the small soccer field at the near corner and continued past a wooden shelter with benches and a rusty barbecue grill anchored in concrete. Just beyond the last pillar, two figures sat together. She recognized the color of Jenny's dress. She moved carefully until she could hear and see them clearly. If he turned in her direction, he would see her, but she counted on him remaining focused on Jenny, who was arching awkwardly away from him as he was tilting his body closer to hers.

"Ben, wait." Jenny's voice was determined. "Don't we want to wait until we've finished our dinner and can be private? You said how upsetting it was to see people doing…that in public."

"You had no problem baring your body for the dyke; how dare you refuse me?" Ben's anger flashed as the sting of her rejection settled on him.

"I'm just so hungry, Ben. You know she never took me out to eat or did anything like what you've made us here." Jenny was cleverly trying to harness his anger for Syd or Lillian's partner or whoever he was focused on.

Syd was proud of her. She prayed Jenny would fight with

everything she had before she let him touch her like that, though she had no intention of letting it get that far. Syd felt sick when he ran his pudgy fingers over her breast, and she fought the urge to run at them, abandoning her carefully planned strategy.

He seemed to shift his concentration from her body to her words.

"I told you she could offer you nothing. She is trash, and she turned you into a whore." Ben's voice was engulfed with the disdain he felt for his perceived girlfriend's paramour. "You don't know how good it would feel to slide this knife between her ribs or between her legs." He stared far across the lawn as he fondled the hilt.

The words pricked at Syd's skin. *A few more seconds*, she said silently.

When Jenny managed to force a smile, Syd heard his satisfied reply.

"You are finally appreciating me for what I have to offer, aren't you?"

Jenny simply nodded her response.

"Ben!" Syd made her voice intentionally deep as it penetrated the dusk. The sound vibrated through the trees, and the leaves rustled in the wind that seemed suddenly harsh.

Ben grabbed Jenny by the hair and pulled her to her feet, holding the knife at her throat. Jenny seemed to search in vain for others walking with or behind Syd.

"What the hell do you want?" Ben trembled with what looked like rage.

"Ben, your last note said you wanted to deal with me. Is that right?" Syd walked deliberately toward the duo. She hooked her thumbs in her pockets, intending her casual, confident demeanor to enrage him even more.

"You turned my Lillian into a whore. You kept her from me and told her lies to make her go with you. I *will* deal with you, bitch."

"Why don't you come over here and do that. Deal with

me now," Sydney taunted, hoping to gauge the ease of his manipulation. She thought she saw him falter as he stepped off the blanket, Jenny's neck pressed under his forearm.

"You just want to lure me away from her. You think you can corrupt her again."

Sydney thought his reaction was promising. She knew she had started a train that she couldn't stop now, and she prayed her instincts were right.

"I'm just here so we can talk, right? That's what you wanted." She shrugged at him and held her palms up. He didn't move away from Jenny. He seemed to feel safe in his position hiding behind his victim. Sydney wanted to derail him, move him emotionally until it devoured him. Had Jenny's life not been balanced on that fine line, she would have enjoyed the game of it.

"Actually, I *want* you here. With us." His voice was demanding but disturbingly calm. "I want Lillian to watch as I punish you for what you've done. You deserve to see her take pleasure in your final destruction."

He was too committed, too fixated on his end game. He needed to have his attention shifted, and Syd thought she knew exactly how to accomplish that. There was no going back now.

"Ben, I want her back with *me* now. You can't keep her from me, you know." Sydney hoped the strategy was the right one and just enough to shift his attention from Jenny to her...just long enough. Syd knew if he let Jenny go for only a few seconds, a shooter could take him.

"You filthy dyke. You have *no* right to be here. Lillian is mine." He shoved Jenny roughly forward and walked a few feet from the blanket. He circled her, teasing the knife around her body and ensuring, unintentionally, that no one would risk Jenny's life in an attempt to incapacitate him. He eyed Sydney, mocking her as he skimmed the blade dangerously near the skin left bare by Jenny's summer dress.

Sydney felt the shift she had hoped for. She advanced farther, keeping her hands in clear view and stopping approximately thirty feet from him. She could see figures near the trees in the wood line shift as they transformed into rifle-wielding officers. They sidestepped to keep up as the subject moved closer, always maintaining cover and sight line.

"Are you so scared I could take her from you?" Sydney felt the sting of anticipation and adrenaline. She made her voice still deeper and darker, and she embarked on a tactical approach from which she knew there was no retreat. She took a deep breath and began. "I mean, take her from you *again*? Are you afraid that she remembers how good it felt to have my mouth on her, Ben? How good it felt when I held her hot, naked body against mine?" Syd taunted him and saw him pause as the images found purchase in his disturbed mind.

He pointed the knife at her in a furious gesture. "You shut the fuck up! You cannot talk about her that way. She told me she *hated* you touching her. She told me it would never happen again!" His voice trembled with fury and indignation as he continued to shake the knife in Sydney's direction, forgetting his prisoner.

Sydney saw Jenny step incrementally behind him as Ben zeroed in on Syd, the object of his wrath. She knew that if officers could retrieve Jenny, they would wait for the opportunity to take him into custody. She took slow, measured steps to her left, edging closer to the trees and the waiting police. He unconsciously mirrored her moves, and she carefully calculated the next step in her game.

"You know that isn't true, Ben. You watched me in the car, didn't you? You watched my hands slide over her smooth skin. You saw how much she liked it, how aroused she was. You saw how good I am at making a woman feel satisfied. You couldn't hear it, but she begged for more." Syd laughed tauntingly at the enraged man and watched Jenny freeze in place, obviously terrified to move in the event Ben turned around to find her.

Syd calculated that he was nearly six feet from Jenny, and she needed him to move a little farther toward her, which he did suddenly and all at once as he charged toward her with the knife leveled in front of him.

"Are you remembering it? Can you see it in your mind? Are you picturing my hands all over her, Ben? Stroking her body? You can't decide whether or not you loved to watch, or you're pissed that a woman like me can do it better than you, make it better for her." A dark figure pulled Jenny into the shade of the woods and disappeared. Syd felt her body relax a millimeter. She wouldn't let herself lose focus, however.

"I'm just going to stand here and let you think about that, Ben." Sydney was letting anyone who could hear her know that she would no longer try to move him any farther. Their next moves would be calculated on his current position. At least, she hoped that was the case. He'd stopped and was staring at her, the knife still raised. She felt ice course through her veins when she pictured Lillian describing her repeated rape at the hands of this despicable man who'd chosen Jenny as his next victim. She squared her shoulders and held his gaze. In her mind, this was no longer a battle; this was the last move at the end of a war that Ben Barrett would soundly lose.

"Are you still thinking about it, Ben?" She slowed her voice to get him to stay focused on her as four helmeted figures moved up behind him. She continued talking so his attention stayed on her. "Are you wondering what I have that you don't? Can you picture it? Can you see us together? Are you wondering what I'm doing when I make a woman scream my name, over and over again? I make them satisfied, Ben. You just make them pity you." Syd would admit that she was deriving a little perverse pleasure from taunting him. A molecule of satisfying verbal revenge on a man she would cheerfully dismantle with her bare hands.

Ben screamed and shook the knife, suddenly lunging toward her.

He cried out as he was propelled to the ground almost instantly, the knife wrenched from his hand. His arms were jerked into cuffs behind him, and Syd heard the team lead's voice, "One in custody. Clear."

Syd finally exhaled fully and bent over, bracing her hands on her knees in an attempt to still her racing pulse. She listened to the voices of the team as they moved Ben to the parking lot, his screams of rage and vitriol filling the air. Syd thought for a moment that the residual silence now swirling around her seemed somehow louder than the chaos of the past few minutes.

She walked slowly back toward the makeshift command center. She couldn't see Jenny, but she knew she was okay. The buzz of the adrenaline flush still obscured the periphery of her vision, and her movement was still a little unsteady. She tried to remember when the adrenaline dump had last affected her so drastically.

"Syd." Parker's breathy voice was a welcome sound as she approached the lot. Syd lifted her up as Parker wrapped her legs around Sydney's waist and held on.

"Hey, you okay?" Sydney buried her face in Parker's hair.

"Are you?" Parker wouldn't let go.

"I'm fine. It was quick." She realized the words were true, but it didn't help her unsettled state of mind. She needed her pulse to slow before she faced what would be a furious police command and potentially angry Mack.

"Where is Jenny? Did Mack get here?" Syd scanned the lot. Parker slid from her arms, and Sydney thought the void created by the separation was painful.

"They're over here." Parker dragged her in the direction of the commotion.

"How did they take it when they figured out what we were doing?" She knew she was in hot water, to say the least. If she got on the wrong side of the department, she might never see another evidence reconstruction contract again.

"We? *We* had *nothing* to do with that." Parker's stern words, obviously intended to scold, were clearly overshadowed by relief.

"But it worked. I heard everything. You did it. I couldn't believe what you were saying, but it *worked*. I think several guys are going to have to go take cold showers after all your dirty talk, but you did it. I'm so proud of you. I thought Mack was going to pass out, Syd." Parker skimmed her fingers over Sydney's face as if to trying to reassure herself that she was in one piece.

"I guarantee you that she did better than I would have. I couldn't have done it if it was you out there." Syd breathed into Parker again and closed her eyes. Parker clutched against Sydney, seeming to know intuitively that she needed the grounding embrace.

When Mack saw Syd, she didn't speak. She simply hugged Syd tightly, fighting tears of relief welling in her eyes.

"Thank you." Mack held her tightly. "Jenny's in the van with the detectives. She'll want to say thank you herself."

Sydney skimmed an arm across her forehead to wipe away the perspiration born of the past intense moments.

A very angry-looking Sergeant Lu stared at Sydney as he approached. "What the fuck was that, Hyatt?"

She shrugged. "I knew from his letters that he was pissed because he had been taken out, in his eyes, by a woman. He thought I was her, or I represented her, whatever. I had to piss him off so much that he couldn't help but focus on me. Besting him in the eyes of a woman that he thought was his is what made him go off the rails to start with." She pointedly avoided the details they'd gotten from KC and the real Lillian.

"You violated every tenet of proven hostage negotiation. You put my people and the hostage in danger—"

She doubted she had heard the last of it, but she cut him off anyway. "So, what you're saying is, you don't think I have a future with the department, Hank?" She counted on their friendship getting her a little bit of a pass.

"If you worked for me, I'd make sure you spent the rest of your career guarding the student lounge at a remedial junior high." He made a disgusted noise and turned toward the remaining assembly of officers.

"Promise me you wouldn't, Syd. I don't think I could take it." Parker placed a firm hand onto Sydney's chest.

"Hell, no. Clearly, there are too many rules." She smiled at Parker and feathered a kiss over her temple.

EPILOGUE

Six months later

Parker threaded her fingers through Syd's and reclined against her in the back seat of Mack's SUV, lulled by a ridiculously simple drive down a country road.

"Did I tell you what happened in court today?" Mack addressed the passengers—her wife, Syd, Parker, and Mia.

"I didn't get a chance to tell Parker either, so go ahead." Syd sounded happy at the news.

"Well, apparently, the DA heard from an *unnamed source* that Leanne Mason had been one of Ben Barrett's victims. He went to Maclean and convinced her to testify at trial and at a subsequent trial for her rape. He filed a series of other charges as well. She's also filing a civil suit against him because the same someone appealed for a pro bono deal on her behalf. Turns out that the little slime ball has a family trust fund worth about five million."

"Nice work." Parker knew that the "someone" was Sydney, who couldn't stand to let an opportunity for justice go by without a fight. "He won't be in a position to hurt her or anyone else again."

"Let's hope not." Jenny still sounded raw from the experience and her recent testimony.

Mack held her hand and pulled their SUV into the lot. "You were awesome, by the way. Half the jury was crying, and the other half was furious."

Syd reached up and squeezed Jenny's shoulder. "I'm on the stand Monday. Hopefully, the trial will wrap up soon."

Jenny ran an appreciative hand over Sydney's, but her usual snappy replies had been absent since the ordeal.

It was weeks before Jenny had slept through the night. Nightmares had kept a good night's rest out of her reach. Syd knew the trial threatened to bring it all flooding back. Most days, though, she was close to feeling like her old self again.

"Are you two sure about this?" Mack looked dubiously at Parker and Sydney when they had all piled out into a lot in front of a lonely, dimly lit strip of shops.

"Yes. We'll be fine, you chicken." Syd laughed at her. "Parker's hung out here before, and she says it's great." She winked at Parker, who just shook her head. She'd come to terms with the crazy that had invaded their lives again. Syd was learning to hover less obviously, and Parker was learning how to appreciate that Syd would always be there to shield her from monsters and bad guys—and goose bumps.

They approached the bar, and Syd ordered a round of drinks from a man in his late forties. She handed him a fifty-dollar bill on a twenty-five-dollar tab. He looked tired and grumpy before the ridiculously generous tip transformed his attitude. Syd passed out drinks and caught someone moving toward them. Parker stepped forward and hugged Charlie, who fisted a wad of keys and a bottle of Stella's vodka.

"Jenny, you remember Charlie?"

Jenny smiled and reached out her hand. "Of course."

Parker pointed at Mack, holding Jenny's other hand firmly. "This is Mack Foster, Jenny's wife."

"It's a pleasure, Mack. Welcome."

Parker turned and grabbed Mia's hand, pulling her toward

the front of the group. "And finally, Charlie, there's someone I would like you to meet," Parker said happily.

Mia pushed a springy red curl behind her ear and held out her hand when Parker tilted her head in Charlie's direction.

"Charlie Harris, this is Mia Wright."

About the Author

Cass Sellars is a certified fraud examiner and criminal justice professional. She has led white-collar criminal, corporate and financial fraud, and theft investigations. Formerly an editor of a small magazine, a creative journalist, and a public speaker, she's always been a writer at heart. The Lightning Series has allowed her to explore the world of romantic suspense fiction.

After life-changing experiences as a victim of corrupt "justice," she felt compelled to write about powerful lesbian characters who have the opportunity to fight for those who have been victims and seek justice where money and politics are not always the only winning assets.

Sellars grew up in the Midwest and England, but spent much of her adult life on the East Coast. She currently lives near San Francisco. She dabbles in interior design, event planning, singing, travel, and women's music and works at being a vital part of the lesbian and creative communities.

Visit her website: http://www.casssellarsauthor.com.

Books Available From Bold Strokes Books

A Chapter on Love by Laney Webber. When Jannika and Lee reunite, their instant connection feels like a gift, but neither is ready for a second chance at love. Will they finally get on the same page when it comes to love? (978-1-163555-366-6)

Drawing Down the Mist by Sheri Lewis Wohl. Everyone thinks Grand Duchess Maria Romanova died in 1918. They were almost right. (978-1-163555-341-3)

Listen by Kris Bryant. Lily Croft is inexplicably drawn to Hope D'Marco, but will she have the courage to confront the consequences of her past and present colliding? (978-1-163555-318-5)

Perfect Partners by Maggie Cummings. Elite police dog trainer Sara Wright has no intention of falling in love with a coworker until Isabel Marquez arrives at Homeland Security's Northeast Regional Training facility, and Sara's good intentions start to falter. (978-1-163555-363-5)

Shut Up and Kiss Me by Julie Cannon. What better way to spend two weeks of hell in paradise than in the company of a hot, sexy woman? (978-1-163555-343-7)

Spencer's Cove by Missouri Vaun. When Foster Owen and Abigail Spencer meet, they uncover a story of lives adrift, loves lost, and true love found. (978-1-163555-171-6)

Unexpected Lightning by Cass Sellars. Lightning strikes once more when Sydney and Parker fight a dangerous stranger who threatens the peace they both desperately want. (978-1-163555-276-8)

Without Pretense by TJ Thomas. After living for decades hiding from the truth, can Ava learn to trust Bianca with her secrets and her heart? (978-1-163555-173-0)

Emily's Art and Soul by Joy Argento. When Emily meets Andi Marino she thinks she's found a new best friend, but Emily doesn't know that Andi is fast falling in love with her. Caught up in exploring her sexuality, will Emily see the only woman she needs is right in front of her? (978-1-163555-355-0)

Escape to Pleasure: Lesbian Travel Erotica, edited by Sandy Lowe and Victoria Villaseñor. Join these award-winning authors as they explore the sensual side of erotic lesbian travel. (978-1-163555-339-0)

Music City Dreamers by Robyn Nyx. Music can bring lovers together. In Music City, it can tear them apart. (978-1-163555-207-2)

Ordinary is Perfect by D. Jackson Leigh. Atlanta marketing superstar Autumn Swan's life derails when she inherits a country home, a child, and a very interesting neighbor. (978-1-163555-280-5)

Royal Court by Jenny Frame. When royal dresser Holly Weaver's passionate personality begins to melt Royal Marine Captain Quincy's icy heart, will Holly be ready for what she exposes beneath? (978-1-163555-290-4)

Strings Attached by Holly Stratimore. Rock star Nikki Razer always gets what she wants, but when she falls for Drew McNally, a music teacher who won't date celebrities, can she convince Drew she's worth the risk? (978-1-163555-347-5)

The Ashford Place by Jean Copeland. When Isabelle Ashford inherits an old house in small-town Connecticut, family secrets, a shocking discovery, and an unexpected romance complicate her plan for a fast profit and a temporary stay. (978-1-163555-316-1)

Treason by Gun Brooke. Zoem Malderyn's existence is a deadly threat to everyone on Gemocon, and Commander Neenja KahSandra must find a way to save the woman she loves from having to make the ultimate sacrifice. (978-1-163555-244-7)

A Wish Upon a Star by Jeannie Levig. Erica Cooper has learned to depend on only herself, but when her new neighbor, Leslie Raymond, befriends Erica's special needs daughter, the walls protecting Erica's heart threaten to crumble. (978-1-163555-274-4)

Answering the Call by Ali Vali. Detective Sept Savoie returns to the streets of New Orleans, as do the dead bodies from ritualistic killings, and she does everything in her power to bring their killers to justice while trying to keep her partner, Keegan Blanchard, safe. (978-1-163555-050-4)

www.ingramcontent.com/pod-product-compliance
Lightning Source LLC
Chambersburg PA
CBHW030514020726
47494CB00004B/1091